CRYPSIS

Edward J. McFadden III

Trident Media

ISBN-13: 9798319361530

For more information go to: http://www.edwardmcfadden.com

Printed in the United States of America

10 9 8 7 6 5 4 3 2 1

*For Snoop and Skittles, who showed
me the true meaning of stealth.*

CONTENTS

1

As the sun peeked over the rim of the world the river shimmered like a ribbon of diamonds, its silvery waters winding through the vegetation beneath the shadowed canopy of ancient cypress trees. Birds squawked and hollered, and the boat's outboard gurgled as wary alligators fled, leaving wakes of churning whitewater crisscrossing the river. A plane streaked overhead, its muffled roar the only reminder that civilization was near. The earthen scent of swamp rot permeated the air, and smokey fog wavered and undulated two feet above the water.

Evan Thorpe stood in the bow of the Searcher II, mist coating his tanned face, his mid-length curly blonde hair pulled back and secured with a rubber band. He wore board shorts, flip-flops, and a blue T-shirt. The blonde and gray stubble that covered his face itched, and his stomach burned, the anticipation of a discovery making his nerves jump. Thorpe needed to find something on this trip. Badly, and not just for the money. Since his failed attempt at being a biologist, the treasure hunting business hadn't treated him well. If he didn't find something… anything, on this trip he'd have to go work for his uncle selling medical aids. The thought of it turned his stomach, hardened his resolve, loosened his ethics, and raised his expectations.

The growl of the motor fell to a low hum, backfired, and went still, the nasty scent of burning gasoline carrying over the river.

Thorpe rolled his shoulders and cracked his neck as a tremor of nervous pain ran to the tips of his fingers and toes. He wiped his brow and reigned in the urge to rip Harding's head off. It wasn't his fault. The vessel was a rental.

"Sorry about that, boss," Finn Harding said as he joined Thorpe.

The boat floated free, the current tugging the vessel steadily south. There was a sharp bend in the river ahead, and Thorpe said nothing as he gazed down into the green water.

"We'll be at the spot in a minute," Harding said. "I'm going to grab the anchor and dive buoy."

Thorpe nodded and began checking and pulling on his gear. The operation was on a need-to-know basis, so he'd ordered Harding to tell no one about what he'd found while conducting an excursion for tourists. This meant no deckhands, no divemaster, no help at all. As an added precaution, the pair left Harding's charter boat in its slip and rented a boat because Thorpe didn't want to be seen leaving the marina. The goal of the hunt wasn't gold or jewels but something potentially more valuable, and there were always eager eyes.

The rumble of a chain being dragged over fiberglass rose above the argument of two gulls as Harding deployed the anchor.

"How did you find this place?" Thorpe asked. The pair was north of High Springs in the middle of nowhere.

"I bring the more experienced divers up this way," Harding said. He tossed the dive buoy over the side and tied it off on a cleat. "Folks who don't want to see other people. The river is busy, but not so much up this way."

"Why didn't you take the find for yourself?" Thorpe asked. He didn't care what the reason was, but the portion of his brain in charge of skepticism was always working overtime.

Harding laughed. "I could have, but then what? Anything found on this section of the river is supposed to be reported to the staties. I had tourists with me, and if I reported it they'd take it, and all I'd get is my name in the paper and maybe a mention in some academic journal nobody reads."

Thorpe harrumphed. The guy made some

good points. "Why tell the authorities anything? Why not come back alone? I haven't seen a rabbit ranger since we've been out here."

"I've made a few mistakes since we last worked together," Harding said. "If I got caught selling illicitly obtained fossils or artifacts— Shoot, I wouldn't know where to start anyway. I'd end up getting ripped off or arrested. With you at least I'll get a piece. Besides, permits are required for any dig, and I knew you wouldn't want that."

The river contained the spectral remnants of many ancient predators, their forlorn bones mingling with the rushing water. Thorpe nodded as he suppressed a smile. He didn't buy everything Harding was selling, but he bought enough to assuage any concerns.

"What's our depth?" Thorpe asked. The twenty-one-foot center console Boston Whaler had spun around and the anchor line off the bow was taut. Ribbons of whitewater eddied around the boat as it was held fast in the flowing current, and tiny fish leaped from the water.

"Eighteen feet. Because we're just upriver of the bend, the bottom below us is muddy and the sludge drifts can be several feet deep in spots. Around the turn, where we're going, the river bottom is sandy and mostly firm, but the water moves faster."

"You didn't mark the location, right?" Thorpe asked.

Harding pointed at his head. "Only in here. Not even on the map."

Diving in eighteen feet of water wasn't much of a challenge, but people regularly drowned at shallower depths, and diving in rivers provided unique challenges. That was why Harding insisted on following all safety protocols, except for one of the most crucial rules which they were ignoring.

Thorpe was taught that there should always be someone on the boat while divers were in the water. This wasn't a hard and fast rule, but more a strict guideline, though it was one Thorpe preferred to follow when possible. In this case, he'd judged the risk of loose lips was greater than a mishap on what amounted to a vacation dive during bad weather in the Caribbean.

Harding pulled on his dive vest and fought the weight of the tank as he pressed to his feet, the Whaler listing and swaying, the river popping against the hull.

"I think the best way to do this is for you to wait here while I find the location of the fossil. I'll drag a lead line that you can follow. The water here is cloudy from the strong current and boat traffic, but the dope in the governor's office hasn't opened the floodgates lately, so the water isn't that warm, seventy degrees-ish. I'd wear booties, though. The river bottom can be rough on the feet," Harding said. "The weather is clear but always remember the current. Keep hold of the lead line and you should be fine. I'll make sure you're anchored. If you find yourself being tugged down river, and you can't fight the current, come to the surface and I'll help you."

The heat of anger spread over Thorpe. He was an experienced diver, so he was only half listening as Harding went through the pre-dive safety check, ensuring all equipment was functioning.

A black hard case held the underwater communication units along with their wireless base station and battery. Harding handed Thorpe one of the lightweight transmitter and receiver units to attach to his full-face dive mask. "The system operates on advanced wireless technology, using a radio frequency. Clip it to your mask. It's got a high-quality microphone and speaker, so we'll hear each other even over the hiss of the current and the puff and pull of the mask's regulator."

Thorpe clipped the comm device onto his mask and said, "Should we test it?"

"We're still too close to each other. Their signal strength is set high because it has to penetrate the water. Keep the unit off until you're wet." Harding adjusted some knobs on the base station before attaching his communicator to his mask and sitting atop the gunnel to pull on his booties.

Thorpe pulled on his water shoes, fastened his weight belt, and checked his buoyancy control device. All was in order. He slipped on his mask, took a deep breath to ensure the regulator was working, and gave a thumbs up. His heart was racing, the tips of his fingers tingling with the thrill of the hunt.

A gull shrieked at Harding as he grabbed a mesh dive bag and clipped it to his belt. "I've got plastic trowels, brushes, gardening-sized shovels, and a Dustbuster-type device that can clear a small area."

Thorpe fiddled with his vest straps as his gaze strayed back and forth from the river to the shotgun in its scabbard on the side of the command console. He didn't see any gators loitering about on the surface, but there was a good chance the prehistoric beasts were out there. Nothing a few shotgun blasts into the water wouldn't resolve.

Harding noticed Thorpe looking at the gun and said, "Yup. It's about that time."

With the blasts still echoing through the surrounding forest, the birds braying and bitching, Thorpe asked, "That's enough to scare them away?"

"The gators don't love sections of the river where the water moves fast. But no worries. Take this." He handed off a loaded speargun. "Just don't shoot me with it by mistake. It's going to be hard to see down there."

Thorpe nodded and gave another thumbs up.

"O.K., then," Harding said as he picked up a length of rope, gave one end to Thorpe, and attached the other to his vest via a carabiner. "I'll give it three tugs when I'm in position and then you can follow the line down. Once you're in the water don't forget to turn on your comm."

Thorpe gave a third thumbs up.

Being careful not to get tangled in the rope, Harding dumped himself off the boat into the river. Bubbles exploded above him as he sank, a knot of whitewater churning on the surface, the lead line trailing into the depths behind him.

The water calmed, the wind whispered, and the plop and tinkle of tiny fish jumping from the water leaked over the river. Five minutes slipped away before the lead line jerked three times and Thorpe entered the water, the rope attached to his dive vest.

Thorpe half swam, half sank into the depths, green water backlit by sunlight filling his field of vision. As he descended through the murk, he kept an eye on his depth gauge and adjusted his buoyancy control device, a wake of bubbles trailing behind him. He breathed easily as he activated his comm and said, "Harding, do you copy?"

"Copy, loud and clear, over."

"On my way." Thorpe pulled himself along the lead line, the mint-colored sediment-filled water limiting visibility to less than five feet.

The bottom was muddy, but as Thorpe followed the lead line the water cleared, the current picked up, and the river bottom became sandy. He pushed through the gloom for several minutes before his partner materialized out of the green haze.

Harding was anchored to the bottom via a hook and was clearing away sand.

When his feet were planted on the shifting sands, Thorpe slung the speargun over his shoulder and dropped to his knees beside Harding. With the silken depths of the Santa Fe River sliding by, the duo worked to uncover their prize.

The pair fell into a coordinated rhythm as they worked, the current constantly pulling and tugging on them. "How deep is the specimen buried?" Thorpe asked.

"It was partially exposed when I found it," Harding said. "So I buried it under a couple of feet of sand, but the way the current rips around the curve here, see—"

Even with the rush of water clogging his ears Thorpe heard the distinct tap of plastic hitting something hard.

Harding broke out the sand-sucker and began clearing the area.

At first, there was nothing but what looked like a whitish-colored rock, but as the anomaly was uncovered a skull materialized out of the silt and sand.

Thorpe's breath caught. It was just as Harding had said it would be.

The Smilodon skull had a mottled patina of

earthy browns and grays, the broad arches of its cheekbones flaring outward like wings, framing the empty eye sockets darkened by the murky water. Though the lower mandible had broken away, the skull was remarkably well-preserved, with the joints between the bones still faintly visible like the seams of an ancient puzzle. Thin cracks crisscrossed the bone, and the nasal cavity was broad, a reminder of the powerful sense of smell that guided the Smilodon as it hunted.

Thorpe smiled as he focused on the trio of massive, elongated canine teeth that had endured the relentless passage of time. Two of the teeth were fangs that jutted out prominently from the upper jaw, their once razor-sharp edges dulled by eons of erosion. The third tooth was smaller and broken, and all the teeth had been stained yellow by the minerals of the riverbed.

Harding wiggled the skull, clouds of sand obscuring the find as he pulled it free and handed it off.

Thorpe cradled the skull in both hands. The teeth were still firmly embedded in the skull's upper jaw, and he rubbed them with his thumbs. He may have failed out of college, but he hadn't forgotten everything. The dense structure of teeth could preserve genetic material for millions of years, and in the dark, empty eye sockets of the ancient predator, Thorpe saw dollar signs.

2

C had Mercer climbed from sleep, the sharp whine of his cellphone echoing through the room. Light pulsed through the darkness as he reached out, feeling around on the nightstand for his phone. Pain knotted his head, and weariness leaked through him, his muscles heavy. Mercer felt like he hadn't slept more than an hour.

Jenni mumbled, rolled over, but didn't wake.

He found his phone and pressed the power button to stop the trilling and light show as he girded himself for whatever the call would bring. Nobody he cared about was pregnant or in the hospital, so unless it was a wrong number, the call was bad news. Bad news that involved him.

Mercer rolled onto his back as he stared at the glowing screen. It was Twerp and that couldn't be good. The big guy had never called Mercer at home before. Whenever there was a problem at the facility Jinx or one of her people called, and on rare occasions, Rocco.

"Yes, sir," Mercer said as he tapped accept call. "Is everything alright?"

"If everything was alright, would I be calling you in the middle of the night?" asked Evan Thorpe. The CEO of Evolve Enterprises, Inc. sounded aggrieved and belligerent.

Mercer said nothing. If he'd learned one thing in the Army, it was to keep his piehole shut when a superior had a head full of steam.

"There's been an incident down at the facility," Thorpe said.

Mercer waited. Follow-up questions in the early stages of Twerp's speeches could prove deadly.

"I'm unsure of the details," Thorpe continued. "I need you to get down there and find out what's going on."

"Got it," Mercer said.

"Call me as soon as you know something. First. Not second, first. Report to me only until further notice."

"Yes, sir," Mercer lied. The connotation was clear: call me before the law, but Mercer would cross that bridge when he came to it.

His stomach churned with worry as Mercer snuck from his bedroom with his clothes and went about putting himself together.

In the bathroom, Mercer gripped the edges of the sink, his tired reflection staring back at him in the mirror. Short brown hair, damp from a quick rinse, clung to his forehead in uneven strands, and his olive skin, usually sun-kissed with life, looked pallid under the fluorescent light. Shadows enveloped his brown eyes, deep creases lined his brow, and a hollowness had settled beneath his cheekbones—subtle signs of stress that made his reflection feel like a stranger's.

Mercer swallowed hard, forcing down the unease that clawed at his gut, and fifteen minutes later, with a steaming cup of microwaved coffee in hand, he slipped out into the fading night.

Tall Pines was quiet, all the houses dark, and the streetlights cast puddles of light over the blacktop road. The Evolve Enterprises complex was north of Camp Meeker, so Mercer made a right on Morelli Lane, which took him to Bohemian Highway where he made another right. Trees and underbrush pressed in on the edges of the road, the Jeep's headlights driving away the blackness, the right side of the road rising into the mountains, the left side falling away into darkness.

A chain-link fence surrounded the entire four-acre complex of Evolve Enterprises, and Mercer arrived to find the front gate closed. He pulled his ID, waved the card before the access control reader, and the gate swung open.

The facility's driveway wound through thick forest, an occasional young redwood peeking its five-hundred-year-old head above the black oaks and evergreens. Another fence, this one topped with concertina wire, provided secondary containment around the Evolve building.

Tony, the nightguard, opened the gate and waved Mercer through. The parking lot was empty, and as he pulled into the Director of Security's reserved space, he saw Jinx waiting for him outside the building's main entrance.

An owl cooed as Mercer exited his car as if issuing a warning. The parking lot lights were at forty percent to conserve energy, and Jinx's shadowy form appeared and disappeared as she made her way toward him, passing through the stone pillars that lined the main walkway. The monuments were etched with pictures and text recounting various Evolve Inc. successes.

Mercer sipped his coffee and didn't break stride. He said, "Morning. Who called you?"

"Ozzie," Jinx said, but Mercer knew she was lying. Twerp had probably called her. Probably before him. Mercer's number one looked put out, her frizzy black hair in a knot atop her head, her brown face free of its usual light sheen of makeup. Dark greasy bags hung beneath her eyes, and she was strapped, her Glock Nine on her hip. Mercer's Sig Sauer was locked away in his desk.

When the pair reached the building's entrance, Jinx held the door open for Mercer, and the duo stepped into the dark lobby of Evolve

Enterprises. "What've we got?" Mercer asked as he sipped his coffee.

"Your guess is as good as mine," she said. "What I do know is a specimen escaped."

Mercer stopped walking, causing coffee to slosh through the hole in the cup's lid. "Come again? The big man didn't mention anything about that."

Jinx said nothing.

"Has the facility been searched?" Mercer asked as he looked over his shoulder. Suddenly the certainty that he was the smartest and strongest creature in the land didn't feel so certain.

"My people are going through the entire building. Nothing yet," Jinx said. "In the meantime, most of the alarm zones are activated and all security systems are online, except for where we'll be heading, and the locations being searched."

"Which lab did it escape from?"

"Four."

As Mercer flashed his ID and passed through a door secured by an electronic lock, he asked, "Who made the discovery?"

"One of the night lab techs. Holloway."

Mercer knew the guy. He was competent, smart, and didn't make foolish mistakes.

The pair made their way down a long hall of offices, passed through another locked door, and entered the heart of the lab complex. LED light glared down from above and the temperature dropped as the perpetual hum of the building's undercurrent filled the silence. They passed the cage-washing room, the incinerator facility, and the cleanrooms where DNA cocktails were mixed before reaching the labs and containment areas, where Evolve's products either became viable or ended up in the burn chamber.

Holloway sat outside the entrance to lab four. He looked up when Mercer and Jinx arrived. "Morning. Sorry..." he said.

Mercer nodded. "What happened?"

"I was doing my rounds," Holloway said. "Routine checks. When I entered lab four, I saw the containment chamber's door was ajar. All the specimen's bio monitors were offline, as was its camera and monitoring device."

"Wouldn't all that show up on your main screen?" Jinx asked.

"Yes, but I was doing my rounds," Holloway said.

Mercer had so many questions he had to take a breath to order his thoughts. He stalled by asking, "What about the other specimens?"

"All secure and accounted for," Holloway said. "No anomalies reported."

Mercer nodded toward lab four's open door and said, "Has anyone else other than you and Jinx been in there?"

Holloway shook his head.

"Did you touch anything?"

"No."

"Wait here." Mercer pulled his phone, opened his camera app, and entered the lab with Jinx in tow. "What about the security footage?" he asked his second in command.

Jinx harrumphed. "Doesn't show much. Given the specimen in question, it's not much help, but there are a few things of note."

Mercer couldn't recall which specific biological creation was being tested and trained in lab four, but none of the company's projects involved creating softer and kinder kittens. "What about the security log for the electronic lock on the containment chamber's door?"

"There's a log, but we won't have it until Dax gets here at 8:30," Jinx said.

The two thousand square foot lab was standard fare. Banks of LED lights hung from the ceiling and reagent shelves and benches filled the space. On the far wall, there were two fume hoods with supporting lab benches on either side of a metal enclosure with a transparent, reinforced polymer front. The paddock's door was ajar, just as Holloway had said. High-definition cameras with night vision and thermal imaging provided constant monitoring of the organism, and Mercer knew the data from these cameras fed into a central monitoring system that used AI to analyze the specimen's behavior and health. The enclosure was also equipped with an advanced climate control system that maintained optimal temperature, humidity, and air quality, and the scientists adjusted the light cycle to push the limits of the creature's circadian rhythms.

Embedded sensors within the cell collected data on the organism's physiological parameters, such as heart rate, body temperature, and movement patterns. Mercer thought the interactive tasks to engage the specimens, which were connected to feeding stations and other training-specific stimuli, were the cleverest part of the company's testing. The changeable puzzles also provided mental and physical stimulation. The computers atop the lab benches were equipped with advanced analytics software, allowing scientists to view live data, historical trends, and predictive models. The workstations also controlled the tranquilizer system, which remained inactive.

"What about the power?" Mercer asked as he tried to think of a way the door to the enclosure could have been opened without human intervention.

"There was a blip," Jinx said. "But backup provided immediate power transfer, within milliseconds. None of the critical devices in the facility missed a beat as far as I can tell."

Mercer examined the open paddock door and its locking mechanism. The electronic lock had a physical key override. If the key wasn't available, the redundant lock could be released electronically via a series of codes entered into the central security system by at least two high-ranking Evolve Enterprises personnel. There were no scratches on the lock and no signs of tampering, even though smears of saliva covered the inside of the enclosure's door.

The door had opened because of a malfunction, or... someone had set the specimen free. "Can you cue up the security footage on one of these computers?" Mercer asked.

Jinx nodded. "It'll take a couple of minutes for me to log on and download the files, but yeah."

Mercer abandoned his empty coffee cup on a bench and took the opportunity to spend a few minutes alone with Holloway, who still sat dutifully in the corridor. "What time do you clock out?" he asked.

"Supposed to be seven," Holloway said. "Do you want me to hang out?"

"Would you mind? The cops are going to want to talk to you. Probably Twerp."

"Cops?"

A lava bug crawled from Mercer's stomach to the small of his back. "Who did you call? Dr. Ozzie or Dr. Miranda?"

"Ozzie."

"What time?"

Holloway rubbed his chin and studied his hand. "I don't remember."

"Check your phone."

Holloway nodded. After a few swipes, he said, "I called at 3:49 AM."

"Thanks." Mercer sucked in a deep breath. "Do you have any thoughts on where… it might be? Or if it's still in the facility?"

"Most of the building has been searched, so I —"

"That's not what I asked," Mercer said.

Holloway hiked his shoulders. "I don't know where it is or what it's capable of. That's way above my pay grade, though I'll say it wouldn't stun me if the creature was still in the building. If it got out, how and where?"

"Anything else you can tell me?"

"Not really, unless you want the basics about the creature."

"I do, but that can—"

"Got it Mercer," came Jinx's voice from the lab.

"Coming!" Then to Holloway, "Go to the cafeteria, grab some food, and come right back here."

Holloway nodded and pressed to his feet.

Jinx sat on a lab stool before one of the workstations, her face twisted in a knot of confusion and worry. Mercer fell in behind her.

The monitor showed the lab in darkness, equipment indicator lights and the glow of displays creating white halos in the blackness. Infrared light was invisible to the naked eye, but it was picked up by night vision cameras. The specimen was framed at the center of the screen, its huge, distorted, cat-like form undulating in waves of white, red, blue, and black. A red light flashed on the paddock lock, then turned green. There was a blur of motion, a kaleidoscope of colors moving with the fluidity of water.

What had the bigheads at Evolve done? He knew the researchers who worked at the company stretched the boundaries in their goal to create new and superior organisms. But none of that mattered. He had to call the police and notify them of the escape. The potential danger. But what would he say? He didn't know yet what exactly had escaped.

And it wasn't just the cops. Evolve got money from the feds all the time and the company had several contracts with the Department of Defense. All that came with oversight, though Twerp did his best to keep the entire operation well below everybody's radar. Hence its location in the middle of nowhere outside Occidental, not far from Santa Rosa and Sacramento, both of which were close to military bases and supplied a diverse workforce.

He pulled his phone to call 911.

"Chad?"

Mercer turned to find Drs. Ozwald and Miranda Maleficar, Evolve's head scientists and the conductors of the company's biological symphony. They'd both met Twerp at college.

"Freeze that, Jinx," Mercer said.

The image on the screen darkened, the creature a rainbow-colored blob.

"Can we go somewhere private to talk?" Dr.

Ozzie asked.

Mercer looked at Jinx, whose gaze strayed to a speck on the linoleum floor. She already knew what the upcoming discussion was about. "No," he said. "Jinx was just leaving."

"What about the video?"

"I'll call you if I need you."

3

Mercer shared what he knew and got nothing in return, but it wasn't like he had a choice. Other than Twerp, O&M was in charge, and depending on where you were in the building, even that hierarchy could be debated.

"Do you mind if I ask you a few questions?" Mercer said.

Dr. Miranda said, "I can't imagine what—"

"Like what time did Holloway call you?" Mercer pushed.

"Chad," Dr. Miranda said. "I think you might be confused as to who works for who."

"Whom," Dr. Ozzie said.

Dr. Miranda sighed. "You were watching the security footage when we arrived, I presume?"

Mercer wanted to tell the woman to bugger off, but he was on his last chance. If he blew it at Evolve, he didn't know what he was going to do. Jenni might even bail on him. "Yes," he said.

"Then let's see it," Dr. Ozzie said.

Mercer unfroze the security footage with the tap of the mouse, and the undulating mass of colors began moving through the darkness again.

"May I?" asked Dr. Miranda.

Mercer relinquished the mouse.

Dr. Miranda went to work, and the image onscreen froze as she zoomed in, and the picture got brighter. The closeup provided by the high-resolution cameras stripped away most of the distortion, and the creature could be seen, the wall of its cage looming in the background.

The creature's eyes were yellow, and they gleamed with menace in the darkness. Its head was huge, and a thick mane of brush-like hair ran down the center of its head and diminished in length as it trailed down the beast's back. No fur covered the specimen, its skin smooth, though Mercer couldn't tell what color the creature was. Despite the dark, the beast's canine fangs glowed white, and its rippling muscles made it appear as though a swarm of ants crawled over its body.

"I'm switching to the recorded feed from the specimen's collar device," said Dr. Miranda.

The image on the screen shifted, and the interior of the lab came into view as the trio saw what the beast had seen. Lights flashed, screens glowed, but the image distorted as the creature moved its head up and down rapidly. The status light on the containment chamber's door glowed green.

"It's slamming its neck and the side of its head into the side of the enclosure," Dr. Ozzie said.

Dr. Miranda added, "And as you can see, and I'm sure it will be verified by the official log, the paddock's door lock is disengaged." She switched back to the security video, adjusted the zoom and clarity, and the beast's shadowy form stood on its hind legs, forelimbs planted on the side of the paddock as it slammed its neck collar against the wall, faint sparks dancing through the darkness like fireflies. She paused the video and said, "That's when the specimen's tracking device and camera went offline."

"Are you telling me the thing intentionally damaged its monitoring device?" Mercer asked.

"It would appear so," said Dr. Ozzie.

Dr. Miranda started the video again, but there wasn't much to see until the beast pushed open the door of the enclosure and slipped through, activating the motion sensor and turning on the lab's lights.

Mercer suppressed a groan.

The creature's muscular cat-like body was hairless except for a dark mane running down the center of its back. Its grayish skin was smooth, and it shimmered and shifted as the beast moved. As it dropped to all fours its color changed, and Mercer's breath caught in his throat when the creature's rear flank blended into the metal of a cabinet and appeared to vanish. Its head was disproportionately large compared to its thick, muscular body, and its deep-set, yellow eyes exuded a cold, calculating intelligence. Though it advanced with the fluidity of water, the creature's movements were unnatural, as if its body was slightly out of sync with the environment around it. The beast disappeared from the camera's eye.

Dr. Miranda changed the camera feed and the POV showed a shadowy form leaving via the lab's main door as an alarm sounded, a strobe light turning the lab into a disco.

"The door can't be secured from the inside for safety reasons, but they can be alarmed," Mercer said. She switched the feed to the hallway camera just in time to see claws rake across the lens before the screen went dark.

"And it wasn't picked up anywhere else?" Dr. Ozzie asked.

"Not yet," Mercer said. "All the video needs to be reviewed, and the logs checked. The biggest issue as I see is that you both did your jobs too well. The creature wasn't picked up by the motion sensors. The lab lights and the hallway lights came on because of the motion of the opening doors." He wasn't sure of that, but it made sense based on what he'd just seen.

"We've got a real problem," Dr. Miranda said.

"No shit," Dr. Ozzie said.

"What is it and why can I barely see it?" asked Mercer.

"We call it Saberonis," Dr. Miranda said.

Mercer bit his lip, the maggots in his stomach churning, but he said nothing.

"Mr. Thorpe thought the name was flashy. You know, for marketing. The greenies love drama and cool names," Dr. Ozzie said.

Mercer waited.

"What is it? Why can't you see it too good?" Dr. Miranda shook her head as she smiled. "Because, as you said, we're good, no, great at what we do, and the Saberonis was supposed to be the future of this company. Fulfill our major contract with the—"

"That's not helping now, dear," Dr. Ozzie said. "Chad needs the facts so he can catch this thing."

Mercer's head jerked back like he'd been punched, but he let the comment slide for the moment.

Dr. Miranda sighed. "The Saberonis is one of our greatest creations. Simply put, it's a stealthy, fast-moving, killing machine, that's seventy percent prehistoric Smilodon, twenty-nine percent chameleon, point five percent elephant, and point five percent planarian."

"At first, we considered attempting to de-extinct the Smilodon, but there were too many problems with the DNA sequencing," Dr. Ozzie said.

"Plus, we wanted to add other traits to the specimen, so we filled in some of the gaps with DNA from complementary creatures," Dr. Miranda said. "The Smilodon, often referred to as a saber-toothed cat, was a formidable predator that roamed the Americas during the Pleistocene epoch, approximately two point five million to ten thousand years ago. The creature is best known for its massive canine teeth, which could grow up to seven inches long."

"I saw that," said Mercer.

"However, unlike modern big cats, Smilodon had a more robust and muscular build, with a stocky body, short limbs, and a powerful neck. This anatomy allowed it to wrestle large prey to the ground, and its forelimbs were particularly strong, equipped with retractable claws. Smilodon adapted to a variety of environments, from open grasslands to forests, often coexisting with other large predators such as dire wolves and American lions. However, its reliance on large prey like bison, camels, and even young mammoths made it vulnerable to environmental changes. As the Ice Age came to an end, many of these large herbivores began to disappear, leading to the eventual extinction of Smilodon around ten thousand years ago."

"Where did you get the Smilodon DNA you used to make your stew?" Mercer asked.

Dr. Ozzie chuckled. "If we knew, we'd be breaking our confidentiality agreements by telling you."

"The choice of the chameleon is obvious, no?" Dr. Miranda said.

Mercer stayed quiet.

"A chameleon's camouflage is primarily achieved through the manipulation of specialized cells in their skin called chromatophores, which contain different pigments," Dr. Miranda said. "Beneath these cells, there's another layer of cells called iridophores, which reflect light. By expanding or contracting these pigment cells, chameleons can change the color of their skin to match their environment."

"And the color change isn't only used for camouflage but also for communication, thermoregulation, and signaling their mood or intent to other chameleons," Dr. Ozzie added.

Mercer, feeling like an undergrad in a doctorate course, said, "The addition of elephant DNA for size makes sense to me, but refresh my memory. What's a planarian?"

Dr. Ozzie nodded. "A type of flatworm belonging to the class Turbellaria, known for its remarkable regenerative abilities."

"It can heal itself?" Mercer asked.

"A planarian can be cut into pieces, and each fragment has the potential to regenerate into a complete, fully functional organism," Dr. Ozzie said.

If Mercer understood what O&M was telling him, they had created an overlarge, saber-toothed cat with the ability to change the color of its skin and heal itself at an advanced rate.

And it had escaped.

"The planarians have this extraordinary ability due to the presence of pluripotent stem cells, known as neoblasts, which can differentiate into any cell type required for regeneration," Dr. Miranda said. "This remarkable trait has made the creatures a subject of extensive scientific study, particularly in the fields of developmental biology and regenerative medicine."

"Put it all together and you have the perfect apex land predator," Dr. Ozzie said.

Mercer could think of plenty of people— governments, who would pay big dollars for such a creature. "And all this is why the creature is so difficult to track and see." It was a statement, not a question.

Dr. Ozzie nodded. "Crypsis was one of the primary characteristics requested by the... potential customers."

"It's a form of genetic camouflage that allows an organism to avoid detection by other animals, typically predators, by mimicking the surrounding textures, colors, and shapes," Dr. Miranda said.

"There are many examples in nature," Dr. Ozzie said. "A leaf insect looks remarkably like a real leaf. Snowshoe hares turn white in winter to blend in with snow."

"And certain species of octopus and cuttlefish can change their skin color and texture to match their surroundings," Dr. Miranda added.

It all made sense to Mercer, but his mind worked in an orderly, logistical way. He asked, "How the hell did you plan to control it? Those lame collars?"

Dr. Ozzie chuckled sardonically. "The collar is temporary. Its purpose is to provide a GPS locator signal and camera view. If the creature advances to a... sellable state, a cranial interface will be implanted, but this can't be done until the creature's brain has fully developed."

"And now that GPS and camera aren't functional," Mercer said.

"You saw the same video we saw," Dr. Miranda said.

"But we'll get Dax's people on it," Dr. Ozzie added. "Maybe they can repair the device remotely or at least ping it for a signal."

"How did it know to do that? Break the tracker, I mean."

O&M shrugged, but Dr. Ozzie said, "Intelligence was another modifier. It's smart. And most likely sees everything as a threat."

"It can't get the collar off," Dr. Miranda said.

"Can't?" Mercer said. So far, based on what he'd seen and heard, he didn't think anyone knew what the Saberonis could or couldn't do. That's what the researchers at Evolve were in the process of determining.

Dr. Ozzie chuckled.

"O.K.," Mercer said. "We need to call the police, the feds, and get them to start looking for the thing before someone gets hurt, or worse."

O&M shook their heads. Dr. Ozzie said, "We can't do that."

"As much as we'd like to," Dr. Miranda said.

Mercer wasn't that surprised, but O&M's wishes changed nothing. "Come again?"

"All this must be kept secret. What we do here…" said Dr. Ozzie.

"Skirts the edges of the law," Dr. Miranda finished. "Plus, Mr. Thorpe will kill us. Probably you also, and maybe even your wife."

Mercer was stunned by the casualness of the accusation. "A bit of an exaggeration," Mercer said. "No?"

O&M said nothing.

"Look, I understand this can be bad for the company," Mercer said, "but wouldn't it be worse if this thing goes on a killing spree? The community needs to be notified so they can take precautions."

"What's your opinion about employees not informing prospective employers about past crimes?" Dr. Miranda said.

Mercer's heart sank. He'd lied a little on his resume and omitted a few embarrassing facts, but it wasn't enough to allow an apex predator to roam his turf. He laughed, but there was no mirth in it. "You think because I exaggerated on my resume you've got something on me?"

"Not really, but that allegation when you were in the military," Dr. Miranda said. "That was some ugly business."

Mercer felt the weight of his years. How the hell had they found out about that? He knew

Thorpe had money, but that shameful tale was classified. He tried to act as though he didn't feel like he was going to fall on his face. "So what?" he said. "Jenni knows all about it and this job isn't that great." At least the first part was true.

"Then there's the incident when you were a police officer," Dr. Ozzie said. "Does Jenni know about that? And why you were forced to retire?"

An icy chill crept over Mercer. No, Jenni didn't know the real reason he'd been fired from the cops, or about the encounter that had led to it. It had been one time, yet it ate at Mercer like a cancer because he knew if Jenni found out, she would never be able to forgive him. Despite his angst, he'd always known the real problem was he couldn't forgive himself.

"You need to help us," Dr. Ozzie said. "You have no choice. That's why Mr. Thorpe chose you."

"Plus," Dr. Miranda said. "Isn't it the right thing to do? Kill it and the company is saved."

"And what can the locals do, really?" Dr. Ozzie added. "This will all be over for better or worse by the time they get their heads out of their asses and the feds mobilize. You can respond faster, better."

"We know what you're capable of," Dr. Miranda said.

Mercer didn't believe that, but he couldn't get what Dr. Miranda had said about Thorpe killing them all, including Jenni, out of his head. She was all he had, and he couldn't lose her.

They had him. Unless he was willing to blow up his life, and start again, if that was even possible, he had to go along to get along. So far nobody had been hurt. Maybe he could hunt the thing down before there was any collateral damage and the whole affair would fade away like a bad dream.

4

"**C**an either of you think of anybody who might want to sabotage the company? This project in particular?" Mercer asked. He'd do his job until... There was no sugarcoating it. He was across the line, and his past was coming back to take a chunk out of his ass. At best.

"You mean beyond the religious zealots and their numerous houses of God, the conspiracy theorists, quick buck artists, reporters, the government, the local authorities, and the public?" Dr. Ozzie said.

"Point taken," Mercer said.

"I see where he's going though, honey," Dr. Miranda said. "It seems clear the Saberonis had help."

"We need to question and check out every employee, even the ones who didn't have access to the labs," Dr. Ozzie said.

Mercer hiked his shoulders. "That would be standard procedure, but I don't think it will yield much. If it was an employee, said person would know that any trail could lead to them, so they would sell the information, but even that is extremely unlikely. The codes to the high-security area are changed every twenty-four hours."

"You can cross two names off your list. I can assure you it wasn't me," Dr. Miranda said.

"And I was with her all night, and there are cameras all over our property that prove we never left the house," Dr. Ozzie said.

Mercer believed them, but that didn't mean the scientists had nothing to do with the escape, though he couldn't see what the couple would gain. "How was it going with the Saberonis? How far were you from… marketability?"

"We were beyond our promised demonstration date by a year, and pressure was building, but…"

"But what?"

To that, O&M had nothing to say, and that told Mercer the married scientists knew more than they were letting on.

"Chad, you have to understand," Dr. Miranda said. "Much of what we do is trial and error. We take a…" Dr. Miranda's gaze strayed to something Mercer couldn't see.

The room was silent save for the hum of the HVAC and the steady beeping of an offline biorhythm monitor. Mercer glanced over his shoulder.

Evan Thorpe, AKA Twerp, eased into the room. The overconfident windbag paused like

Darth Vader and put his hands on his hips as his head swept side to side atop his skinny neck. When he saw O&M, he said, "What happened here?"

"I was just about to call you, sir," Mercer said. He hadn't expected to see the boss so soon.

"Certainly, you were." Twerp wore jeans and a golf shirt—a pink Polo, of course, and thin cracks of fatigue creased his tan face. His curly blonde hair was matted on the sides of his scalp, but a growing bald spot, sunburned and freckled, shined with an unnatural glow under the harsh stare of the LEDs. He sighed as if he was the only one on Earth that made any sense, and said, "Get Holloway and Jinx in here. Does anyone else know the details?"

"Not yet, but when the data crew comes in the word will spread. I need the logs from the—"

Twerp put up his hand like Mercer was a child. "We'll deal with that in a minute."

Jinx and Holloway joined the party, and the fivesome stood before Twerp like they were facing the firing squad. If Thorpe's eyes were guns, Mercer and his colleagues would've been bullet-ridden.

"Let's have it then," Thorpe said.

Each member of the team told their part, and Thorpe was shown the relevant security video, and when it was done the boss wandered around the lab as if the benches, reagent shelves, and equipment would inspire him. He examined the enclosure, its door, and its lock, but he said nothing, the tension in the room building, which was no doubt what Twerp wanted.

Thorpe didn't have that nickname for no reason. Though nobody knew much about his personal history, most folks thought he was a Grade-A asshole. He had no patience, didn't know what he didn't know, and was arrogant to the point of annoyance. It was well known that he had no loyalties to anyone, not even O&M, and he was a womanizer with shifting morals and a borderline capitalist criminal. O&M knew him back in college, but any questions about Twerp were met with silence. The man had a diploma on the wall, but Mercer had checked, and the record showed he graduated, but there was something about an Honorary Degree, and he knew those were bullshit. There were also rumors that Thorpe had once been a treasure hunter of a kind, but Mercer couldn't see it.

"What's the plan for when employees start showing up?" Thorpe asked.

That hour wasn't far away. Twerp hadn't asked about, or even mentioned law enforcement, and Mercer judged the boss didn't even want the topic brought up, so Mercer kept his mouth shut.

Air surged into the lab, and the equipment beeped, but nobody spoke.

"No recommendations? What the hell do I pay you all for?"

Mercer was impressed. Holloway, Jinx, and O&M were smart enough to stay quiet.

"Clean up in here," Thorpe said. "Jinx, sequester all relevant electronic data, video, and documents for legal hold and have the copies transferred to my secure account."

Jinx nodded.

"Then... sequester the data in the system," Thorpe said. "This is standard procedure when the security of the information is paramount, for legal purposes, confidentiality, and preservation. This information is sure to be involved in legal discovery, so we must take all precautions." Then he locked eyes with Jinx and the unspoken message was clear; remove all traces of the creature and its escape.

Jinx nodded.

Mercer almost laughed. Precautions? Wiping away all history of the incident could be perceived in other ways. He almost suggested placing security clearance levels on the data, but he knew the boss would give him a ten-minute speech about how hackers were constantly trying to break into the Evolve Enterprises servers to steal their intellectual property.

Thorpe's face twisted, and he shot Mercer a look that could've wilted lettuce as if the boss had read Mercer's mind. But there was no mind reading taking place. It was only common sense.

"Mercer, do what you need to do. Find it," said Twerp.

Mercer licked his lips and nodded. Twerp's ass was on the line and Mercer could save it, but did he want to? No. But he had to. At least he needed to try.

Mercer held an impromptu staff meeting with Jinx, Mercer's real number one and third in command, Declan McAllister, along with the Cleaning Supervisor, Colette "Coco" Greer, and Facilities Manager, Rocco Tridadoni. The tale Mercer told had holes big enough to drive a truck through, but his people knew the deal. Silence was golden.

When he was done relaying the skeletal basics, Mercer called in the IT Supervisor, Dax Rhett, and the timeline was laid down.

"Breakout, if we can call it that, occurred at 3:26 AM," Dax said. "An open door alarm popped up on the main control screen, but Holloway was on his rounds. He discovered the specimen was missing at 3:49 AM when his call log shows he called Dr. Ozzie."

Mercer was called at 4:41 AM and he made a mental note to question Twerp and O&M about the almost one-hour gap.

"As to the creature, the electronic lock log shows the series of doors the creature used to escape the building. The alarm was already tripped, and the doors can't be locked from the inside per fire code, and the doors the specimen used had crash release bars.

Mercer stared at a map of the building, a yellow line tracing the path of the beast through the facility. "It had no trouble finding its way out?"

"Hard to tell," Dax said. "The regular cameras throughout the facility don't have the same capacity as the lab cameras and the specimen... evaded the camera's eye. How it did that is above my paygrade, but—"

There was a knock at the conference room door and the receptionist stuck her head in. "Mercer, Alex Brantley is here to see you?"

"Plant him in my office and tell him I'll be with him in a minute," Mercer said. Alex was a close friend and a retired sheriff who also happened to be the best hunter Mercer knew. He'd asked for his help, keeping the facts to a minimum and saying only that he needed to catch a pest on Evolve's extensive grounds.

The receptionist nodded as she retreated.

"Jinx, start the process of interviewing the staff. Go easy, nice cop, but make sure you remind them all of the NDA they signed," Mercer said. "Dax, tighten the timeline and get that tracker collar online. In the meantime, I'll take Alex and Declan, and we'll search the outside of the facility and the surrounding forest and see if we can pick up a trail. If we do, we can put together a bigger party to—"

Dax's phone screamed, "Answer me, answer me, answer me." The IT man looked to Mercer

41

for permission and said, "That's the emergency ringtone."

"Take it," Mercer said as he pushed to his feet and glanced at his watch. It was 12:06 PM. He felt like he'd been up for days and the Saberonis had a head start.

Dax nodded and gave Mercer a thumbs up. He killed the call and said, "My people were able to ping the creature's GPS device, and they got a location."

"The collar is working?" Jinx said.

"No, but making contact was a big step."

"Where is… it?" said Mercer.

"Outside the facility," Dax said. "My tech said it looks like the specimen is just beyond the tree line on the southern side of the building."

Everybody went for the door like someone had yelled fire, and Dax held the door open for Mercer and his people as they surged out into the hallway.

Mercer's office was on the west side of the building overlooking the parking lot and the main walkway with its series of monuments. He broke into a jog, and open office doors fleeted by, the worried faces of employees staring at him.

At the end of the hall, he made a left, went through a security door with a buzz, passed the cafeteria, copy and storage rooms, then made a left when he came to the Vice President for Marketing's suite. He entered an emergency stairwell and climbed to the second floor, and he exited into a passage that led to the CEO's cathedral-like conference room. The room had huge windows with electronic shades, and as Mercer and his entourage entered he found the shades open.

Mercer sprinted around the long conference table and stood before the row of windows, Jinx, Declan, and the others on his heels.

It was a sunny day, not a cloud in the sky. There was a strip of green grass dotted with pathways, stone benches, and plenty of local flora. Beyond the manicured grounds, a dense line of evergreens loomed like a wall. Mercer couldn't see the secondary fence which he knew was just beyond the trees, and a long way beyond that, the outer fence surrounded the entire property.

Mercer pulled his phone, swiped to his binoculars app, and used the device to scan the edge of the forest. His companions followed suit, and soon the Evolve employees were holding up their phones and staring like they were at a concert.

At first, Mercer saw nothing, the shadows beneath the dense tree canopy thick. Then something moved, an amorphous absence of light, and a large shadow reached out from the forest. There was a blur of movement, and the beast appeared for two heartbeats.

Jinx let out a slow breath.

The Saberonis was huge, and as it rose onto its

hindlegs it appeared to be staring at the building, its yellow eyes pinpricks against the shadowy background.

A collection of employees had gathered at the open conference room door and Mercer shooed them away.

"I need to go get Alex… and my gun," Mercer said.

"We're coming with you," Rocco and Coco said as one.

"No, we have to keep this quiet," Mercer said. "I'll contact you if I need your help."

Rocco grabbed Mercer by the elbow as he headed for the door and said, "Chad, if you do get a shot at it, empty your gun."

5

Mercer headed to the loading dock, stopping by his office first to grab his Sig Sauer and swap his loafers for boots. Declan picked up a rifle, while Alex carried his old service pistol—a Smith & Wesson Model 10, a six-shot .38 Special double-action revolver —tucked away in a pancake holster. The loading dock was on the east side of the building, but exiting that way allowed the trio to avoid drawing attention, especially from the creature.

It was just after 1 PM and the late spring air was thick and steamy. Jinx was at the security desk manning the cameras, but just to be safe Declan wore a bodycam not unlike the collar the beast wore. It transmitted Declan's POV to the central station, and it had a GPS that tracked his location to within ten feet. Mercer led the way along the back of the building as a gentle breeze stirred the vegetation, the midday sun baking the landscape. When he reached the corner of the building, he stopped and raised his binoculars.

The Saberonis was still crouched just beyond

the tree break, its yellow eyes floating six feet above the ground in the shadowy darkness beneath the thick canopy. Based on what he'd seen so far, that told Mercer the beast was down on all fours. The creature's head swung right, then left, before its gaze locked on Mercer and his companions.

"Can you see it, Declan?" Mercer asked. They were close enough to take a shot at the creature with the rifle and far enough away that the threesome could retreat into the building if the beast charged.

The Saberonis rose onto its hind legs, its camouflage momentarily fading and shifting as the creature moved.

Mercer felt his confidence drain, his muscles heavy from lack of sleep. The thing was huge. "Give me the rifle," he said as he stuffed his Sig Sauer into his waistband and let the binoculars swing to his chest on their leather strap. He accepted the rifle and put his eye to the scope but pulled back.

The Saberonis was gone.

"We blew it," Mercer said as he handed the rifle back to Declan and surged forward. He was halfway across the manicured grounds, the tree line looming like a wall, when he slowed. The creature could be hiding in the flower beds or behind the decorative bushes that flourished with firework tops of blue, white, and red. He paused at the edge of the woods and waited for his partners, the forest's shadow reaching into the gardens.

The forest surrounding Evolve Enterprises was comprised mainly of towering Douglas-fir trees, their dense, pyramidal foliage of dark green needles blocking out the sun. Patches of black oaks dotted the forest, their green leaves glossy, their bark almost black, and small glades of young redwoods hid among them.

Pinecones and bronze pine needles covered the hardpan beneath the forest canopy, and thin pricker vines clogged the ground between the thick tree trunks, pulling and grabbing at the companions as they tracked the Saberonis.

Alex led, rifle stock pressed to his shoulder as he scanned the ground. If he was following a trail, Mercer couldn't see it. Clouds of gnats filled the air, and ants, squirrels, and insects fled before the hunters.

The Saberonis was nowhere to be seen.

When the party was fifty yards into the forest, they came to a halt. A thin glade of oak trees, short when compared to the redwoods and evergreens, stretched out before them, the underbrush thicker due to the thinner canopy.

If sight and touch fail, let sound lead the way. A deep, hollow clicking, like a huge rattlesnake issuing its warning, echoed through the forest followed by an unnatural cackle-like scream.

"Alex?" said Mercer.

A cloud of Chickadees sprayed from the

greenery, the tiny birds a blur of motion, their black-capped heads, white cheeks, and brown backs ruffled. Brown feathers streaked white floated in the air as Alex sprang into action, heading straight, but he'd only gone twenty feet before he stopped and dropped to a knee.

"Whatever we're chasing…" Alex spared a glance at Mercer. "The thing might be almost invisible, but it doesn't float above the ground." He pointed at two patches where the pine needles had been dug up, and within the dirt patch, there were round impressions and slash marks indicating the pads and claws of feline feet.

The hunters pressed on until the forest thinned, revealing the inner fence. A barren, thirty-foot-wide gap extended along both sides of the barrier, and it wasn't only a maintained fire break. It was also a way to keep the tall trees from falling on the fence, though the inner perimeter was regularly patrolled at night and randomly during daylight hours.

"Damn," Alex said.

There was a hole in the fence at ground level, as if a swirling ball of wire cutters had rolled over the hardpan and bored through the chain-link.

Mercer raised his Sig Sauer, and the three companions inched forward, the ground covered in cut weeds, mosquitoes and flies filling the air.

Nothing moved in the forest beyond the slash in the fence, but still Mercer's nerves poked at the underside of his skin, his stomach a nuclear knot.

The tear in the fence was roughly six feet high, and the poles on either side of the opening were bent inward despite the reinforced steel posts being set in concrete. The fence itself was an interwoven diamond-shaped pattern of metal wire made of galvanized steel, which was coated with a layer of zinc to protect against rust and corrosion. Heavier gauge wire was strung through the diamond pattern, and tension bars and steel bands that added rigidity and strength were connected to the posts. These reinforcements, along with the chain-link, had been blown out.

Around the hole, the fence was bent outward, with some of the cut wires having jagged ends, while others appeared to have been cleanly snipped. The razor wire atop the fence was undisturbed.

"Looks like its claws cut through the fence like butter," Declan said.

Alex examined the slashes, tracing his fingers over the cut metal as he said, "What the hell are we chasing here?"

As Mercer squeezed through the hole he said, "Let's go."

Declan and Alex didn't follow.

"What?" Mercer said. He understood his friends' concerns, but time was of the essence. They were on the creature's trail, with a successful resolution and his own survival within reach.

"Shouldn't we get back up?" Declan held up the rifle as evidence of their lack of firepower. "We can have Thorpe call in more people to walk the perimeter of the fence," he finished.

"Screw that," Alex said. "You've got to call the rabbit rangers, the police. Shit, the feds. Whatever this thing is, it's far from harmless. It ain't gonna be easy to hunt, and based on this fence, it's dangerous. Really dangerous. You got anything to say? Partner?"

Declan, who knew the deal, leaned forward and pointed his bodycam at the ground.

"Alex, I'll fill you in as much as I can when we have time. But my NDA is a killer... Plus, you don't want to know."

"Really, but I do," Alex said. "If you want me to put my ass on the line I need to—"

Mercer put up a hand. "I need you."

"You need me? Or they need me?" He waved a hand dismissively in the direction of the Evolve Enterprises offices.

"Me," Mercer said. "Help me. Not for the company, not for your ex-constituents. But for me. I need this."

"Need?" Alex said. "Why?"

Mercer remained silent. Though Alex was a friend, he was unaware of the darker mistakes.

"Yeah, got it," Alex said.

"Please." Declan was no tracker, and Mercer

hadn't hunted in years. If he was going to find the beast, he needed his friend.

"O.K.," Alex said. "But you've got no idea how big you owe me."

"Fine. Now come on." Mercer crossed the strip of cut weeds and plunged into the forest. The temperature dropped ten degrees, and the thick scent of pine and eucalyptus filled his nostrils.

"How could you let this happen?" Alex demanded as he brushed past Mercer and took the lead.

Mercer and Declan exchanged a glance as they fell in behind him.

"What? You think I don't know how you evolve hidden away out here in the forest?" Alex said, with extra emphasis on evolve. "What I don't understand is how the thing escaped. Did you forget to set the alarms? Write the security company a bad check?"

Mercer said nothing. He didn't know the answer to that question. The timing of the entire escape event was like a choreographed play. The beast beating its monitoring device, the door unlocking while Holloway was on his rounds. It all stank of an inside job, specifically Twerp. He could've hired a hacker, provided codes, and with access to all the building systems he could easily have planned the orderly escape. But why? If the creature had become a liability, why not send it to the burn chamber? Why all the drama? He didn't know, but he'd bet everything he had money was involved.

The snap of a tree branch carried through the woods and Alex changed direction as he tracked the sound. Evergreen branches whipped Mercer and pricker vines tore at his clothes as he threaded through the underbrush, expecting to come head-to-head with the Saberonis in every dark patch of shadow. The Sig Sauer suddenly felt heavy in his hand. He hadn't been to the range in… he couldn't recall how long, though he'd always been a steady shot, even before he was properly trained.

Mercer's knees throbbed as he jogged, sweat staining the underarms of his shirt, his boots chafing his feet. He felt his phone vibrate against his chest and he pulled it just long enough to see it was Twerp calling before dropping the device back into his pocket. He'd call the boss when he was good and ready. Either Twerp was watching Declan's bodycam feed, or Jinx had told him about the hole in the fence. If he spoke to the boss now, he would insist on sending help, and that was the last thing he wanted.

Alex stopped to examine a broken tree branch. There were three deep claw marks in the bark, and he lifted the hanging branch, which still clung to the tree trunk by sap-saturated bark. He said, "It's not far." He aimed his gun at the underbrush ahead, his gaze sliding back and forth as he scanned the forest.

Pain settled in Mercer's lower back. They were

missing an opportunity. He could feel it. "Should we split up to cover more ground?" he asked, because that was the first thing he thought of, though he knew immediately it was a bad idea.

"No," said Alex.

The sound of vehicles echoed through the woods, and Mercer figured they were getting close to the outer fence. Bohemian Highway ran along the western side of the property but the road bent east as it meandered south, making up part of the property's southwestern boundary.

Mercer and his partners reached the outer fence, with the road barely visible through the narrow strip of woods beyond it. There was no hole in the fence and there was no sign of the Saberonis.

Alex paced along the fence. "We need to walk the entire perimeter."

"But which way do—" Declan stopped speaking, his mouth falling open as his eyes grew wide.

Mercer followed his gaze.

Seventy yards to the south the Saberonis tore at the chain-link fence, the shriek of its claws tearing metal and the grunt and wheeze of its exertion filling the stillness. It stood on its hind legs, its smooth gray skin shifting color as it moved, its short tail a blur as it cycled back and forth.

"Declan, do you have a shot?" Mercer asked.

Mercer's number one licked his lips, his eyes

fluttering like he'd forgotten about the rifle. Declan nodded, raised the weapon, and put his eye to the scope.

Ancient Smilodon, of which the Saberonis was a distant genetic relative, was a primordial creature that scientists believed had a powerful sense of smell that guided it as the beast hunted. At least that was what Mercer's fast internet search had revealed. Perhaps it was this heightened sense of smell or some other extrasensory perception, but the creature turned its head, its yellow eyes finding the companions as its jaws slid open, its long curved fangs glinting in the sunlight.

Declan fired. The shot pinged off the fence, and a spark knifed through the air as the bullet ricochetted and thumped into the ground. He ejected the spent shell casing and jacked another bullet into the firing chamber, but the beast was too fast.

There was a blur of motion and an inhuman roar. The Saberonis was on the move.

6

His feet frozen to the ground, **Mercer** stared at the area where the Saberonis had been as he waited to see if the beast was running away or charging him. He raised his gun but aimed at nothing, the wind whispering through the fir trees, brown pine needles swirling across the hardpan.

Just beyond the strip of forest that separated the road from the fence, a car rumbled down Bohemian Highway. If the driver saw what was unfolding, he or she knew better than to get involved.

Nothing moved on Mercer's side of the fence. Pine needles, leaves, and twigs had drifted against the chain-link, and in spots, thin hair-like strands of lichen clung to the galvanized metal. Mercer judged the party was a quarter mile southeast of the main entrance.

A flash of light ahead, a large blur of color, and the smooth gray skin of the Saberonis could be seen as the creature darted back into the woods.

Alex was the first to break free from the group's collective paralysis. He ran along the fence, his gun aimed at the forest, though the Saberonis had disappeared into the greenery.

Mercer and Declan trailed after, and Mercer stopped briefly to examine the fence. The chain-link was stretched, and several of the diamonds were torn and some of the wires had been cut. If given a few more minutes, the Saberonis would have broken through.

His phone vibrated in his pocket again, and he regretted suggesting the bodycam. Thorpe was probably watching along with Jinx, and like the owner of a football team, he thought he knew what plays to call.

Back in the forest, Mercer found Declan and Alex hiding behind a redwood tree. The majestic specimen was a baby, only six feet around and no more than a hundred feet tall, its bark a rich tapestry of deep russet hues, rugged and grooved from decades of weathering. Its trunk tapered as it climbed into a thick canopy of evergreen needles, and its branches spread out in every direction, each one a strong, sinewy arm supporting clusters of dark green foliage.

The air reeked of cedar, damp wood, and the earthy scent of moss, and a thick layer of fallen needles made a rust-colored carpet beneath Mercer's feet.

"It's there," Alex said. "In front of that thicket of pricker bushes."

The vegetation Alex was referring to was fifty yards distant, a thick beam of sunlight illuminating a small clearing that was created when a giant oak had given up the ghost.

At first, Mercer couldn't see it. The patch of shrubbery was thick, and the bushes had thin brown branches and tiny yellow-green variegated leaves that constantly shifted and swayed in the gentle breeze. Though he was close, Mercer pulled his binoculars to get a better look as Declan tried to get a bead on the thing with the rifle's scope.

The first thing Mercer saw was the eyes, those yellow piercing eyes that never seemed to blink. Then he noticed the collar, its white band wrapped around the creature's thick neck, its device still attached. The Saberonis was massive, its limbs proportionately shorter than those of modern big cats, giving it a powerful, stocky appearance. It was standing on all fours, and still, the creature stood five feet tall, and Mercer recalled that O&M said the specimen weighed over a thousand pounds.

Huge jaws dominated its broad, powerful head, while elongated upper canine teeth arced over its gums and hung menacingly, extending a foot below the beast's mouth. The creature's shoulders were heavily muscled, supporting its large head and adding to the strength of its forelimbs and the effectiveness of its retractable claws.

As the vegetation shifted, so did the color of the Saberonis. The creature's advanced crypsis abilities were astonishing. O&M had done amazing work, and as the beast blended into the vegetation Mercer realized just how outmatched he was. The beast was genetically engineered to kill, and Mercer and his companions were just another potential meal in its newfound territory.

The Saberonis surged into motion. It was fast, nothing but a smear of muscle and shifting gray skin.

"Shoot!" spat Alex. "What are you waiting for?"

"There's tree trunks and too much underbrush in the line of fire and I..." The tip of the rifle dipped. "I don't see it!" Declan shrieked.

The sound of galloping feet, a cry, like tearing paper, and the beast lunged from the undergrowth, jaws flexed open, curved fangs on display, short tail out straight as the Saberonis attacked.

Mercer dove to the side, narrowly avoiding the creature. The beast's claws sizzled through the air where he had been, slicing leaves and branches. He rolled as he hit the ground, gripping the Sig Sauer tightly.

Like a cat dropped upside-down, the Saberonis twisted as it sprang and seamlessly changed direction. Its skin, a shifting distortion of color, provided camouflage so effective that the creature became nearly invisible as it locked in on its next victim.

Declan barely had time to react, and he

brought up the rifle in a desperate attempt to fend off the attack, but it wasn't enough to stop the beast's momentum. The force of the impact knocked Declan off his feet, and he hit the ground hard, the rifle skittering out of reach.

Alex pressed his back to the redwood, his gun held in a doublehanded grip as he searched for the Saberonis. The creature was moving fast, and firing would put his companions at risk.

The beast roared in fury, the sound echoing through the trees, a primal cry that made the knot of pain in Mercer's neck stomp down his spine and settle in his lower back.

Mercer got to his feet and staggered back, the beast's shifting as its skin attempted to adjust to the chaos of color surrounding it.

Alex fired twice, but if the shots hit the creature, it made no sound.

Time slowed, everything moving so fast Mercer felt like he had slipped a few seconds behind the rest of the world.

The beast's powerful jaws snapped closed as all four of its powerful paws, claws extended, dug into the hardpan, and the Saberonis changed direction.

Declan pushed to his feet.

The creature recovered quickly, its eyes narrowing in anger as it prepared to take another shot at Declan.

But Mercer's number one was already moving, and the creature's claws raked the air behind him, narrowly missing his legs.

A blur of grey skin as the beast twisted and lunged at Declan like an arrow.

Alex fired three fast shots that tore through the vegetation.

The beast's momentum carried it forward as one of the bullets smacked into the upper thigh of its right hindleg. The other two shots hit tree trunks.

With a stuttering cry of pain, the beast lashed out at Declan as it flew past.

Declan dropped and rolled into the undergrowth, narrowly escaping the creature's off-balance strike.

Mercer aimed his Sig Sauer, but he didn't have a shot.

The Saberonis swung its baseball-mitt-sized paw, claws searching for flesh as it reared back onto its hind legs, its jaws opening to reveal fangs like white scimitars. Declan screamed, claws raking over his midsection, blood leaking from his arm and chest where the beast had slashed him. Mercer's number one flopped to the ground, holding his stomach as he writhed, blood spraying the vegetation.

Alex, who now had a better angle from his position next to the redwood tree, squeezed off two shots but it was too little too late.

The beast's bottom half disappeared as the creature blended into the green underbrush. Branches snapped as the birds stopped singing and an ominous silence fell over the woods.

Mercer ran to Declan's side, firing into the forest where he'd last seen the creature, the pop and crack of the shots and the hammering of his heart the only sounds. His ears rang, and Mercer shook his head as he stared after the creature, but he could no longer see it.

Alex stepped from cover and started after the beast, a trail of blood drips marking the way.

"Wait!" Mercer said. "Declan is wounded, and his safety is more important than... He's just more important and you can't go alone. Plus, the creature might circle back."

"Wild animals don't really do that," Alex said.

"Do wild animals damage their monitoring devices before they escape? And find their way out of a high-security building?" Mercer said.

Alex grunted and spit.

Mercer barely had time to pull his phone from his pocket before the distant wail of a siren echoed through the forest. He called the command center and got Jinx on the line. "I assume you called the ambulance?"

"10-4. We couldn't see what happened to him. Is he O.K.?" Jinx asked.

As if on cue Declan moaned, and Mercer stripped off his shirt and used it to staunch the man's wound. "His intestines aren't hanging out, but he's lost a lot of blood. I'll send Alex to the road, and he can flag down the ambulance and they can cut the fence."

A pregnant pause, then: "Negative on cutting the fence. I'll be to you with my people in two minutes, and Declan can be transported to the front gate and taken from there."

Mercer wanted to tell Jinx—Twerp, to piss-off, but he had to admit the big man had a point. A hole in the outer fence would raise tons of questions and it could be seen by outsiders, and even getting it repaired could start the rumor mill churning about a beast that ate metal.

With Alex standing watch, Mercer tended to Declan the best he could. His shirt wasn't doing much to stop the bleeding, so Mercer applied as much pressure as he dared.

Declan's eyes had glazed over, and when they slid closed Mercer shook him and they opened. "What? What?" sputtered Declan.

"Stay with me," Mercer said.

Declan squinted as if he could no longer see. "Mercer?" Then the man found his second wind. "Mercer, tell Stephanie I love her," Declan said. "Tell her—" He coughed up blood.

Mercer and Alex exchanged glances. There was nothing either of them could do about internal injuries, broken ribs, and loss of blood.

"Tell her I love her and the boys. Will you do that?" Declan asked.

Mercer wanted to say no and give the guy a pep talk. Tell him that he could do that himself when he survived, but instead, he nodded. Upsetting the man served no purpose, and the way things were looking he might have to carry out Declan's wishes.

Jinx and several of her guards arrived five minutes later and used a stretcher and a golf cart to bring Declan to the front entrance where they were met by an ambulance. Mercer wanted to go with him, but there was more pressing business.

Two of Jinx's guards rode to the hospital and would stay there and assist Declan's family as needed and report back to Jinx.

Mercer and Alex walked up the main drive, and his friend peeled off toward the parking lot when they exited the barrier forest. The walk seemed longer than usual, but he figured that was because it had already been a long day, and it was only getting longer.

"I'm heading home to eat, rest up, and get better prepared," Alex said. "Night vision, guns. Call me when you want me to come back."

"Thanks, man," Mercer said. "Really. I owe you one."

"Yes. Yes, you do."

Mercer's day got worse when he saw Twerp waiting for him. The boss sat on a stone bench next to the final pillar that lined the pathway. When Mercer reached him, the man was staring up at the monument, which had text and the picture of the company's incorporation papers stamped into the stone. "I remember that day. It seems so long ago now. You weren't with us then. You were still out there." Twerp tossed his head, indicating the outside world. "Well, you're here now."

Mercer said nothing.

"Why didn't you answer your phone?"

"As you undoubtedly saw, I had my hands full."

"We saw very little, though I'm sure once the video is scrubbed and enhanced it will tell the story." Twerp sighed. "I'm hiring... specialists to help us out."

"Specialists?"

"Bodies, weaponry, technology, and expertise," Twerp said.

"Will I report to them?" Mercer asked himself why he cared only to have the question ground under by the meat-churner of his ego.

"You work for me. So you will work with them because you and your team don't seem up to the task."

"Sir, you know what we're dealing with, and the beast caught us unprepared. We need to—"

"Exactly. Unprepared. Unlike you," Thorpe said. "Not what I was expecting when I chose a man of your... unique background."

Mercer's stomach sank. There it was again. The threat to blow up his life if he didn't keep his mouth shut and do as he was told. "Which specialists?"

Twerp smiled and said, "Top people."

Mercer nodded and bit his lip.

Thorpe must have felt the heat of Mercer's

hatred because he added, "But stay on the case. If you kill it, there'll be no need for them. But make it fast."

The beast had evaded him, but it was still inside the fence line, so there was hope.

7

Evolve Enterprises, Inc., Occidental, California, U.S.A.
1:12 AM PST, Day Two

Mercer couldn't go home because things were moving too fast, and he didn't want to see Jenni. It wasn't that he didn't want to be with his wife, but he didn't want to answer questions, or hear her concerns, all while suffering the guilt of his newly exposed betrayal leaking from every pore. So, he left a message after he knew she'd be asleep, a true coward move. He rubbed his eyes, tapped his phone, and said, "We got a hit on one of our trail cameras in the forest."

"On my way," said Alex.

Mercer sat up and searched for his boots.

Evolve security guards were patrolling the outer perimeter fence, but no holes had been found so far. Everyone agreed it was only a matter of time before the beast realized it could easily climb over the fence, and the security personnel had been instructed to look for any signs of damage to the chain-link or the fence's accompanying supports or enhancements.

Nothing had been found thus far, so unless they'd missed something, the Saberonis was still on Evolve Enterprises grounds. He'd been dead on his feet when he crashed on the couch in his office, only to be jerked from sleep for the second time in twenty-four hours by the trill of his phone.

He slipped on his boots, gathered his weapon, phone, and spare magazines, and headed for the door.

The update on Declan wasn't great but he was still alive. He was on the intensive care floor in critical condition, and the doctors said he had a fifty-fifty chance of making it through the night. If he survived, the odds he would live would begin to climb.

Mercer had called the man's wife—he'd made such calls before when he was in the military and on the PD, but somehow this one struck closer to home. Declan was a friend, and it was partially Mercer's fault the guy had been slashed like prices after the holidays.

Jinx and Mercer met on the loading dock. She had two of her top guards with her: retired Marine Ricky Cokely and retired police officer Freddie Rameriz. Both men were strapped like they were going to war, and both guards wore bulletproof vests. Mercer didn't think he'd ever heard either man speak. Jinx's radio erupted.

"Jinx, come in."

"Go ahead," she said.

"We just let Alex Brantly through. I told him to pull around and park at the loading dock. He's got a trailer on the hook."

"10-4." Then to Mercer, "A trailer?"

Mercer hiked his shoulders. Alex said he was going home to prepare. "Where's the boss?" He wanted to know if Twerp was going to be watching.

"Asleep in his office," Jinx said. "I convinced him it was too dangerous out there. Same goes for Dr. Ozzie and Dr. Miranda. They went home."

"Good," Mercer said. "What about the hired help?"

"Thorpe is giving us until sunup. If we don't get the thing whoever he hires will be here by lunch."

"Great."

Alex's pickup appeared pulling a trailer carrying two ATVs. His brakes squeaked and an owl hooted, the sounds echoing through the enclosed parking area as he exited the cab. "Morning… evening… whatever." Alex grabbed an Army green duffle from the truck's load bed.

"What are we going to do with those?" Jinx said as she pointed at the twin Hondas. Mercer had ridden the ATVs several times with his friend.

"Sorry?" Alex said. "I know there are no trails in here, but being able to move around fast could be helpful, no?"

Jinx laughed like Alex was an idiot. "They're too loud. The creature will hear us coming a mile away."

Alex laughed, full and hard, going all out, bending over and slapping his knee. "There are so many funny things about that statement I don't know where to start. First, the beast is likely to hear us coming even if we tape cotton to the bottoms of our feet, and have you considered that the noise might draw the creature in? Ever hear of curiosity?"

Jinx didn't look convinced.

"Then there's the real purpose I brought them," Alex said, pausing to hold his audience, but Mercer ruined it for him.

"We can use them as decoys to help us surround and drive the creature," Mercer said.

That made Jinx stare at the ground, and Mercer felt shame in drawing pleasure from her embarrassment. Jenni was right, he really could be an asshole sometimes, but Jinx could be unjustly cocky, so no harm no foul.

"Cokely. Rameriz. You ride the ATVs," Mercer said.

Without a word, both men slung their AR-15s over their shoulders and went to the quads.

"Not that it matters, but where did you get the hit from?" Alex asked.

"Southeast quadrant," Jinx said. "Not far from the big redwood, I think."

The ATVs came to life and Mercer gave orders for Cokely to go to the fence line in the east and slowly patrol the perimeter, heading south, and Rameriz would patrol in the opposite direction.

"Questions," Mercer asked via his headset comm. "Be sure of your shots. I can't have a friendly fire situation out here."

Cokely and Rameriz wore bodycams, and as Alex put on his night vision goggles Mercer felt left out.

"Lead on, Jinx," Mercer said when the threesome was ready, and the ATVs had disappeared into the darkness.

"How many sensors do you have out here?" Alex asked as he trailed after Jinx. The trio were making their way across the manicured grounds to the forest, where they'd use the hole in the inner fence.

"There are about forty trail cameras, and roughly thirty of them are functioning at all times. Batteries die, et cetera, but we get good coverage. All the cameras are wirelessly linked to the command station, and the motion sensors activate the cameras which send out a notification if something of the appropriate size is detected. We get plenty of good pictures of deer, bears, birds, and there's a fox den somewhere on the property."

"Did the cameras in question capture anything useful?" Mercer asked.

"Not really," Jinx said. "A white cloud of light,

then two glowing eyes floating six feet from the ground. Eerie as hell."

"Why didn't the trail cameras pick anything up yesterday?" Alex asked.

"They did," she said. "We got some good pictures of you as well."

Mercer's stomach grew hot. Now it was a certainty that the boss knew he'd blown him off... twice.

Owls hooted, birds cooed from within their hiding places, and beneath it all the steady buzz of crickets and the bleat of lizards and frogs. Moonlight angled through the dense tree canopy, the evergreens disappearing into the blackness above. The party marched single file, Alex and his night vision leading, followed by Mercer, and Jinx served as rearguard.

The Evolve Enterprises property extended into the wilderness in all directions except to the west where it ended at the Bohemian Highway. Beyond the company's land, the vast forest was sparsely populated by homesteads, farms, wineries, marijuana fields, and young redwood groves. Further to the east were the towns of Graton and Barlow, and beyond them Santa Rosa, a thick tapestry of farms and residential neighborhoods in between. Most of the regular Evolve staff lived in Graton or Santa Rosa, but the execs and scientists tended to live locally in Occidental or had lavish homes by the Pacific Ocean to the west.

Mercer didn't want to think about what would happen if the Saberonis reached a residential neighborhood.

The trio crossed the fire break, passed through the rip in the inner fence, and delved into the forest. As they trekked, Alex looked over his shoulder and saw that Jinx was almost out of earshot, and whispered, "How's Jenni? I haven't seen her in a bit. You two still trying?"

Pain knifed through Mercer. He had loose lips when he was drinking and his buddy, though he knew little of his past, knew most of his present, and a bit of his future. He said, "She's O.K."

"And you? Do you feel the same way? Does she?" Alex was a widower, and his two boys were grown and had their own families.

Mercer wanted a kid—now, and Jenni was in perpetual stall mode, the fear of taking care of an infant paralyzing her. "We haven't talked about it lately." They hadn't talked about anything lately.

Jinx said, "Command tells me we're almost to the camera."

Alex let the topic drop, at least until the next time they were sipping whiskey, and said, "We're here. Hold up so you don't disturb anything."

Mercer and Jinx stopped walking as Alex advanced, peering at the ground through the night vision goggles.

The trail camera was attached to a thick Douglas-fir ten feet from the ground where it had a commanding view of a tight clearing filled with tall weeds.

Alex moved away from the camera to where a section of weeds had been flattened. "No sign of blood," he said.

Mercer was certain—it had been verified via video, that the beast had been hit at least once, yet the trail of blood left by the Saberonis had petered out after a hundred feet and Jinx's team had been unable to find so much as a drop beyond that.

"Hold up," Jinx said. "Cokely is calling."

Mercer took the opportunity to take a drink of water. His neck ached from sleeping on his office couch, and he felt nauseous from the cafeteria sandwich he'd scoffed down.

"Got it," Jinx said. "On our way."

To the south, the roar of an ATV pierced the stillness.

"Cokely found something," Jinx said.

"A tear in the outer fence?" Alex said.

"No."

"What then?" Mercer said.

Jinx said, "Let's go see. He said he's by marker eighty-one, almost due east of our position."

The small party double-timed it through the forest, but it was still slow going. The underbrush was dense and leafless pricker vines and depressions hid within the shadows, and rocks, dead tree branches, and roots threatened to trip them up with each footfall.

Headlights cut through the trees, the ATV's

engine roaring as Rameriz came from the south, riding along the fence. There was yelling and screaming, and then both the ATVs fell still with a gurgle.

Alex slipped off his night vision goggles as the threesome exited the woods. Cokely and Rameriz stood just beyond the trees, their flashlights trained on a broken branch that lay atop the fence.

"Well, shit," Alex muttered as he lowered his rifle.

Mercer holstered his Sig Sauer and dropped to a knee, turned on his flashlight, and trained its beam on the ground.

Clear prints marked the creature's passage —circles created by the beast's footpads and slashes from its retractable claws.

"This branch wasn't down when the last patrol rolled through here," Cokely said.

It was obvious that the branch had recently broken because the wood was fresh, the oak a clean white, strands of sap still dripping from the break. The branch was a foot in circumference, and Mercer figured in a pinch it could've held the weight of all present.

"I thought the trees along the outer fence were trimmed regularly?" Mercer said.

"They are," Jinx said. "Twice yearly. This is the outer fence after all, and normally we don't pay much attention to it. We… the royal we, always thought the threat would be someone trying to get in, not out. Plus, without the razor wire, my grandmother could climb a six-foot chain-link fence."

"Your grandmother was taught what climbing was at the park when she was two years old," Mercer said. "The Saberonis has lived its entire life in a cage without a jungle gym."

"True," Jinx said. "But it seems to learn pretty fast, based on its escape and all. Plus, weren't you the one bitching about the tree trimming budget?"

"Fair enough," Mercer said. Technically everything security related was Mercer's responsibility, but he delegated many aspects of the day-to-day running of the operation to Jinx. That was what Twerp preferred, Jinx being his inside person, though the big guy wasn't aware that Mercer knew that.

There were claw marks on the tree the beast had climbed, and the bronze needle-covered carpet was disheveled. It didn't look like the tree branch could have extended over the fence, but as he peered down the length of the fence, his flashlight slicing through the blackness, he saw other branches reaching for the fence.

Mercer sighed and rolled his shoulders. "Jinx, call Thorpe and wake him."

The series of upcoming decisions were above his pay grade, but he felt Alex's eyes boring into him, and he heard his friend's words in his mind: we need to call the cops. Alex had signed an NDA

—that was the only way Twerp would allow his involvement, and though the boss didn't have anything on his friend other than the threat of financial ruin, he was an Evolve slave for the duration.

Mercer stared through the fence at the disturbed ground on the opposite side, the tall Douglas-fir trees standing like ominous silent sentinels. If the trees could talk, they would tell how the beast had been smart enough to identify a branch of the appropriate thickness and use its weight to cause the branch to break and provide it with a bridge over the fence. Why the beast didn't just break through the outer fence as it had the inner, he didn't know. Could it be the beast didn't want to make noise and draw attention to itself?

He wasn't sure exactly why the beast had escaped the way it had, but in his opinion, there was one undisputable fact: the Saberonis was free.

8

Cokely and Ramirez abandoned the ATVs and the fivesome climbed the chain-link fence and left the Evolve Enterprises property behind. Shadows writhed under the Douglas-firs, the ground hardpacked dirt covered in tan pine needles. Pinecones dotted the forest litter carpet like cracked Easter eggs, but there were no discernable tracks. No drips of blood. No sign of the Saberonis at all. Even its musky scent was gone.

The team searched the area in a grid pattern going out as far as a mile in every direction, and they found nothing of note.

"Let's head back," Mercer said.

Cokely and Rameriz took the ATVs, and due to the dense underbrush, they rode along the fence line. When it was just Jinx, Alex, and Mercer trekking through the forest, Alex asked, "What are you gonna do now? Stand down to these people... the specialists Thorpe is bringing in?"

Mercer had been wrestling with that question since the moment Thorpe told him about his plans. Thing was, there really was no decision to make. Twerp owned his ass. So what the boss wanted, the boss got.

Twenty minutes later Mercer was helping Alex put the ATVs on his trailer when Twerp appeared on the loading dock.

"Chad, may I have a word?" Thorpe said.

The lava rock in Mercer's stomach doubled in size because Twerp never used his nice voice unless he was about to deliver a thick shit sandwich. Mercer didn't respond, but simply got off the ATV and started for the loading dock.

Alex whispered, "I'll stay at the ready."

A delivery truck was unloading compressed gases, and Mercer waved to the driver as he climbed the steps to the loading dock.

"I saw the body cam footage," said Thorpe. "Another rough outing."

Mercer knew the man was just trying to stoke his frustration because the body cameras, regardless of the video's quality, couldn't do a great job in the dark with flashlights creating deep shadows and white blind spots. Still, he was sure Jinx had already given a report, and probably Cokely and Rameriz as well, so there was no sense fighting the inevitable. "Yep. It gave us the slip. I guess your creation passed its test and the company was successful, at least with this product."

Thorpe's eyes widened for half a heartbeat like a flaring flame, and then he smiled much like a snake might. "Come with me. I want to tell you something and I don't want you to hear it from anybody else."

So there it was. The rotten sandwich.

The pair pushed through two large swinging doors and walked down a long hallway with no doors. At its end, the pair got on an elevator that took them to the second floor and the hallowed executive wing.

"Are you in need of refreshment?" Thorpe asked.

"Coffee'd be nice."

Twerp nodded, and when the bell sounded announcing they'd arrived on the second floor, Mercer said, "I need to hit the head."

"Of course," Thorpe said, but the man looked like he'd just eaten moldy cheese. "Meet me in the conference room."

Mercer nodded.

The executive bathroom was like entering another country. The facilities on the lower level were pedestrian, but Twerp's throne room put the Ritz Carlton facilities to shame. The hand wipes were thicker than Mercer's bath towels, and every surface shined, the scent of cleaning fluids thick in the air.

As Mercer relieved himself, he checked in with Alex.

"Everything alright?" Alex asked.

"I guess. Listen, I need a favor."

"Another one?"

"Point taken," said Mercer. "We can discuss

how much I owe you at a later date, but right now I need you to call your local contacts. Reingratiate yourself at the local watering holes —a major inconvenience for you, I know. Call your pals still in the Sheriff's Office. I need to know about… any unusual calls or sightings in or around Occidental. That's the only way I'm going to get a handle on this now."

"I can do that."

Mercer killed the call without saying goodbye because a suit entered the bathroom. He finished up, washed his hands, and tiptoed to the conference room.

The first thing that hit him upon entering the palatial space was the intense scent of fresh coffee, and it made his stomach rumble.

Thorpe was seated at the far end of a long table, and as if he'd heard Mercer's stomach complaining, he said, "I also took the liberty of retrieving some leftover donuts from yesterday. Sit."

Mercer strolled by the fancy leather chairs, his gaze straying to the photographs on the walls that depicted Evolve Enterprises employees performing various tasks in labs and offices, each poster highlighted with a motivational phrase.

"Milk? Sugar?" asked Twerp.

"Black is fine." Mercer snatched a chocolate glazed donut and killed half of it with one bite as he sat.

There were no paper cups here, and Thorpe

poured coffee from a fancy urn into a bone-colored Chia cup and handed it to Mercer.

"Thank you," Mercer said as he finished the donut with a second huge bite and took a pull of coffee. He brushed crumbs off his shirt as he grabbed a second belly-buster, this time a sugarcoated jelly donut.

"I've made a decision," Twerp said.

Please say you're calling the cops. Mercer bit into his second donut.

"I consulted select board members and Tippi Flaridy offered her father's company's services."

Mercer struggled to keep his expression steady. Rumor was the boss was involved with Ms. Flaridy, which seemed hard to believe because she was... aesthetically challenged. But then he reminded himself how money could enhance someone's physical appearance.

"As I know you're aware, her father owns Excalibur Security Services and I can count on them to keep things on the QT," Twerp said.

Mercer stayed silent, anger building in him like a storm.

"I can tell you're upset. Don't be. I've given specific instructions. ESS will pick up the trail where you left off, but their focus will be turning over every rock on our grounds."

Mercer wanted to tell the man that he'd already basically done that and that Alex was one of the best trackers in Northern California, but he said nothing.

"I have a more important job for you," Thorpe said.

The rock in Mercer's stomach turned to ice like the cooling of molten steel.

"You have all the local contacts, and you know the terrain intimately. The communities around our site are your backyard," Twerp said.

Mercer licked his lips, finished his jelly donut, and considered having a third donut, but decided against it because he knew he'd already done enough damage.

"My thinking is the ESS people can track the specimen from the inside out, and you can hunt the beast from the outside in. Does that make sense?"

It did. Mercer didn't want to admit it, but he nodded. The entire affair was going off the rails at breakneck speed, and there was no way he was stepping in front of the train.

"Great." The boss stood.

Realizing he was being dismissed, Mercer got to his feet as he downed the last of his coffee.

"Go get some rest," said Twerp. "The ESS people will be here at 1 PM and I want you there. Everyone is forming up on the loading dock."

Mercer eyed the donuts but kept his pie hole shut and his hands in his pockets.

"Don't disappoint me, Mercer," Twerp said. "You're a valuable employee, and replacing you would be a hassle I'd rather not deal with. *Comprende?*"

Mercer nodded and left the room.

It was Wednesday, which meant Jenni would be working a double at the clinic, but he checked in with her anyway. The conversation was difficult because he couldn't tell her anything more than there'd been a classified emergency in one of the labs and he needed to see the problem through to completion. When she asked when he would be home, he promised her that he'd be home that night, though he didn't know if he'd be able to keep that promise.

Mercer ate, caught a catnap, and by 12:45 PM he was standing on the loading dock with Twerp, Jinx, and a cadre of her people. The guards were locked, loaded, and fully decked out in bulletproof vests and woodland camouflage fatigues.

The ESS vehicles pulled into the enclosed parking area before the loading dock at 12:58 PM, led by a black Tahoe with fully tinted windows. The black guard transport vehicle looked like a cross between a bus and a tank. As the hired stormtroopers in full battle gear and helmets, their faces hidden behind shields, poured out of the truck, Mercer couldn't help but think of sales meetings and marketing brochures. It was an impressive display of force and organization. The hired guns formed up like they were preparing for an inspection, and when the small paramilitary force was standing like statues, a man exited the Tahoe.

The guy wasn't what Mercer had expected. He wore a dark suit with a light blue tie, and he moved with the ease of a man who had never struggled for anything. He wiped his brow with a handkerchief like the heat was oppressive—it was a humid seventy degrees, hardly hot. The man walked a line before his men, eyeballing them like they were steaks, and he was looking for the choicest cut. "At ease," he screeched. It sounded like a bird getting a rectal exam.

With practiced ease, the stormtroopers spread their legs and shifted their assault rifles, holding their barrels in their right hands with the butt touching the concrete and the muzzle pointed forward, their left hands behind their backs.

The leader noticed his audience and transformed from a poser military leader to a salesman. "Mr. Thorpe?"

"Yes." Twerp trundled across the loading dock and down the steps to meet the man, Mercer and Jinx in tow.

"Tyson Grey," said the suit as he held out a hand.

The men shook.

Mercer's stomach went sour.

"I've read all the briefing materials, so unless there are any questions, the creature already has a head start," Grey said.

"Let me introduce you to my team," Thorpe said.

Introductions were made all around, and Grey introduced the leader of his ground force, Cherline "Cheri" Glanville. "The goal is to work together and share all information and together we'll get this thing," Grey said. "We're here to support your existing efforts in any way we can, and hopefully we can explore some new avenues. The terrain is..."

Mercer tuned the guy's canned speech out. Despite the salesmanship, and the nick to his ego, the ESS force looked more than competent, and he needed the help. Badly. So what if they got the credit for killing the creature? For starters, he'd be off the hook, at least for the moment. Mercer hadn't had an opportunity to consider the future, but he figured a job search was coming regardless of how things went down with the Saberonis. He didn't think he could live with the day-to-day stress of Twerp having something on him. But that was for another day.

When Grey was done with his pep talk, Mercer asked, "Who do I call if I find something?" He knew that question stretched the boundaries of reasonableness, but he felt it needed to be asked. Firemen and cops got into fights on the street all the time about who was in charge of a fire-related emergency.

Grey looked at Thorpe, who said, "Call me first, Chad."

Twerp and Grey shared a knowing glance. Mercer might be calling Thorpe, but seconds later he'd call Grey, who would be making the decisions. Shoot, the mercenary would probably be listening in as Mercer reported to the boss, but still, the answer was better than he'd expected.

"O.K., then. Unless there are more questions, let's get to it," Grey said.

The meeting broke up, and Twerp and Grey disappeared into the building as Jinx and her people joined the ESS folks. Assignments were given, and goals and schedules were set.

Mercer watched from the loading dock. He felt like he'd been pulled from the game—a game he'd never asked to play. But now that he was on the sidelines, he felt his value plummeting, and when he became worthless... His phone vibrated.

It was Alex.

9

"**E**xcuse me?"

"Alex, I'll call you right back." Mercer swiped at his phone like a senior citizen and looked up to find Grey's number one standing before him.

Cheri was dressed in woodland camo and black combat boots, and an AR-15 hung from her shoulder. Her face shield was up, and strands of red hair fought to escape her helmet, her eyes so blue Mercer wondered if they were contacts. Freckles dotted her sunburned cheeks, and a thin scar ran up the right side of her face. She was a knot of controlled energy, and she tapped her finger on her rifle's trigger guard as she shifted on her feet. Even with all that, she still looked beautiful, and he felt a twinge of attraction.

"New information?" she said as she thrust out her chin indicating Mercer's phone.

He held up his cell like he'd been caught watching porn in church, and said, "Is there something you need?"

Cheri frowned. "We're supposed to work together."

Mercer smiled.

"Can I have your cell number in case I need you?" the squad leader asked.

"I think it's best if you go through the command center," Mercer said. "That way everyone knows what everyone else is doing, the coordination will be better, and nothing will slip through the cracks."

"If that's how you want it," she said. "Are you coming with us?"

"No," Mercer said a little too fast. How much should he tell this woman—easy question, nothing.

"Mercer, I know how you feel."

"You do? Why don't you tell me?"

"I will," she said. "You're pissed and insulted that the boss brought in outsiders, and you still can't understand how the creature escaped, who helped it, and why? You're on your third strike, and—"

"Got it. Thanks."

"All I want is the specimen dead, Mercer," she said. "It doesn't matter who gets it. We get paid either way, but you... Are you sure you don't want to join us? There's always room for another good shot, though, you did miss the thing a few times already."

Mercer bit his lip and said nothing, his anger building, but he wouldn't allow himself to be sucked in.

"Can we at least exchange contact information

so I can tell my boss we spoke?" Cheri asked.

Mercer gave the woman his cell number and she shared her number.

"See you around then," Cheri said. She skipped the steps and instead jumped from the loading dock to the parking area. "Let's go!" she screamed as she broke into a jog, all the hunters falling in behind her like eager ducklings.

Mercer called Alex back, his neck aching and his stomach churning as conflicting questions clogged his mind. Questions he didn't want to think about for too long for fear of their answers.

"You're the luckiest son' bitch I know," Alex said.

"That's debatable," Mercer said. "What's up?"

"I made a few calls, but the one that struck gold was my old pal Rita who sits dispatch on weekdays. She just called and told me about a deputy responding to a call at a house just east of the Evolve property. Something about a dog being mauled."

"On my way."

Mercer met Alex at his house, and they took his pickup and left behind the Evolve Enterprises car with its wave logo on its side. Mercer carried his Sig Sauer, and it wouldn't leave his person until the specimen was caught or killed. Alex had a rifle in the pickup's rear window gun rack, and he had his old revolver.

"Do you know the people who live at the

address?" Mercer asked.

"No, but Rita filled me in," Alex said. "The house is owned by Mr. and Mrs. Iverson, though Mr. Iversen passed on recently. COVID. Mrs. Iversen lives there alone now. She called complaining about her missing dog at 2:14 PM. Then she wandered out back of her house, found the remains of an animal, and called again at 2:27 PM."

The road wound around several sharp turns as it ran through a thick forest of scrub pine, an occasional redwood peeking through the thick canopy. Traffic was light, and the few people who lived in the area were at work or already back from morning errands. There were no houses visible, but an occasional mailbox appeared along the edge of the road indicating a driveway or business.

Alex brought the pickup to a stop next to a mailbox labeled 321 – Iverson. He made a right and crept along the dirt driveway, rocks and twigs crackling and popping beneath the tires.

The pair arrived at the Iverson house and found a dented white Honda parked out front. Behind it, there was a white Ford Explorer with "Sonoma County Sheriff" written in bold green letters and a gold badge insignia on its side.

A huge woman wearing a tent-like blue muumuu who Mercer assumed was Mrs. Iverson pushed out the house's front door and stood on her porch, hands on hips, flaps of fat hanging from her arms, an old rifle slung over her shoulder.

Alex and Mercer exchanged a glance, and Alex grabbed the rifle as both men checked their weapons before getting out of the truck.

"Who are you all? Whatever you be selling, I ain't buying," the woman said.

Alex made sure his revolver could be seen as he flashed his retired star. "My name is Alex Brantley, and this here is Chad. We came to help look for your dog."

Mrs. Iverson smiled, and the expression made her liver-spot-speckled face look even older.

"What's your dog's name?" Mercer asked.

"Her name is Peaches."

"Did you hear anything before you noticed Peaches was gone?" asked Alex.

"Sure did," the woman said. "A loud screech followed by a yelp."

"What type of dog is Peaches?" Mercer asked.

"A mutt. White and black."

"Did you get a glimpse of what took her?" said Alex.

She shook her head no.

"Did you look for Peaches?" Mercer pushed.

She let the rifle drop from her shoulder into her waiting hands. "Sure did. I went out back and found—" She sniffled, and a tear slid down her cheek. "Thing is, I'm not sure what I found. A mess—that's what I found. And a blood trail that leads into the forest."

The wind stirred the vegetation, the rattle of pine needles drowning out the sound of arguing birds.

"I started to follow the trail but the lady at the Sheriff's Office said not to. She said to go back to the house and lock the door. Which is what I did."

"Where is the deputy that responded to your call?" Mercer asked.

"He's out back. Told me to stay put."

"How long has he been gone?" Alex asked.

"'Bout fifteen minutes, but I ain't no Timex."

"Stay put," Mercer said.

The woman frowned and it looked as though her face was melting. She turned without a word and went back inside.

Mercer and Alex worked their way around the side of the house where they found a cracked concrete pathway that led to an open gate. Tall weeds swayed in the gentle breeze, and sunlight angled through the tree canopy like a dying flame.

A natural stone patio gave way to what appeared to have once been a lawn that ended at the edge of a thick forest, but the manicured grass was long gone. Tall weeds lined the edges of the backyard, and a large square had been mowed at its center. The area reeked of dog shit and piles big and small, hard and soft, dotted the ground.

The duo traversed the crap minefield and found a pile of bloody viscera, a hairy black and white leg, and a black ear. Mercer covered his nose as the scent of waste fled and the coppery scent of blood filled his nostrils.

A blood trail ran into the forest, clumps of fat, gristle, and shreds of what looked like intestines mixed within.

"Head on a swivel," Alex said as he put the rifle's stock to his shoulder and eased into the cool confines of the woods. Tall evergreens blocked out the sun, and the chatter of the birds fell still.

The blood trail was easily followed, the crimson puddles and drips easy to see atop the bronze pine needles.

"A bloody footprint," said Mercer as he pointed.

"The Deputy," Alex said.

"Should we call out for him?" Mercer asked.

Alex laid a finger over his lips and whispered, "No. We have no idea what he's dealing with. He could be hiding from the creature. He or she could have the thing in their sights. Who knows?"

Exactly, but Mercer figured his buddy was right.

The sound of rustling leaves and snapping branches carried through the forest, and Alex and Mercer followed the noise.

Alex was on point, Mercer right on his heels, Sig Sauer at the ready, a bullet in the firing chamber. Thin deer paths crisscrossed the woods and drifts of needles marked their edges. Gray lichen hung from many of the lower branches, and the tree canopy was thick, the undergrowth sparse.

A shrill cackle bark echoed through the woods, and the pair came to a sudden stop.

"That sounded close," Mercer said. Too close. He looked back over his shoulder, and he couldn't see the house. A cold sweat leaked from his pores, his heart galloping. The Saberonis was near. He could feel it, like a dark cloud or a bone-chilling cold. A sense of menace consumed him, and for the first time, he considered quitting the hunt. Quitting it all.

What the hell was he doing out here? What did he have to gain? He was no monster hunter, and why the hell did he even care? He could leave Evolve, and he and Jenni could move and start fresh. But even as the fantasy took shape in his mind, he knew that it was nothing more than that. A fantasy. Jenni had finally found a job she liked, and she would demand reasons. Questions would have to be answered, and if she ever discovered what he'd done, it would be the end of them, and probably the end of him.

"You in there?" asked Alex.

"Yeah, sorry."

The blood trail had grown thin, and there had been no further sounds worth tracking.

"Do you think it took the dog somewhere to eat it? You know, how cats do?" Mercer asked to make conversation.

"That's what I figure," Alex said. "Not uncommon. I assume the specimen eats in... a normal way?"

Mercer harrumphed. "It's always been given a special balanced diet. I know raw meat was used as a reward, but to the best of my knowledge, Peaches is the creature's first kill. If the dog is dead, which seems likely."

A crow shrieked and Mercer jumped.

The forest was thinning along with the blood trail and Mercer was beginning to despair when his phone vibrated. "It's Jinx," he said.

"Answer it. Quietly. She might have news."

"What's up?" Mercer said as he answered the call.

"What's not? Where you at?" she asked.

"Did you call for a reason? I'm kinda busy."

"I wanted to keep you abreast of our progress, of which there's been little," Jinx said.

"What's the little?"

"We confirmed what we already knew," Jinx said. "The specimen has broken containment and is no longer on the Evolve grounds."

"No shit? Did they find its trail?"

"No."

Mercer waited, his frustration growing.

"I also wanted to update you on Declan," she said.

The anger drained from Mercer like his heart's plug had been pulled.

"He's going to make it, but he'll be in the hospital for weeks and his full recovery will take a couple of months," said Jinx.

Some of the guilt that had been eating at Mercer faded. His friend was going to live. He wouldn't have to go to Declan's funeral and face his family. A great weight lifted from Mercer. "Thanks. Anything else?"

"Do you need help?" she asked.

Mercer was getting the feeling he was being pumped for information. A surge of anger piped through him, but he stayed polite and professional. "I'll call you if I need you." He hit 'end call' and said, "No progress back at Evolve."

"Not a surprise," Alex said.

"Bunch of jackrabbits with guns," Mercer said.

"That's a bit of a stretch, no? You better reign it in or you'll get yourself in hot water."

Mercer shook his head. At that moment he didn't care about the price of his insolence, but at the same time he knew he was running out of chips, and soon he'd bust.

10

The worms of unease were beginning to wriggle in Mercer's stomach when the deputy appeared in the forest ahead. Mercer's first instinct was to call out, but he kept his lips pasted shut. Standing still as stone, the deputy waited within a thick tangle of thorny branches with tiny green leaves. No birds sang, and a gentle whisper of wind barely stirred the pine needles that blanketed the ground. The forest had grown sparse, the Douglas-fir trunks thicker and taller.

"What's he doing?" Mercer whispered.

"I don't know," Alex said. "Use the binoculars."

The deputy was only a hundred feet away, but there was a knot of branches clogging the line of sight. Mercer retrieved the binoculars from a pouch on his belt and pressed them to his eyes.

It took a few moments for him to focus the field glasses and pick his line of sight through the greenery, but when he did, he saw that the man had his back to him, and he still hadn't moved. Mercer stared as he counted in his head.

When a thirty count had slipped away, Alex

said, "What's going on? What do you see?"

"Nothing. He's just standing there like a statue."

"Let's go find out what's up." Alex surged forward, following the blood trail.

Mercer stowed his binoculars and checked his Sig Sauer as he followed.

Using the thick tree trunks as cover, the pair slipped through the forest, skipping over roots and easing around stubborn pricker bushes that had somehow taken root in the hardpacked dirt. Sunlight cut through the canopy far above and cast errant spotlights on the forest floor, illuminating ants, beetles, and a garter snake.

The deputy was deep within a patch of undergrowth. He'd followed the trail of blood, broken branches, and crushed vegetation. Mercer and Alex stopped when they reached the edge of the thicket, the deputy twenty feet away.

"Hey. Hey," Alex whispered. "Psst."

The deputy made no sign he'd heard the calls.

"Deputy. Deputy." Mercer raised his voice as loud as he dared and still the lawman didn't acknowledge the pair's presence.

Alex rolled his eyes and began picking his way through the brush, following the trailblazed path.

The deputy was stooped like he had an intense backache, and he was still facing away from the pair, his right hand holding his service weapon pointed at the ground, the trail of blood running through his legs. His left arm was bent upward, as if his hand had been on its way to his mouth but never made it there.

Mercer's breath caught as he rounded the man and saw his face.

The deputy's nametag read Webster, and his face was frozen in a rictus of terror, his eyes wide, his mouth hanging open. Salt and pepper eyebrows blended into the lawman's closely cropped hair, and though he was clean-shaven, a five O'clock shadow covered his chin. His hat was missing, and his tan uniform shirt was torn, the replica of his star embroidered above the left pocket smudged with dirt. A comm handset hung from his right breast pocket, a black wire trailing down to his radio.

"Deputy Webster?" said Mercer.

The guy stared into the distance as if frozen in time.

Mercer followed Webster's gaze.

The Saberonis crouched thirty feet away at the edge of the thicket, its piercing yellow cat eyes staring into the dense vegetation. As the specimen moved its skin shimmered and shifted, nothing more than a smudge on the air as the beast blended into the brown and emerald.

This time there was no hesitation. No delay. Mercer raised the Sig Sauer and fired. And he kept firing as he eased through the thicket, thin branches with thorns ripping at his clothes and exposed skin, the scent of burnt sulfur thick in the air. Bullets tore through the vegetation, cutting off branches and knifing through leaves.

The Sig Sauer clicked empty, and Mercer got low as he reloaded, the sound of metal sliding on metal echoing through the forest as he jacked a bullet into the firing chamber. He popped up and aimed, but the Saberonis was gone. He held the gun out straight in a singlehanded grip as he fumbled for the binoculars, but he stopped when a gravelly roar carried through the forest.

"I can't see it," Alex said. "We need better cover."

Though Alex had said wild animals rarely backtracked, Mercer guessed based on what they'd seen that no longer applied to the Saberonis.

As the pair fought their way back through the thicket to Webster the scent of urine filled the air. Mercer glanced over his shoulder every two seconds expecting to find scimitar fangs searching for meat, but there was nothing but the wind and rattling leaves.

Webster's tan shirt had sweat stains beneath the armpits, and Mercer noticed a damp spot on the crotch of his Army-green uniform pants— he'd pissed himself. He was still standing frozen, his gaze locked on where the beast had been as if the Saberonis was a distant relative of Medusa.

Mercer arrived to find the deputy trembling.

"We need an ambulance," Alex said.

"No," murmured the deputy as if from far

away. "I'm O.K."

"I don't think you're—"

"Please!" Webster squeaked. "I'll never live this down. And I'll probably be fired."

Mercer nodded. This was good for Evolve because if Webster insisted on an ambulance or backup, the cat would be out of the bag.

"What did you see, deputy?" Alex pressed.

Webster's face twisted, "It was... horrible. A ghost, but not a ghost. A nightmare. It had what was left of Mrs. Iverson's dog hanging from its jaws."

"Did it attack you?" Alex asked.

"No. It toyed with me."

Mercer and Alex exchanged a glance and Mercer rolled his eyes. "Toyed with you?"

"It looked into me. Does that make sense? Like it was sizing me up and it decided I wasn't worth the time."

Mercer did know what the man had felt. He'd had the same feeling. Like you were outmatched, like riding a bicycle in a race against a Ferrari. He needed to get this bike back on the road and settle things down, or he'd lose control of the situation and wipe out. "When was the last time you checked in with dispatch?"

Webster's tall forehead wrinkled as he bit his lip.

"Your radio!" Alex yelled.

Mercer jumped and Webster jumped higher.

"The Sabero—animal knows where we are. We

can't stand around bullshitting," Alex said.

Mercer nodded.

"Webster, call in and tell dispatch you're still investigating but you're alright," Alex said.

The deputy stared at Alex like he hadn't heard him.

Alex pulled the radio handset from Webster's chest and said, "Report back. Now."

Webster did just that, and with the cavalry held at bay, the pair convinced the deputy to sit down and gather himself while Mercer and Alex tracked the Saberonis.

"Don't move," Mercer said. "We'll be right back."

Webster had returned to Lala Land and he stared up at Mercer like he'd never seen him before.

The birds had resumed their serenade, and the thumping of Mercer's heart had eased when his phone vibrated. "It's Cheri." He hit accept call.

"Mercer?"

"In the flesh."

"How are you making out?" Cheri asked.

"I'm not. What's up? Where are you?"

"I think we found the specimen's trail. We're roughly four miles southeast of Evolve."

Mercer covered the phone with his hand and whispered, "The ESS crew is just west of us." Then into the phone, "That's a 10-4. Keep me up-to-date."

"What are you doing?" Cheri asked. All

politeness had drained from her tone.

"Talk later." He killed the connection.

"What happens when they find the silent man back there?" Alex asked.

Mercer hiked his shoulders. "Ask me if I care."

After half a mile of trekking through sparse evergreen woods, the partners were forced to change direction when they reached a jagged cliff face where the land had cleaved. Climbing wasn't an option, though the rock wall was only twenty-five feet tall. Many hollows likely hid a plethora of insects, snakes, and birds, all waiting to poke, pinch, and bite anyone who disturbed their domain. Plus, much of the stone was covered in slippery moss. The mountains rose in the distance on the eastern horizon, and it occurred to Mercer that the cliff face was the first of many natural obstacles that awaited him if he continued on his current course.

"Which way should we go?" Mercer asked.

Alex scanned the forest floor and then panned his head from north to south as he examined the thick strip of vegetation that separated the woods from the cliff face. He sighed and said, "I don't know."

Mercer slowly turned in a full circle and pressed his back against the cliffside, facing the forest. Could the beast be watching them even now? He said, "Do you think we passed right by the specimen in the forest?"

"That's a distinct possibility," Alex said. "I

don't know about you, but I wasn't looking up. The thing is bound to figure out its part cat at some point and start climbing. It's got genes from the sabertoothed cat family. And when it starts to realize its potential…"

The heat of indecision spread through Mercer, and he was about to say that they should head back to the deputy when there was movement to the south along the tree line.

Alex put his rifle's stock to his shoulder, fired, and grunted. With the ring of the shot still hanging in the air, he said, "I couldn't get a bead on the thing. But it's not far. Are we going on or heading back?"

"I need this over," Mercer said as he surged into motion, threading his way along the thin gap between the forest and the overgrowth at the base of the cliff face.

When the pair reached the spot where they'd seen the Saberonis, the beast's tracks were easy to see. It left a trail of broken branches and stomped vegetation behind, and Mercer thought he heard the beast growling, but then realized it was his stomach.

The height of the cliff face diminished as the ground angled upward. Thick brown telephone pole-like tree trunks created a wall to the right, and bird's nests and snake holes filled the stone wall to his left, the undergrowth falling away as the gap between the forest and the disappearing cliff face narrowed to nothing.

When the escarpment was nothing more than a six-foot high cut in the land, Mercer climbed on a rock and peered east.

An abandoned farm stretched out before him on a twenty-acre plot notched like a giant step into the side of the mountain. Fields overgrown with weeds and unkempt shrubbery surrounded a house that Mercer was surprised was still standing. The dwelling was bleached white, whatever color it had been lost to time. All the windows were broken, and graffiti marred the cracked and broken shingles.

An old barn, half caved in, sat beside the house, and the structures were surrounded by the remnants of a wooden fence. Beyond the fence and forlorn fields, the forest of evergreens boxed in the property.

The place looked like nobody had cared about it for a long time.

Alex climbed onto the boulder, stood next to Mercer, and said, "I've never been up here. I didn't even know this place was here."

A hawk screeched and a shadow fell over the notch in the land.

Mercer looked back into the woods, expecting to see two orbs of yellow light sizing him up, but there were no eyes, and nothing moved.

"That's something," Alex said.

When Mercer turned his attention back to the old farm Alex was pointing.

To the north, the tall weeds blanketing what

had once been growing fields were bent and broken as if something huge had pushed through them.

"Looks like a trail," Mercer said. His palms itched as he glanced over his shoulder, his thoughts going to the deputy.

"He's fine," Alex said, reading his mind. Then, sensing his friend was still vacillating, added, "This might be our last chance at the thing. At least without a lot of company."

Mercer worked his way to where the rift in the land ended, and the companions were able to easily step up onto the plateau that contained the abandoned homestead.

From their new elevation, the pair saw the roof of Mrs. Iverson's house, though the old woman and the deputy couldn't be seen.

Tall weeds whispered and sighed as a gentle breeze stirred the vegetation. A sharp clicking noise Mercer had come to associate with the beast carried over the field. The duo reached the section of flattened weeds and dropped into a crouch, both men trying to see into the dense morass of green.

Shadows danced and writhed beneath the weeds, and clouds of gnats, flies, and mosquitoes filled the air. A gray mini-vampire with black stripes alighted on Mercer's arm, its proboscis piercing his flesh. He slapped the creature flat, a thin spattering of his blood spraying his forearm.

When Mercer looked up the yellow eyes of the Saberonis were staring back at him.

11

The specimen came at the duo through the ten-foot weeds, crackling vegetation, and snapping stalks marking the beast's passage. Mercer planted his feet and aimed his weapon, but the creature was a blur, and the greenery was thick.

Alex tugged on Mercer's elbow as he backpedaled to the forest and the safety of the Douglas-firs. The rifle was slung over his shoulder, and he fired his revolver randomly into the weeds, the crack and pop of the shots ringing over the field, and for two heartbeats the day symphony went still.

Mercer followed, the chaos of birds arguing and insects singing like sawblades slowly building. When the two men were behind tree trunks, their weapons at the ready, Mercer listened hard, eliminating the forest chorus, the push of the wind, and the tinkle of pine needles. The field ahead was as silent as it ever would be.

A crow cawed, the sound crawling up Mercer's spine and settling in his neck. Webster was sure to draw attention soon if he hadn't already.

Whether it was the ESS crew, dispatch not receiving an update, or a fellow lawman coming to check on the deputy, their time as the lead hunters was almost up. When that happened, Twerp wouldn't need him anymore, or he would find a worse task for Mercer to perform. Or he might do nothing, and somehow that seemed like the most painful option, letting him marinate in his shame and worry.

Mercer scanned the overgrown field ahead with the field glasses, and nothing moved except swaying weeds and the occasional flutter of a bird.

A screech, like the largest chicken ever born was being throttled, carried over the field.

"Sounds like it moved off," Alex said.

Mercer and his friend stared at one another. It was gut-check time... again. How far was Mercer willing to take this? He didn't want his life blown up, but he also didn't want to be dead.

Alex reloaded the rifle and put fresh cartridges in his handgun. "I'm game if you are. Two rules, though, and both are nonnegotiable."

Mercer said nothing. He could feel time slipping away along with the beast and his comfortable life, and questions or protests would only slow the process.

"When I say we're done, we're done." Alex locked eyes with Mercer who returned his stare. "I yell retreat, and you retreat. Regardless of the situation, where I am, what I'm doing. Got it?"

"I'm not sure about that, Alex. I think may—"

"Don't think. I'm an old man. You're a young man."

Mercer grew cold.

"Don't look all doughy-eyed," Alex said. "Nobody's throwing their life away. Do you agree?"

Mercer nodded almost imperceptibly like he was making a promise with his fingers crossed.

"Second, call in the cavalry. Now." Alex let that one hang in the air like a fart on a crowded bus.

"O.K.," Mercer said. He saw the logic in it and had been considering making the call since he'd found the deputy. At best the ESS crew was a half-an-hour away, and if he didn't get the beast by then, at least his ass would be covered and the boss couldn't say he wasn't being a team player, whatever the hell that meant these days.

Mercer called Cheri, relayed his coordinates, and gave her the homestead as a marker.

"We're twenty minutes out," Cheri said. "Should I call in air support?"

Mercer looked at Alex who lifted his eyebrows. Air support? Mercer must have been tuned out during that portion of Gray's speech. "Say again?"

"I can call in the chopper. They've got big guns. Heat-seeking missiles, thermal cameras, all the new stuff."

Aside from the attention it would draw, Mercer couldn't see the downside. And who would pay attention to an abandoned house burning down in the middle of nowhere? Mrs. Iverson wouldn't care when he explained they brought in the firepower to kill the animal that murdered her beloved Peaches. Anyone else who saw the copter would most likely ignore it, and with the Sheriff's Department stretched thin he thought the chance of interference from them was minimal. Plus, the ESS pilot was sure to be an ace if what he'd seen of the unit so far held true.

Mercer said, "Call them in and give them the same information I gave you. Just make sure they know we're down here. Don't blow anything up until I give the O.K."

"That's a 10-4. ESS out."

Mercer's heart hammered, and he thought perhaps he and Alex should just wait it out. But something told him if they did that the beast would slip away, and there would be nothing for those thermal cameras to see and nothing for the heat-seeking missiles to hit.

"Lead on," Mercer said.

Alex darted through the vegetation that separated the forest from the overgrown field. He hit the opening in the weeds at a run, rifle over his shoulder, Smith & Wesson out before him sweeping back and forth.

Weeds whipped Mercer's face, his feet getting caught up on roots and dead plants as he ran down the path the specimen had trailblazed.

The overgrown field gave way to a hardpacked

tracker trail. Alex and Mercer spilled onto it, both men tripping in the knot of grass that ran down the center of the utility road. To the south, the house filled the mouth of the trail, to the north it ended in a wall of evergreen trunks.

Alex crouched and examined the hardpacked ground, which looked recently scuffed. Slashes from the beast's claws along with the oval-shaped pockmarks from its foot pads could be seen in the dirt. The ground was hard and parched, and Mercer wondered at the amount of weight needed to make the impressions.

The pair followed the tracks, the blood trail only an occasional drip now. Alex was on the right side of the path and Mercer on the left, a strip of vegetation between them. Weeds swayed and whispered, and the sun glared down, the humidity now a thick soup that soaked Mercer's shirt through. Perspiration dripped into his eyes, and his leg muscles protested under the strain of dehydration. Mercer wasn't in bad shape, but he certainly wasn't in good shape, and he hadn't worked out in ages.

The distant *womp womp* of airfoils pounding the air echoed over the field.

Mercer's phone vibrated, but he didn't answer it. The trail came to an end and the pair paused at the edge of what appeared to have once been a lawn.

The yard surrounding the farmhouse had been overtaken by nature, the fence nothing but an occasional freestanding section of split-rail and forlorn posts. Weeds and wild grasses encroached upon the foundation, and a rusted water pump stood nearby, its handle frozen. Next to the house a dilapidated barn leaned heavily to one side, and a rusted swing set with no swings stood forlorn in the overgrowth. A deep melancholy washed over Mercer. At one time children had played in this yard, and he heard their spectral laughter and thought of Jenni.

The house was covered in faded asbestos shingles, which were a mottled patchwork of pale, chalky hues, with some areas bleached white by the relentless sun, while others retained the darker, almost ghostly shades of their former color. Like old skin, the shingles clung to the house, some curling at the edges where the material had grown brittle, revealing small gaps where the elements had breached the once-solid defenses. Moss and lichen grew in the crevices, adding a muted green to the palette of decay.

Thick vines climbed to gutters clogged with debris, and many of the downspouts were rusted and had broken away from the structure. All the windows were smashed, and shards of glass jutted from their rotted frames like broken teeth. Curtains, long since faded and frayed, blew gently in the breeze. The roof had several holes and was missing many shingles, leaving exposed patches that revealed weathered and decayed wood.

A trail of crushed overgrowth led to the house's porch, and the front door creaked as it swung in the breeze. The thumping of the approaching helicopter grew louder as the partners worked their way toward the house, Mercer's nerves poking at the underside of his skin.

The porch was covered in a layer of silt and dust, and huge cat-like pawprints trailed across the old boards toward the open door. Mercer saw no drops of blood. Tilted precariously to one side, the porch looked like it had been added long after the house was built. Its wooden floorboards creaked and groaned, some of the boards so weakened by rot that they threatened to give way. The posts supporting the roof were similarly compromised, with large sections of paint peeled away, revealing splintered wood beneath. A solitary rocking chair, its woven seat long gone, sat at one end of the porch as if waiting for someone who would never return.

Alex paused on the door's threshold and looked over his shoulder at Mercer, a silent question framed in his expression. That look said this was the point of no return.

The air hummed with the thunderous roar of the approaching helicopter, but the whirlybird still sounded a few minutes out. Minutes that could be the difference between killing the creature or losing its trail entirely.

Alex swept into the house, gun up in a doublehanded grip.

A loud crack reverberated through the room as a floorboard gave way. Alex's right foot disappeared into the hole as he tripped and tumbled to the floor. His gun discharged, and a bullet punched into the ceiling, old plaster raining down on him, white dust filling the air.

Mercer helped his mate up, swinging his gun around as he searched for a target, but if the beast was there, he didn't see it.

Alex dusted himself off as he advanced, his ego more damaged than his body.

A low gurgle carried through the house, and the scraping of claws on wood sent the invisible worry ants scurrying up his spine.

Mercer examined the house's front door, thoughts of locking the creature in the house and retreating flitting through his mind only to be beaten back by the reality of broken windows and a backdoor. But maybe there was another way.

"Wait," Mercer hissed as Alex surged toward the beastly growl.

Alex looked back in frustration, worry, and pain creasing his face.

"What if we patrol the outside of the house? Keep the thing in here until the chopper arrives and blows the house to hell with the Saberonis inside." The plan had several holes, but given he'd just pulled it out of his ass, and it didn't involve him or Alex going toe-to-toe with the creature, he thought it was solid.

Alex's face softened and he nodded slowly.

The partners left the way they'd entered, avoiding the broken floorboard and easing through the open door and down the porch steps. Mercer went right, and Alex left, both men facing the house, the aim of their guns shifting from empty window to empty window.

Mercer went to the corner of the house and peered around back. Nothing moved except the weeds and a weathervane atop the decrepit barn. He made an about-face and marched along the side of the house until he reached the front. There he waved to Alex and then repeated the process. When he was in a comfortable rhythm, Mercer contacted Cheri, who picked up on the first ring.

"Everything O.K.?" she said.

"Hunky-dory," Mercer yelled into the phone. "We've got the target trapped in the abandoned house I told you about."

"Good, but we're still a ways out. I can hear the chopper."

The pounding of airfoils carried over the fields, the air puffing and thudding with vibration.

"It'll be here in a minute," Mercer said. "Can you patch me into the pilot?"

"Affirmative," Cheri said. "Give me a second."

Mercer's phone trilled and vibrated. It was

Twerp. He ignored the call as he continued his patrol.

"Mercer, I've got Winger," Cheri said.

Static filled the line for a second, and then, "Mr. Mercer. Instructions?"

Mercer glanced at the house and then at the dead vegetation surrounding the house. An explosion would surely cause a fire, but still— the pumping station wasn't far, and he could call them in as soon as he got off the phone with the whirlybird pilot. "Do you have my position on your GPS?"

"Yes, sir. We'll be to you in thirty seconds," came Winger's gruff voice over the comm.

"The specimen is inside the house, so blow it to hell," Mercer said.

There was a long pause as if the pilot was getting permission and all Mercer heard was the mechanical whirring of the copter's engine and the pounding of its airfoils. The pilot's voice tore through static, "That's a 10-4. Get clear. I repeat, get clear."

"Copy that." Mercer tore around the corner of the house and found Alex staring at the incoming helicopter.

"Did you call for..." Alex said.

Mercer didn't stop running as he headed for the fields. "They're going to blow it."

The shriek of breaking glass and splintering wood rose over the copter's rotors, and a blur of color burst through one of the windows, shards of glass clinging to the form like diamonds.

A sleek gray body, two burning yellow eyes, and long, curved white fangs framed against railroad spike-sized teeth charged forward at full speed, heading straight for Mercer.

12

Mercer felt a surge of air press into him, and he dropped to the hardpan.

The creature's shifting form sailed over him, its front claws out and searching for flesh, its jaws open in a wicked smile.

As the creature's momentum carried it passed Mercer the beast's tail brushed his chest and the air sizzled. He felt the heat of the beast's breath on his face, smelled the rot of its breath, and drips of saliva splattered his face. He rolled and pressed to his feet, but as he swung the Sig Sauer, he held his fire.

Like a flash of light, the Saberonis bounded across the yard, shifting and zigzagging, before disappearing into the tall weeds to the east.

The growl of the helicopter shook the air as the chopper came in low over the forest, its black fuselage awash in sunlight. Mercer had seen the Army's version of the modified MD 530F, though he'd never been up in one. The one-person chopper was tailored for light attack and reconnaissance missions, and the nose of its reinforced composite fuselage was equipped with advanced avionics. A digital glass display in the cockpit provided the pilot with real-time data, including navigational charts, enemy positions, and weapons systems status.

Alex ran, and when his friend sprinted past him, Mercer took off in pursuit.

The MD 530F was armed to the teeth, with hardpoints on its stubby, side-mounted pylons carrying an array of weapons. Dual M134 miniguns, capable of firing up to six thousand rounds per minute were mounted on either side, and two missiles completed the arsenal—at least what Mercer could see of it. Beneath the helicopter, an infrared camera system worked in tandem with laser designators, enabling the helicopter to mark targets for itself or other aircraft and ground forces.

Alex changed course, heading for a tractor path that ran through the fields.

Mercer's knees threatened to come unhinged. He looked over his shoulder as the chopper swept over the tree line, flattening the overgrown fields with its rotor wash. Mercer put his head down and ran down the right rut of the truck path, tall weeds engulfing him on both sides. It was too late to halt the attack—Mercer's voice would be lost in the chaos, unheard over the bedlam.

Beneath the thunder of the helicopter, Mercer thought he heard sirens, and he remembered he had to call the fire department and report a fire that hadn't started yet.

A sharp whistle, like the biggest balloon ever made was slowly releasing its air, rose above the chaos. There was a brief pause and Mercer blocked out all sound except his racing heart.

An explosion rocked the ground beneath his feet, and Mercer glanced back and saw a giant orange and black fireball. A wave of heat pressed through the fields of dry weeds and some of them caught fire as Mercer was driven forward by the hot blast of air. He managed to stay on his feet, but now the vegetation all around him was ablaze, fire licking at the overgrowth at the center of the utility road as flames tore across the fields.

Smoke clogged the trail, and he no longer saw Alex ahead on the path. Mercer wanted to pull his phone and call for fire support, but as the copter wheeled away, and the roar of the pounding airfoils faded, the shrill sound of emergency sirens rang through the day.

Mercer figured the ESS folks had called the fire department, which was well-equipped because they handled forest fires.

Alex appeared ahead, a wall of flame skittering across the path and blocking his way forward. He spun around, smoke swirling around him, the crackle and pop of fire drowning out the ringing in Mercer's head.

When Alex saw Mercer, he ran toward him.

Mercer searched for an escape route, but all he found were angry flames that spat at him.

Alex arrived, and the two men needed no discussion or debate.

The partners stumbled down the left rut in the tractor path, every step a battle, the searing heat at their backs, the flames licking at their heels. An inferno roared around them, a relentless sea of flames devouring the dry, overgrown fields with terrifying speed. The sky above, which moments before was pale blue, was choked with dark smoke that billowed and swirled like a living entity.

Mercer heard someone shouting over the roar of the fire and the retreating helicopter—it sounded like Webster, but his words were lost in the cacophony of crackling vegetation and the rushing wind that fed the flames. Panic clawed at Mercer's chest, his breaths coming in ragged gasps as he struggled to keep moving, ash and hot embers alighting on his exposed skin and burning tiny holes in his clothes.

Alex surged onward, sweat pouring down his face, as he summoned all his willpower and adrenaline to push aside a patch of stubborn weeds.

Both men knew that stopping, even for a moment, would mean death; the fire was too close, too fierce, and the only path to survival was escaping its reach.

Mercer could hardly see through the thickening haze, his eyes stinging as he coughed and fought for air. He stumbled again, nearly falling, but Alex was there, catching him and pulling him forward. The heat was unbearable, the air scorching Mercer's lungs with every breath, and he felt his strength waning as exhaustion took hold.

The path became uneven, and Mercer felt like he was running through quicksand, every step more difficult than the last.

A jet of fire knifed from the burning weeds and caught Alex like a blast from a flamethrower. He brought up his arms to fight off the flames, but his hair and clothes caught fire. Alex danced around for a few seconds, slapping at his head and clothes in a futile attempt to put out the flames.

The heat of anger and loss filled Mercer as his mind spun back to Elementary School and the assembly he was forced to attend each year for fire safety. "Drop and roll! Drop and roll!" Mercer shouted so loudly his smoke-ravaged throat felt like it was bleeding.

Alex heard his plea, and he dropped to the ground, rolling back and forth in the rut of the tracker path as he tried to put out the flames.

Mercer joined him, patting the fire and using what remained of the man's shirt to smother the flames.

There was more yelling—Webster again, and this time Mercer understood what he was saying. "To me. To me."

It sounded like Webster was to the west, and

as Alex got to his feet, his clothes a charred wreck, something amazing happened. It began to rain.

Except, there wasn't a cloud in the sky other than smoke.

Confusion slowed his reaction time, but Mercer wasn't one to hesitate when opportunity struck. He jerked Alex to his feet, and the duo plunged into the smoking greenery, heading west.

Through the haze, Mercer saw a break in the fire, a smoking stretch of burnt land that was no longer on fire. It was their only chance, so they ran toward the bare patch.

Water sprinkled down from above, and the vegetation sizzled and popped as the fire went out. Mercer smiled when he heard the distinctive sound of sprinklers tapping and spitting water.

Mercer and Alex found Webster hunched over a half-buried sprinkler control box, smoke rising around him like steam, the area damp with water. When the deputy saw them, he surged to his feet and ran to them. "Thank God. I wouldn't have been able to live with myself if…"

"Maybe thank the Water Authority for not shutting down the water," Mercer said.

"It wasn't easy getting the rusted spigot to turn," Webster said, and he raised his dirty hands as evidence. "And I agree, I wasn't expecting it to work, but I didn't know what else to do and I had to do something."

"I'm glad you snaped out of it and are alright," Mercer said. "Let g—"

Alex groaned and collapsed.

As Mercer and Webster tended to him, the fire department arrived with two brush trucks filled with water. With the help of three out of the five sprinkler zones, the flames were quickly brought under control and the fire extinguished.

Webster said, "You can't tell them you left me behind... they'll... You just can't."

"Don't worry on it. You just saved our bacon, and we'll follow your lead," Mercer said. No way he wanted to be the ringleader of the coming circus.

The deputy smiled, pressed to his feet, and strode off to meet the police vehicles that had pulled in behind the fire trucks.

The beast was long gone, and Mercer and Alex watched Webster deal with the locals. Though the story the deputy was telling had a skeleton of truth, Mercer and Alex had agreed to forget Webster's episode if he dealt with his people, which he was doing admirably.

The agreed-upon story was Mercer and Alex accidentally set the fire while running from an unknown beast, and Webster arrived and helped. Though no tracks were found—Mercer said that was because of the fire, and it was assumed that the pair had been chased by a bear. Sure, the story was thin, but Mercer's reasoning held up: no one seemed too concerned about an old house, especially when even the authorities weren't sure who owned it.

Mercer and Alex were sitting in the back of an ambulance when the ESS crew arrived, and things got more complicated.

Cheri and crew burst from the forest, guns up, but when the ESS squad leader saw the controlled chaos, she lowered her weapon and began jogging through the devastation toward the rescue vehicles, her team in tow.

"Where's Jinx?" Mercer asked.

"She headed back to the office. Mr. Thorpe wanted to see her," Cheri said.

There was a brief question and answer period adjudicated by Webster, and Cheri explained how Evolve Enterprises had sent its security force out to aid the locals because Mr. Thorpe had heard about the fire and the involvement of one of his key employees.

Again, this swamp-level bullshit was accepted with few questions. The fire was out, and the weed-laden fields were nothing but blackened smoking ruins, dark smoke swirling in the air. There was no complainant, and Webster had volunteered to write the report.

Mercer had been poked and prodded by the EMTs, and other than some scrapes and cuts, and the ringing in his head, he was given a clean bill of health and he felt O.K.

Alex hadn't been so lucky. His clothes were

charred, and the hair on the back of his head had burned away. A bandage covered the bubbling second-degree burn that would forever scar his head, and despite this, the man was in good spirits, as if he'd cheated death yet again.

Webster was fine, and he was having no trouble singing, talking about how his ankle hurt and he could barely walk because he sprained it while chasing the beast.

Mercer and Alex said nothing.

Webster and his clan were the first to leave, and the fire department left soon after. A fire watch would be maintained for the next twenty-four hours to ensure an elusive ember didn't reignite the blaze, but that only required one person.

Mercer and Alex trekked back to his pickup with the ESS team.

"That's it then," Cheri asked. "I can invite Gray to a Saberonis BBQ on the Evolve back lawn?"

There was no point in gilding the lily, so Mercer said, "It got away."

Cheri stopped walking, and when Mercer kept moseying along, she eased back into motion. "Come again?" she said, her tone filled with derision.

"It got away. Do I stutter?"

"You're sure? I mean…"

"We're sure," Alex said. "We saw it. It almost took a chunk out of both of us. I've never considered myself lucky, but I was today."

Mercer couldn't stop his gaze from straying to the patch of blood at the center of Alex's head bandage. Shame, guilt, frustration, and anger all assaulted his stomach, neck, and lower back. It was his fault his friend had been burned like a firework, and the wounds he'd caused would never truly heal, and it didn't matter that the ex-lawman didn't seem to give a turd.

"What now? Did you see which way it went?" Cheri pushed.

Again, with no reason to lie and several reasons to tell the truth, he said, "The last I saw of the thing it disappeared into the weeds to the east of the house."

"East. Should we check the tree line there?"

That wasn't a horrible idea. The fire department had managed to contain the fire, and other than a few blackened Douglas-fir trunks, the forest had been spared. "Good idea," he said. "Take your crew and check the entire area."

Cheri nodded, and after checking in with Gray she gathered her people and gave orders to bug out.

Seven minutes later Mercer and Alex were alone, the stink of the fire and their failure all that remained.

"Did Webster speak with Mrs. Iverson? Tell her about Peaches?" Alex asked.

"He sent one of his guys to speak with her," Mercer said. The canine's corpse hadn't been found, but given the fire, all the blood, and the ear and leg they'd found, there was no hope.

Mercer's muscles ached, and he was starving. His frustration was reaching its boiling point, and it was barely noon.

13

Mercer dropped Alex off at the health center despite his protests, and when Mercer argued that an infection on Alex's scalp could kill his last brain cell, his friend laughed and relented. The docs were hopeful that he would get some hair growth back, but Alex didn't seem to care and was happy there was no need for surgery. When Mercer left the hospital, his buddy was joking around with the nurses. It didn't make him feel much better because it was Mercer's fault his friend had been barbequed.

Evolve Enterprises was on full lockdown. There was a new guard at the main gate which was closed with a vehicle parked across the driveway beyond the gates. When the Evolve security guard saw Mercer he opened the gate, and as he pulled through Mercer waved as the car moved out of his way. The guard moving the car wore the black of an ESS mercenary.

The ride down the winding driveway wasn't as relaxing as it normally was. Mercer studied the forest and saw the dead trees, hollows, and boulders for the first time as he pictured all the places the Saberonis could be hiding.

As was standard procedure, the inner gate was closed, but today three security guards were loitering about. As he passed through security, one waved him on and the other two watched the gates open. There were two Evolve employees and one ESS. Mercer waved as the gates closed behind him, but none of the guards waved back.

Mercer was certain word of his failure had gotten around. Few people knew about the Saberonis and its escape, but they did know something was very wrong and that Mercer was in charge of fixing it, and so far, he hadn't.

The beast was in the wind, and if things didn't change soon, he would be too.

As Mercer pulled into his parking spot, he saw O&M sitting on one of the benches along the main walkway leading to the entrance of the building, the stelae running along its length catching the midday sun and casting long shadows across the stonework. He sighed. Mercer needed a break badly, but speaking to O&M was at the top of his to-do list.

The married scientists looked like they hadn't gotten a wink of sleep. Ozzie had bags as dark as night beneath his eyes, and his hair was unruly, his shirt misbuttoned. Miranda, normally as put together as you'll ever see a female scientist, wore jeans, a t-shirt, and a sour expression. It all told Mercer that O&M didn't have good news to impart.

"We heard you've had a difficult twenty-four hours," Dr. Ozzie said as the couple rose.

"You could say that."

"We know you're busy... have you been home?" Dr. Miranda said.

Mercer said nothing. His patience for pleasantries was gone.

Dr. Ozzie coughed gently and said, "Can we talk for a bit?"

The wind pushed from the forest, pine needles rattled, branches creaked and cracked, and the day symphony trilled at full strength.

Mercer sat on the bench the couple had just gotten up from. "No time like the present," he said and smiled curtly.

"Here?" Dr. Miranda said.

With a hike of his shoulders, Mercer made a show of looking around. "I don't see anybody, and the minute I walk through those doors Jinx will find me." The implication of all that meant didn't escape O&M, and the couple nodded as if controlled by one mind.

"We've spoken with Dax," Dr. Ozzie said.

"And he's uncovered some disturbing information relating to the specimen's escape," Dr. Mirada said.

That part of the problem had dropped way down his priority list. It didn't matter how the beast had gotten out. In the end, all he had to worry about was killing it. The hows and whys were above his pay grade, at least at the moment.

"Dax told us there was a breach in the firewall that protects all Evolve Enterprises' intellectual property, data, and financial information, as well as the security system," Dr. Ozzie said. "All the systems, including security, have access points for upgrades and virus protection, and a series of high-level codes are needed to access these digital doors. These access points were breached."

"Is Twer—Mr. Thorpe aware? Jinx?" Mercer asked.

"They've both been briefed," Dr. Miranda said. "Someone from the outside hacked our system and managed to unlock the creature's cage."

A crow cawed, the wind whispering about secrets.

"Has there been an analysis of how it was done, exactly?"

"Excuse me?" Dr. Miranda said.

"What level of skill was needed? Are we talking about attacking the Pentagon here or the Ronald McDonald House fundraising database?" Mercer said.

"Come on, Mercer," Dr. Ozzie said. "You know very well that all our systems and databases are double encrypted, and as the person in charge of the security system, you're well aware of all the bells and whistles."

"Codes are changed every twenty-four hours, and the DDI coming into the building is probably more secure than the Pentagon's," Dr. Miranda added.

"In your expert opinion, and Dax's, do you think someone leaked access codes?"

"Dax was unwilling to venture an opinion," Dr. Ozzie said. "But logic suggests that in fact, that is what happened. Though Jinx has had no luck questioning the staff, and the data logs show no unauthorized logins."

Mercer bit his lip. "It's time to start talking to management," he said.

Dr. Miranda's face twisted.

"We'll see," Dr. Ozzie said.

"What did Thorpe have to say?" Mercer asked, pushing the issue, looking for a reaction.

"Not much," Dr. Miranda said. "A speech about how we all need to be more diligent, how the work we do here could be extremely dangerous if the technology was to get into the wrong hands."

"Blah, NDA, blah, blah," Dr. Ozzie said.

"Where are Dax's techs with the specimen's collar?"

"They were able to ping it again, but you were chasing it at the time, so…" Dr. Miranda said.

"What's the prognosis?"

"Dax says the hardware could be damaged beyond remote repair," Dr. Ozzie said.

"Plus," added Dr. Miranda, "Any software patches require time and a solid connection to upload, but they're hopeful."

"Hopeful of what? That we kill the thing so

they can give up?" Mercer said.

"Don't be obtuse," Dr. Miranda said. "If the creature is near a strong Wi-Fi signal that would help."

"Assuming the hardware isn't broken beyond remote repair," Mercer chided.

O&M said nothing.

"Anything else?" Mercer asked as he pushed to his feet.

O&M exchanged a glance but said nothing.

"Go ahead. Out with it," Mercer said.

"Don't take this the wrong way, but... how is it performing? The Saberonis," Dr. Miranda said.

"Performing?"

"You know, it's battlefield skills," Dr. Ozzie said.

Mercer rolled his shoulders, cracked his neck, and walked away without saying a word.

The next six hours were spent waiting, meeting with people who had no control over the situation, and getting updates from the field. Mercer was exhausted, and he ate and splashed water on his face, but he was approaching zero battery power.

Declan's condition had dramatically improved, and he was expected to make a full recovery. That took some of the weight from Mercer's shoulders, but Alex's bandaged head filled his mind, and his imagination went to work creating streets littered with the dead, the Saberonis feasting on human flesh.

Cheri checked in regularly, and though she said her team was on the beast's trail, he didn't believe it. Unease settled in his stomach like bad clams. If the well-equipped, expertly trained, and experienced ESS crew couldn't kill the beast, who could? Shame washed through him because he suddenly felt he was no longer up for the task, if he ever had been.

His meeting with Jinx was uneventful and guarded.

"Why didn't you stick with the ESS team? Wasn't that the plan?" Mercer asked.

"When Thorpe heard the news about how we were hacked, he wanted me back at the office to handle the interviews with the staff as originally planned," she said.

"Did you interview the boss yet?"

Jinx laughed. "Go home, boss. You're delusional."

Was he? From his vantage point, Twerp was the number one suspect. What Mercer couldn't figure out was why. He nodded at Jinx and said, "Yeah, if I don't go home, I might not have a home to go to." This wasn't a new thought. The timing of his absence was poor because he and Jenni were on shaky ground, and he hoped his resurrected guilt didn't show on his face like a birthmark.

He waited for his final check-ins at 7:00 PM, and considered updating Twerp, but figured Jinx had already done so, so he slipped out of the building into the warm night.

There was a storm coming, and dark clouds rolled across the sky, coming in from the west and breaking at the base of the mountains and scaling up them like smoke. He texted Jenni and asked if she needed anything, but she didn't respond.

Occidental wasn't bustling, but it wasn't quiet. The convenience store was buzzing, as was the diner and Italian restaurant, Giuseppe's. Mercer had the windows down and he smelled fresh baking bread and the intoxicating scent of charred meat. He stopped and grabbed a six-pack of Sierra Nevada pale ale, and he popped one open as he drove.

He passed a sheriff's car parked on the side of the road, and he waved, though he couldn't see which officer was behind the wheel. The sun sat like a burnt egg on the western horizon, its orange glow fading into the black clouds.

Tall Pines was alive with evening activities. Bright light spilled from windows and BBQ smoke billowed from backyards as dogs barked. It was a workday and school was in session, and Mercer smiled as he envisioned children complaining about doing homework and brushing their teeth. He wanted to deal with those mundane tasks. It was more important than... whatever the hell he and Jenni were currently doing, which was surviving. He wanted more. Needed more, and so did Jenni, but a knot of worry twisted his stomach with the idea that they both needed something different.

He pulled into his driveway, killed the Jeep, and sat in silence for a few moments as he stared at his two-story, four-bedroom house. It was a nice place, and Jenni had done a stellar job making it look like a home.

Jenni greeted him with a halfhearted peck on the cheek.

"Hi," Mercer said. "Sorry about last night." Best to just rip off the Band-Aid.

"What was so important that you couldn't come home last night?" Jenni asked as she eyed him with suspicion.

Strangely, Mercer felt nothing. Though he wasn't innocent, she didn't know that, and after what he'd been through the previous thirty-six hours the last thing he needed was an argument. Besides, he had always come home before, so she had every right—good reason, even—to be aggravated and concerned, especially since they hadn't been getting along lately.

Mercer couldn't tell her specifics, but he also couldn't tell her nothing. That would just make her ask questions and he'd have to tell more lies. He'd had enough of that. Mercer said, "One of the specimens broke containment." It felt good to get it off his chest and tell somebody who wasn't in the know, someone whose life wasn't directly tied to the company.

Her eyes went wide, and her lips pursed, but

Jenni said nothing as guilt leaked over her face.

"But you're right to be upset," he said, trying to ease his guilt. "I should've come home at least for a few hours. It did me no good sleeping on the couch in my office. My back aches and I'm exhausted because I hardly got any sleep."

"Did you catch it?" she asked.

The rotten feeling of hopelessness returned, and he shook his head no. "I'm on call, but my hope is that the specimen also needs some rest and will find a dark spot to spend the night."

She nodded. "Are you hungry?" Her face brightened at the possibility of performing a task that might help ease his pain and frustration.

Mercer wasn't hungry and he felt horrible, but he smiled and said, "I could eat."

The couple stumbled through their domestic responsibilities; eating, cleaning up, showering, and watching the obligatory hour of TV before shuffling off to bed.

Jenni was asleep in minutes, but despite his overwhelming weariness, Mercer's mind was racing too fast for sleep. Thunder cracked as the light patter of rain pelting the roof filled the bedroom. A concussive blast rocked the house, and the windowpanes rattled as Mercer's skin crawled.

His eyes slid closed, the booming lightning reminding him of Afghanistan and the horrors he'd seen there. He winced, his brain sparking so many thoughts he couldn't put them in order, and as he eased into temporary death he was there again, reliving the nightmare that was a permanent stain on his life.

14

Cacophonous booms and earsplitting shrieks filled the fading darkness. A blinding flash of white seared Mercer's eyes, sending a sharp jolt down his spine as pain cleaved his head.

The sun hung low, casting long shadows across the battered streets of Sangin. Dust clung to the air, turning the dying light into a hazy orange glow that suffocated the world in its warmth. What locals liked to call The Forever War had been going on for years, the drawn-out conflict a central battleground in the Afghanistan War. NATO forces, mostly British and U.S. troops, had been fighting Taliban insurgents because the Helmand Province, specifically Sangin, was strategically significant due to its location and opium production.

But now that the Brits were leaving, U.S. Command was worried about losing control of the region. To address the situation, Mercer's unit was brought in to clean up the mess.

Mercer eased through the crumbling mud-brick buildings that lined the narrow streets of the district. The sounds of gunfire and explosions echoed off the valley walls, a constant reminder that Sangin was still a warzone, even though the order for the Brits to pull out had been given.

His body ached from days of combat, the muscles in his arms and legs screaming for rest that wouldn't come. But it wasn't just physical exhaustion; it was the weight of the place, the crushing sense of history repeating itself, of lives lost for ground that would soon be abandoned.

"Mercer, we gotta move!" Sergeant Major Hister's voice crackled over the comm, slicing through the haze of fatigue clouding Mercer's mind. He stared up at the heavens, trying to gather his strength. The sky was a washed-out blue, the kind that promised another cold night, and Mercer could already feel the chill seeping into his bones.

He checked the missile launcher slung over his shoulder and his Beretta M9. The gear strapped to his body felt heavier than ever, his helmet dug into his forehead, and the Kevlar vest pressed on his chest with each breath. Every step felt like it might be his last in this cursed place, but he pushed forward, scanning the buildings for insurgents.

The wind gusted, and sand, dust, and gun smoke swirled in the air, stinging Mercer's eyes and throat. He surged into motion, his Beretta in a doublehanded grip as he eased down a narrow alley. The ground beneath his feet felt loose and unstable. Sangin was a land of shifting dirt and hidden dangers, every shadow potentially harboring an IED or an insurgent waiting to ambush the squad. The locals knew the terrain better than the foreign forces ever would, and that knowledge weighed heavily in the pit of his stomach as his boots crunched over the debris.

Mercer had seen the extensive network of tunnels and bunkers the Taliban utilized, which allowed the enemy to launch surprise attacks and then disappear like ghosts. More troubling was the insurgent's ability to blend in with the local population, making it difficult for coalition forces to distinguish between combatants and civilians.

He found most of the squad huddled behind the remains of a wall. Hister crouched as he stared at a map on his ruggedized tablet that connected to the Army's Nett Warrior system and provided a digital interactive map of the area. The Sergeant looked up as Mercer approached, a tight nod of acknowledgment the only greeting.

"Intel says our target is still hot," Hister said, his voice low but steady. "We've got air support coming in, but they're several minutes out and command wants us to terminate the target as planned. You ready Mercer?"

Mercer had the missile launcher. He'd been trained to use the weapon and had volunteered for the mission. Frustration and anger ate at his stomach, his patriotic stupidity sucking him in again. If he'd learned one thing in the military, it was that you never volunteer. For anything. Ever. He knew this better than most, and yet he still was the one with the command launch unit over his shoulder. Mercer glanced around at the others, their faces streaked with grime and sweat, eyes hollowed by the relentless pressure of combat. The team was ready in the only way soldiers ever were—because they had no other choice.

"Ready," Mercer said, his voice cracking and barely above a whisper.

The plan was simple—move fast, stay low, and pray that the Taliban weren't watching. But Sangin had a way of turning the simplest plans into nightmares.

Hister motioned for the unit to move out, and they snaked their way through the alleys, using the sparse cover of broken walls and piles of rubble. The air was thick with the stench of burning rubber and cordite, the aftermath of a week's worth of firefights and airstrikes. Mercer's hands were steady, but his mind was racing, trying to keep track of every possible threat, every potential kill zone they passed through.

Open ground loomed ahead, a stretch of dirt and rubble that had been churned up by the fighting. The squad reached the edge of an alley, the open expanse ahead seeming to stretch on forever. He glanced at Hister, who met his gaze with a grim expression.

"Go!" Hister barked, and they were off, sprinting across the open ground like their lives depended on it—because they did.

A shot rang out, the crack of a sniper rifle splitting the air like a lightning strike. Mercer dropped to the ground and rolled behind a chunk of concrete, his breath coming in ragged gasps as the missile launcher dug into his side. Around him, the others did the same, some finding cover, others dropping flat.

"Sniper, two o'clock!" someone shouted.

Mercer got to his feet and peeked around the chunk of concrete, aiming the Berretta at nothing, the rocket launcher swinging on his back.

The surrounding buildings offered too many hiding places, and the sniper was good—too good.

"Suppressing fire!" Hister ordered, and the squad opened up, their rifles spitting out bursts of automatic fire. Bullets stitched across the building, sending tiny puffs of dust into the air as exploding concrete marred the rooftop of the nearby building where the sniper hid.

Mercer's muscles tensed as adrenaline surged through his veins, sharpening his senses. Every sound was amplified—the rattle of gunfire, the hiss of bullets, and the ringing in his head, despite his Mickey Mouse Ears.

"Go, go, go!" Hister shouted.

Mercer ran in a low crouch, zigzagging across the debris-littered ground. The sniper's shots cracked through the air, but he kept moving, kept running, focusing on the cluster of buildings that contained his target.

As he reached a building that had been blasted into rubble Mercer let out a breath he hadn't known he was holding. Metal rebar stuck from slabs of broken concrete like twisted hair, and he took cover behind what had once been a wall but was now nothing more than a few bricks clinging to a crumbling foundation.

"Status?" Hister asked, his voice steady as it came through his earmuffs. The squad had taken up positions behind Mercer in the rubble where they could stay out of the sniper's sights and provide cover fire as needed.

"All good," Mercer replied, though his mind raced, fear and exhaustion battling for control.

The sound of approaching helicopters carried over the fighting, the deep thrum of rotor blades slicing through the air echoing off the devastation. Relief washed over Mercer like a wave, but it was tempered by the knowledge that he wouldn't be extracted until his mission was completed.

Seconds felt like hours as tension coiled every muscle tight. The helicopters appeared, coming in from the south, sweeping over the rooftops, guns blazing as they laid down suppressing fire.

Mercer holstered his gun, swung the missile launcher off his shoulder, and prepared it to fire. With his finger resting on the missile launcher's trigger, he scanned the building ahead, counting and picturing Hister's map and running through his briefing again.

Several members of the fleeing Taliban leadership were hiding in the remains of the house before him, and it was his job to take out the trash.

The weight of Mercer's helmet pressed down on his skull as his comm crackled to life and the order came through like a bad omen.

"Fire on the target." Hister's voice revealed no emotion; nothing, no excitement, fear, or shame.

Mercer checked the unit's status indicator lights, confirming everything was functioning properly—all systems were green. With the unit set to day vision mode, Mercer looked through the CLU's sight and used the control interface to lock onto the target.

He scanned the remnants of what had once been a large home, now little more than a shell. The structure had been reduced to crumbling walls and a half-collapsed roof, barely standing amidst the debris. His breath caught in his throat as he peered through the CLU's sight, trying to make out any signs of movement. The place was silent, save for the echo of gunfire and the steady hum of the helicopters.

A flicker of movement in the shadows inside

the house.

Mercer took his eyes from the scope in a futile attempt to see what the camera mounted atop his helmet was transmitting back to command. They saw what he saw? Didn't they?

"Mercer, what's the hold-up?" Hister's voice was sharp and impatient.

"I'm checking," Mercer replied, keeping his voice steady, even as a knot of unease tightened in his chest.

At first, he thought it was just a trick of the light, a shifting shadow in the dust-shrouded haze. But then he saw it again, more clearly—a small figure, crouched low in the corner of the ruined building. Mercer's heart sank as he took his finger off the trigger.

"Mercer!" Hister's voice boomed through his Mickey Mouse Ears, drowning out the pounding of helicopter airfoils and the ratatat of gunfire.

Smoke billowed over the target, but when it cleared, he saw the child clearly, his dirty face framed between two chunks of blasted concrete.

"I see a kid in there!" Mercer yelled.

"There are no civilians in the area, Mercer!" Hister yelled, and this time the Master Sargeant sounded put out. "Fire your weapon! That's an order!"

Mercer was no newbie. He knew that the Taliban used children not only as enemy combatants but as suicide bombers. The kid could very well be a Taliban soldier, but still...

He'd killed children. He knew there was no way he hadn't—but he'd never looked a young boy in the eye and snuffed him out like a flame.

"Mercer!"

A deep, all-encompassing weariness came over Mercer. He hadn't signed up for killing kids —collateral damage was one thing, but this... Mercer aimed the missile launcher at the ground.

"I'll have your stripes for this, Mercer!"

Mercer wanted kids someday, or at least he thought he did. But could he bring children into this world? A world where he'd been ordered to kill a child? This was more than just being in the wrong place at the wrong time.

There was a chorus of gunfire as suppressing fire was laid down and Hister and the squad advanced on Mercer's position.

"Give me that!" One of the soldiers tore the rocket launcher from Mercer's grasp and he didn't attempt to stop him.

The soldier leveled the missile launcher as he stared down the sight, aiming the weapon at the target house. He flipped the toggle and set the weapon on Direct Attack mode. The launcher beeped as the system locked in the target and the soldier pulled the trigger.

With a hiss, the missile streaked from the tube and ignited once it was a safe distance from the soldier.

Mercer's breath caught as the boy ducked out of sight and the missile struck the remains of the house. A fireball surged into the sky as debris rained down and black smoke clogged the air. Helicopter airfoils pounded, bullets twanged and zipped, and beneath it all the screaming of Hister.

A thunderous boom brought Mercer awake.

Lightning lit the night, whiteness bursting through the bedroom windows as Mercer sat up, sweat streaming down his face. The bombs faded, Mercer's ears ringing, the memory of the boy's face locked in his mind's eye.

"Are you alright?" Jenni asked as she sat up and reached for the light on the nightstand.

"Don't," Mercer said. "I'll never get back to sleep." There was some truth in that, but he knew if she saw his face, more questions would ensue.

"Chad?"

"Bad dream."

"Sangin?" she asked.

"Yeah." Against his better judgment, he'd shared his war stories with his wife, more to ease his own pain than anything else. He'd known as soon as he'd told her it would affect their relationship forever, but she was his wife. He had to give her something. It made Mercer think of getting bounced from the PD, and the truth behind why. That he hadn't shared. "Go back to sleep," he said.

Jenni leaned over and kissed him on the cheek.

"Goodnight."

"Nite." But sleep was a long time coming, and when it came, the fog of regret, shame, and worry filled his dreams.

15

Thick clouds filled the sky, and a light rain splattered Mercer's office window, air piping gently from a vent above his desk when Alex had called. The retired sheriff had gotten another tip.

Barney at the redwood preserve knew most of the local law officers, because the cops often had to chase kids out of the preserve at night or deal with domestic disputes brought on by too much cheer. The preserve had a petting zoo to draw the young children, and a gruesome discovery had been made.

Mercer was thankful for the call. He'd been preparing to go join Cheri out on the hunt, and based on Mercer's new lead, the ESS crew was chasing shadows.

It wasn't easy sneaking out of the office with O&M, Twerp, and Jinx lurking around. Cheri had stopped reporting in because, well, there was nothing for her to report. Then there was

Alex. His friend was bouncing off the walls and insisted that he was fine and wanted to come to the preserve.

Mercer had fought off all attempts to help, a common theme. He figured it was guilt. It always seemed to come back to that.

Occidental Road meandered through the forest, slowly climbing as it cut through the mountains. The land was a series of large steps, not unlike the one where he'd found the abandoned farm. Thick wet undergrowth packed the sides of the road and evergreens towered over a hundred feet.

The land west of Occidental was packed with unforgiving woods dotted with the occasional homestead. If the specimen was the cause of the killing at the preserve, the beast was following an easterly path that was taking it through the mountains and down into the Sonoma Valley beyond.

Mercer was basically following that path now. He made a left onto Sota Way and the road was boxed in by small redwoods that were only a couple of hundred years old.

The preserve's entrance was a seamless blend of natural beauty and a subtle homage to its namesake. As the road narrowed and curved gently, it was flanked on both sides by towering redwoods that had stood for centuries, their thick, rough bark the color of cinnamon. The trees formed a natural archway, their branches intertwining overhead, creating a green canopy that stopped the light rain. Mist hung just above the road, and it swirled and eddied across the ground. A slight breeze stirred the foliage, and the air was cool and carried the rich, earthy scent of moisture, pine, and eucalyptus.

A rustic wooden sign marked the entrance, carved from a fallen redwood, its letters etched deep and filled with a dark stain that contrasted against the lighter, weathered wood. The sign read "Charles M. Schulz Redwood Preserve" in a whimsical yet dignified font, with a small engraving of Snoopy, nose upturned as if sniffing the forest air, subtly tucked into the corner. The base of the sign was surrounded by large ferns and wildflowers that added bursts of color to the lush green backdrop.

The parking lot, covered in redwood bark mulch, was enclosed by bollards with rope threaded through holes at their tops. There were three vehicles in the lot, and several trails dove deeper into the preserve, their surfaces uneven and worn. Large boulders, coated in a fine layer of moss, dotted the landscape, and empty trash cans stood at each trailhead.

To the right of the entrance, a small, unobtrusive visitor center was partially hidden among the trees, a beat-up pickup parked next to it. The building was made of redwood, with a wraparound porch and sloping roof that blended into the landscape. The structure was modest, its exterior walls adorned with simple illustrations of Schulz's beloved characters, each one connected to the environment that surrounded them: Charlie Brown and Linus leaning against a redwood trunk, Lucy picking wildflowers, and Snoopy perched atop a large mushroom.

The entrance was quiet, save for the rustling of needles, the crack and pop of tree branches, and the calls of birds. Mercer parked, shut down the vehicle, and sat staring out the windshield. The preserve felt like another world, where the weight of everyday life faded—a place where worries were left behind, and the raw, enduring beauty of nature took center stage.

"Yo," said Barney as he exited the welcome center. The big man waved, pulled up his pants, and when he saw that the rain had stopped, he started his climb down the steps. Barney would never be accused of being a health nut, but he looked O.K. for a seventy-one-year-old retired veteran who'd settled in northern California because he'd had enough of the hustle and bustle of the East Coast. He wore olive-colored pants and a brown collared park shirt, but instead of a Smoky the Bear Stetson, he wore a red and gold San Francisco 49ers ballcap, which was pushed back on his forehead and slightly askew. Fogged glasses sat at the end of a hooked nose, and a red scar ran along the edge of his right cheek.

Mercer held out his hand as he approached, and the two men shook. Barney was old school, and if Mercer had tried to fist bump or elbow knock Barney would've looked at him like he had five heads.

"How are you, Barney? Long time no see."

"You and Jenni were here for the fundraising festival, right?"

"Of course," Mercer said. Though the preserve had been started and endowed by the famous cartoonist, who was from Santa Rosa, the preserve still required additional funding, and several events were held each year that focused on getting the local community to pony up for a small piece of the park's maintenance. "I'm ashamed to say I haven't been here since Fall Fest." Mercer wasn't sure why. He'd been all around the world and there was nothing more relaxing than a hike in the giant redwoods, which can be found nowhere else on Earth.

"I'm sure you're busy," Barney said.

"No excuse."

Birds argued, a breeze rattled pine needles, and somewhere someone laughed.

"Slow today, huh?" Mercer said as he motioned toward the parking lot.

"Weather. And it's a weekday."

Mercer nodded. He was so bad at small talk he decided to give up the effort. "What did the sheriff's office say about what you found?"

Barney hiked his shoulders. "Not much. We're swamped. Not priority. We'll send someone out, blah, blah, blah."

"Really? And nobody has shown up yet?"

"Nope." Barney didn't sound surprised. "I understand. There's got to be more important things going on than a dead goat."

"I'm not sure about that," Mercer said. The locals were aware of the events at the farm— some of it, anyway. In his opinion the delayed response was negligent given recent events, but what did he know?

Barney looked at him askance as he licked his lips.

"Why did you call Alex?"

"Why?" Barney smiled wide. "Because he asked me to."

"He asked you to? When?"

"A couple of days ago," Barney said. "He called and said he was tracking a huge bear just northwest of here. Said to call if anything odd happened or I saw it."

Mercer nodded. "Can you show me the goat?"

"Yes, come on." Barney headed for the nearest and widest trail which had a sign at its head that read: "Game Farm this way!", and below in smaller type, "Please, only feed the animals the approved food obtained from one of our conveniently located dispensers. This is for the health of the animals. Thank you for understanding."

Mercer chuckled as he passed the sign, recalling a conversation he'd had with one of the preserve's board members. The preserve made almost $10,000 a year selling cracked corn from refurbished gumball machines.

Massive redwoods, some over a thousand years old, lined the path, the wet pine scent both rich and slightly sweet like an intoxicating perfume. Moss clung to some of the trees, and the undergrowth was almost nonexistent, the hardpan covered in bronze needles and an occasional tiny puddle. Stanchions with rope strung between them surrounded the trees closest to the path, and this was to keep visitors from getting too close to the giants. Although redwoods are immense and powerful, their root systems lie close to the surface. Walking on them can cause damage and even kill the trees.

"What happened? Did you hear or see what killed the goat?" Mercer asked.

"I was doing the morning feeding—Jesse is out the next few days, and I saw all the goats huddled in a corner of their pen, braying and screeching like there was an alligator in there. The rest of the animals were all stirred up too—feathers all over the place, the gate broken open. But the beasts were too scared to leave their enclosure."

"What did you do?"

"Not much. There's a lot of blood… I buttoned up the paddock and called the sheriff, and I was waiting around, so I called Alex. He said not to touch anything if I could get away with it. Thankfully there are no school trips today."

"Did the cops say you could clean up?"

"They said I could dispose of the carcass, but that I should take pictures, which I did." He held up his phone as evidence. "But I was waiting for you."

The path ended at the edge of a field, the sign perched above the path reading Shultz Game Farm, with pictures of the peanuts game playing hide-and-seek in the redwoods. A handwritten note was tacked to the sign that read simply, "Closed."

Mercer caught the coppery smell of blood immediately.

Wooden fences boxed in several enclosures, each containing a different variety of local fauna. There was a bird dome, a goat paddock, as well as two rescued bears who had shown no inclination to return to the wild after they'd been rescued. The small park also had a donkey named Icarus, a peacock named Rainbow, and a turtle named Murtle.

The animals were cooing and huffing, their fetid breath stinking up the air and driving out the scent of animal scat. Mist hung over the enclosures and all the beasts fell still as Mercer and Barney approached.

Barney coughed gently but said nothing, an image worth a thousand words.

The disemboweled goat lay twisted and broken on the hardpacked dirt. Its body was splayed open, the beast's white and brown fur matted with dark, clotted blood that soaked the ground beneath it. The animal's belly was torn open, the edges of the wound ragged and uneven. Entrails spilled out in a tangled, glistening mass, slick with blood and viscus fluids. Several ribs were exposed, the flesh torn away in jagged claw mark-like strips. Though still intact, the ribcage was cracked and splintered, as if crushed by a great weight. The goat's head was twisted to the side, its eyes wide in a frozen expression of pain, its mouth slightly open, its tongue lolling out.

All four limbs were sprawled out awkwardly, the joints twisted at unnatural angles. The beast's hooves were caked with dirt and blood as if the animal had struggled fiercely before succumbing to its fate. One of the legs was bent beneath the body, the bone shattered, the skin torn and frayed around the break. Claw marks covered the carcass, and huge chunks of meat were missing from the hindquarters, back, and chest.

Flies buzzed around the corpse, and the smell was overpowering, a nauseating blend of blood, the sharp tang of bile, and the sickly sweet odor of dead flesh. The ground around the goat was stained with dark, congealed blood, and a trail of huge bloody cat prints led to the now-closed gate.

Mercer wiped his forehead with the back of his hand. The brutality was shocking, the remains telling a silent story of suffering and savagery. He said, "I wonder why it didn't attack the others?"

"It?"

Mercer said nothing.

"Maybe it had its fill," Barney said.

"What?"

"You asked why it didn't attack any of the other animals," Barney said. "Maybe it was full."

"Maybe."

"Can I clean this up now?"

"Give me a minute," Mercer said, but he wasn't paying attention to Barney anymore. He was focused on yet another blood trail, and as he considered the prospect of chasing after the specimen, his stomach soured like he'd eaten bad clams. The trail was recent, otherwise it would have been washed away by the rain.

The definition of insanity is doing the same thing over and over and expecting a different result. No way Mercer was running into the forest alone. He wanted to call Alex, but he'd almost killed his friend, and as it was, he was still on bed rest for the next couple of days as a precaution. He pulled his phone and called Deputy Sheriff Webster, who picked up on the first ring.

"Mercer?"

"Yeah."

"I didn't think I'd hear from you. What's up?" Webster said.

"You on duty?"

Webster chuckled. "I clock out at three. Why do you ask?"

"Did you hear about the call-out at the redwood preserve?"

"Ronda is going to head up there after she deals with a domestic. Why, what's going on?"

"Do you want another shot at the creature?"

Silence, and then, "I think I do."

"Call your dispatch and tell them you're responding to the call at the preserve for Ronda before you head home," Mercer said. "You know, being a good teammate and all that rot."

"See you in fifteen minutes. Need anything?" Webster asked.

"A bloodhound would be nice."

"Can't help you there, but I've got a mutt that can track just about anything. I can stop and pick him up on my way."

"Isn't that against departmental protocol?"

"On my way," Webster said, and killed the connection.

16

The rain came seconds after Webster arrived and Barney disappeared into the comfortable confines of the visitor's center.

Webster parked his patrol car next to Mercer's Jeep. When the green and white sedan came to a stop, the door opened, and a white and black dog launched from the vehicle into the rain.

"Name's Rocket," Webster said as he exited the squad car and pulled up the hood of his raincoat. "Found him as a puppy abandoned in the woods. He might not look like much, but his sniffer is topnotch and he's fast as lightning. That's what the wife wanted to call him."

Rocket had a passing resemblance to that bull terrier with the red circle around its left eye that hawked cheap products at low prices. The dog's long snout ended in a nose the size of a chunk of coal, his tiny black eyes shifting from the woods to Mercer. Rocket's ears were pointy and standing straight, the beast a controlled knot of energy and excitement.

"Sit, boy. Sit," said Webster as he approached.

The dog sat, the growing drizzle making the canine blink spasmodically.

Webster was decked out in his rain gear, and he held his rifle at the ready. He swept his gaze around, pausing on the three vehicles parked at the opposite end of the lot. "There are hikers out there? In the rain?"

Mercer nodded. "Barney doesn't know how many."

Webster nodded and said, "We should close the preserve."

"We should?" Mercer said. "We should." Not that he had the authority, but the thought hadn't occurred to Mercer, probably because Barney hadn't suggested it. He wasn't on the PD anymore, but still... Shame washed through him. There were three guest cars in the lot, which meant at least three people were roaming among the redwoods.

The pair wasted no time, and within minutes the foursome of Webster, Mercer, Barney, and Rocket were securing the main gate. Mercer and Webster pulled it closed, and Barney locked it. The Pardon the Inconvenience sign was put out, and the walk-in gate was locked.

"Barney, if the owners of those cars show up, you can let them out," Webster said.

"I'm coming with you," Barney said.

"No," Mercer said. "You're not."

"We need you here in case something goes sideways," Mercer added.

Barney's face scrunched like a pain had knifed through him and he licked his lips.

"Plus..." Mercer tried to find the words but couldn't. Anything he said would sow the seeds of fear.

"Plus, it's dangerous," Webster said. "This is my job, let me do it."

"Why are you here, Chad?" Barney pressed.

"It's personal," Mercer said.

"Personal?"

"The thing almost got me," Mercer said.

"And me," Webster added.

"What almost got you?"

Mercer and Webster exchanged glances but said nothing.

Rocket chirped in annoyance.

"Wait here while I get my gun," Barney said.

"Barney, I can't—"

"What can't you let me do, Officer Webster? Last time I checked, I was in charge around here."

Mercer and Webster stayed silent.

"And as far as it being personal..." Barney chuckled. "Whatever this thing is that you're chasing killed Helen, and she was a good goat. Been here for years."

That took the air out of the balloon, and as Mercer and Webster trudged back to the trail that led to the petting zoo, Barney retrieved his double-barrel shotgun from his vehicle.

The rain let up, mist snaking through the trees like serpents, as the companions trekked back to the murder scene. Rocket led, the beast's nose hovering an inch above the wet ground.

While Mercer was waiting for Webster to arrive, he'd helped Barney remove the disemboweled animal from the goat enclosure. All the other goats were staying clear of the dark crimson stain that marred the muddy ground and stood still with their heads down, braying softly as if in reverence of their fallen mate.

The blood trail was mostly washed away, but Rocket appeared to pick up a scent and bolted down the path.

Mercer started to jog after the beast, but Webster reached out and stopped him. "Let him do his thing. He'll bark when he finds something worth telling us about."

"He can track in the rain?" Barney said.

"Sure," Webster said. "He's part hound, and he has an incredibly sensitive nose that allows him to pick up on faint traces of scent even after rain."

"Didn't know that," Barney said. "I figured the scent would be washed away."

"It is to some extent. Rain can dilute or wash away some scent molecules, but it can also help disperse them, making the scent spread out and easier for the dog to detect."

The sound of fierce barking echoed through the redwoods.

"Now we can run," Webster said.

"Do we have to?" Barney asked, but Webster

didn't answer.

Mercer and Webster sprinted down the trail, slipping on wet needles, fog cycling through the trees, amorphous smoke-like fingers massaging the path.

Rocket stood over a piece of intestines. Saliva dripped from the dog's mouth, his eyes wide and his tail out straight as he barked.

The intestine was white and roughly two inches long, and it looked like an uncooked breakfast sausage. Bile crept up Mercer's throat, the microwaved egg sandwich he'd eaten for breakfast threatening to make a curtain call.

"Good boy. Rocket is a good boy." Webster reached into his rain slicker and pulled free a treat. "Sit."

Rocket sat as if a steak was forthcoming.

Webster gave the dog his reward and said, "Seek. Seek."

The dog walked in a circle as he chewed, nose sniffing, ears standing at attention. Rocket's tail went rigid, and he stopped walking and looked at Webster for confirmation.

"Seek! Seek!" Webster yelled, and the beast took off.

Barney arrived and said, "What did I miss?" When he saw the piece of intestine, he added, his voice cracking, "Helen?"

"Come on," Webster said.

Barney raised his shotgun, his wet face creased with anger as he fell in behind Webster.

Mercer gave the piece of white flesh one last appraisal before he followed. The knot in his stomach had eased, though he had no idea why. Maybe it was Rocket and the beast's ability to follow the specimen's scent. That advantage could be the difference between success and death. He bit his lip as he put one foot in front of the other, gun at the ready. Thoughts of tiny little cats scratching the piss out of huge dogs worked their way to the forefront of his mind.

Another round of intense barking echoed down the path.

Rocket had found a chunk of meat. A treat was supplied, orders were given, and the dog continued his search.

Skin and fur clung to the chunk of fat, the red remains of torn meat clinging to the gelatinous mass.

Barney grunted and said, "Now I want to shoot the son's a bitch."

"Easy," Mercer said as the companions surged back into motion.

Rocket was way out ahead of the humans when he slowly came to a stop like his battery had run dry.

Webster was the first to reach the canine, and he whisper-yelled at Rocket, ordering the dog to stop and sit.

When Mercer reached the pair, Rocket sat beside Webster, the beast shifting and swaying like a coiled spring. Dog and owner stared east into a thick grove of redwoods.

The sounds of meat being torn, jaws snapping, and the grunt and exhale of the Saberonis eating filled the forest. Mist wove around tree trunks and settled in the pricker bushes and ferns that had managed to root in the hardpan. The trees were giants here, massive specimens over a thousand years old.

Mercer felt a sense of awe as he entered the ancient, living cathedral. The towering trunks, dark and massive, rose into the mist, their reddish-brown bark soaked to a deep, earthy brown. Raindrops filtered through the dense canopy, landing softly on the thick carpet of ferns and needles. The air was cool and rich with the scent of damp wood and wet earth, and puddles reflected the towering trees like mirrors. Mercer had been to this section of the preserve many times, and he pictured the glade in his mind's eye, the giants bathed in dappled sunlight. Now that forest glowed with a muted green, the ferns and undergrowth vibrant under the rainfall.

The sounds of eating ceased.

Rocket whimpered and Webster tried to quiet the animal, but the mutt was a bundle of nerves, and Mercer couldn't blame the beast.

The Saberonis was crouched behind a pricker bush that had rooted in a dirt-filled notch at the base of an enormous redwood. Tiny green leaves camouflaged three-inch stiletto-like thorns, but

Mercer saw the beast. Its skin hadn't blended into its surroundings.

"I… I can see it," Webster said as he raised his gun, but didn't fire.

The specimen wasn't far off, but an obstacle course of thick tree trunks, pricker bushes, and stunted ferns was the only protection the companions had.

"What… is it?" Barney asked.

Mercer scanned the woods with the binoculars, but it was difficult to see because the lenses were fogging in the gentle rain.

The Saberonis was wet, its skin shiny, which made the beast standout against the background of brown and green. Its huge cat-like body was gray-black, and the dark mane of hair running down its back shimmered and glowed beneath a coating of water droplets. It stood on all fours, its color changing and shifting, but not blending into the landscape. The creature's head was soaked, its jaws drenched crimson, and pieces of flesh were caught on its long tusk-like fangs.

Mercer smiled. Water droplets were affecting the creature's crypsis capabilities. He recalled O&M saying that water would darken the specimen's camouflage. In shadowy or wet environments, this could enhance the beast's crypsis abilities, whereas in drier climates, its effectiveness could be reduced. "Guess you don't know everything," Mercer muttered.

"What?" Webster said.

"Nothing."

"I'm open to suggestions."

The thought of chasing the beast through the forest—again, was about as appealing as preparing for a colonoscopy, but what choice did he have? The traditional road and safe lane had been disregarded for the passing lane, and now he was moving onto the shoulder.

"Stay back and cover me," Webster said.

The beast turned up its snout and sniffed, its head lulling to the left, its deep-set yellow eyes radiating a cold, calculating intelligence as they found Mercer and his companions. Its short tail swept back and forth as it dropped the remains of the meat it was chewing on. A low growl, like rocks being pulled over rocks by a stream, carried through the trees.

Mercer aimed his Sig Sauer and fired, knowing he had little to no chance of hitting the beast. The bullet took off a hunk of redwood bark and ricocheted before thumping into the wet hardpan.

Everything went still except the pattering of the rain.

Mercer stared down the barrel of the gun, shifting it slightly as he searched for a shot at the Saberonis.

Unlike prior encounters, the specimen hadn't bolted at the sound of the gunshot. It hadn't moved, and the fact that Mercer could still see the thing brought a bit of hope.

But hope is a fickle bitch, and as the beast eased through the forest Mercer had trouble tracking its movements, even though its camouflage was on the fritz. The creature's growl had grown to a raspy hissy shriek that was building toward a roar.

Barney asked, "Should we follow him?" He jerked the tip of his shotgun in Webster's direction.

The deputy was moving through the forest, fast, gun up as he went right at the Saberonis, Rocket out before him, snarling.

"No," Mercer said. "He said cover him, and that's what we're going to do."

"How? I can't see him clearly, and if I can't see him, how—"

The Saberonis screamed, its thin wail driving through the rain and freezing Webster in his tracks. The deputy searched for a shot and fired three times.

Then the warm rain came in sheets, clouding the air and dropping visibility to twenty feet. The crack and pop of water splattering the tree canopy filled the woods and drops leaked through, pelting Mercer's raincoat, tiny rivulets carrying tan needles running between his legs.

He put his back to the tree, facing away from the beast and Webster. Mercer couldn't see what was happening, and leaving himself exposed in the silvery gloom would help nobody.

A boom thundered through the forest and for

a heartbeat, Mercer thought it was lightning. A second shotgun blast exploded over the driving rain and arguing wind, and he peeked around the redwood.

Barney was hunched over, reloading. Using his raincoat to cover the weapon as best he could, he cracked open the gun and shook out the two empty shells. Then he pressed two new shells into their respective firing chambers, and with a flick of his wrist, the weapon snapped closed and was ready to fire.

Webster dropped to and knee, panning his gun around as Rocket growled, teeth bared.

The Saberonis was gone.

17

Panic filtered through Mercer, a raw, primal fear that paralyzed him. He knew the feeling well, the sense of impending doom, and the soul-crushing fear at the inability to act. Rain soaked the towering redwoods, their massive trunks disappearing into the low-hanging fog that choked the understory. Each droplet of rain seemed to echo in the silence of the forest, punctuated only by the occasional distant rumble of thunder.

"I don't see it," Webster said. He shifted on his feet, his boots squelching in the mud beneath the coating of needles. Rocket sat beside him, his head shifting around like a bird.

Mercer looked over his shoulder at Barney, who was wheezing slightly from the exertion of the hunt.

"We need to surround it," Barney muttered, wiping his fogged glasses. "But I can't see more than a few feet in this mess."

Webster said, "We really shouldn't split up." His jaw was set in a firm line. "This might be our best chance. When it stops raining…"

Rocket chirped in agreement.

Barney shook his head. "I've been working these woods for thirty years, never seen anything but the usual—deer, bears. Big cats are rare. Whatever that thing was, it's probably long gone."

"I'll take point," Webster said. "Stay close to me." The deputy crept forward, gun up, Rocket at his side. The pair hadn't gone far before the dog picked up the faint, but unmistakable tracks of the Saberonis. The paw prints were massive, the slashes delineating claws three inches long.

"Ever see anything like that?" Webster muttered.

Barney's face went slack as he bent to inspect the tracks, and his eyes widened. "That's not from anything I've ever seen. Not around here."

Mercer's gaze swept the forest. "It's still close." The wind howled, and a shiver ran through him. He checked his gun—again, and added, "Let's keep moving."

The companions resumed their search, and with each step Mercer took the tension in his muscles grew heavier with the weight of the situation. Rain plastered his raincoat, and Mercer was hot, his t-shirt soaked with sweat. The oppressive silence of the forest was punctuated by the snap of a branch and a loud hiss.

Rocket stopped dead in his tracks, the dog's tail going straight, his nose pointing into the rainy gloom ahead.

Mercer saw nothing but shifting shadows and drooping vegetation. Then one of the shadows moved—a flash of pale gray slipping between the trees like a ghost. "There," he whispered as he pointed.

The forest seemed to close in, the ancient trees like prison guards. Mercer felt like an ant beneath the giants, their sheer size breathtaking and humbling. He'd been to the Grand Canyon, crossed the Rockies, and had been to the edge of the Blake Plateau, but he'd never seen anything that compared to the grandeur of the redwoods in northern California.

Webster and Rocket moved forward slowly, Webster signaling for Mercer and Barney to stay back. Mercer saw the tautness in the deputy's shoulders, the way his finger stayed on the trigger of his rifle. They were out of their element—Mercer was the only one who had seen combat, but Webster had been trained for dangerous, unpredictable encounters, and Barney had years of experience in the woods and was an ex-soldier.

The creature appeared again—closer this time. It slinked between the trees, low to the ground, its massive paws making no sound on the rain-soaked earth. Muscles undulated beneath its slick skin, and its yellow eyes glowed as the beast searched the woods. Its mouth was closed, yet thick fangs jutted from its upper jaw, gleaming even in the dim light—long, curved, and saber-like. The specimen was enormous—its head the size of a boulder, and it was framed by the strip of thick black fur that ran down its back.

The Saberonis growled, low and guttural, the sound vibrating through the trees. It took several steps toward the companions, moving with terrifying grace, muscles rippling beneath its wet skin.

Rocket squeaked and Webster slipped the dog a treat, never taking his eyes off the specimen as it advanced.

Mercer raised the Sig Sauer, his hand trembling.

"Now that we can see it," Webster said, his voice calm but urgent, "don't make any sudden movements. Rocket and I will go straight. Mercer left, Barney right. Let's see if we can box it in."

Barney was breathing heavily, his eyes wide with terror. "I've only got two shots."

Mercer said, "We need to put it down before it attacks. If you have a shot—even if it's not a good one, take it."

Webster nodded as he started forward, and Mercer and Barney fanned out on either side of him.

The Saberonis stopped advancing and crouched behind a fern, its eyes fixed on them now, pupils wide. Mercer felt the intelligence behind those eyes, a predatory focus that sent the imaginary ants scurrying down his spine. The creature was calculating, measuring its prey.

With a suddenness that almost made Mercer squeeze the Sig's trigger, the specimen's growl deepened as the Saberonis surged through the greenery.

Webster reacted first and he fired a shot. The gun cracked through the forest, the sound deafening in the rain. The specimen veered off course, the bullet just missing the beast as it punched into the ground with a thud.

"Move! Move!" Mercer shouted.

Rocket darted forward, a white flash of muscle and teeth.

Webster loaded another bullet into the rifle's firing chamber and put the stock of the gun to his shoulder, his eye pinned to the scope.

Mercer fired twice, but he was off balance and the Saberonis had vanished into a thicket of undergrowth. His heart raced, the sound of the rain and his heavy breathing filling his ears.

"Did we hit it?" Webster asked, breathless.

Mercer shook his head no. "It's still out there."

Barney wiped his glasses with shaking hands. "It's impossible. It shouldn't even exist…" He looked at Mercer, fire in his eyes. "I suppose that's really why you're here, Chad? Is this thing an Evolve… creation?"

"Doesn't matter," Mercer said, scanning the forest with a grim expression. "It's real enough. And it's hunting us."

The rain let up, but the knot in Mercer's stomach grew, the heat of worry spreading through him like a disease. The tension was palpable, the air thick with the scent of wet earth and pine.

Barney's glasses were fogged again, and rainwater streamed down his wrinkled face, but it was the terror in his eyes that concerned Mercer the most.

Webster and Rocket didn't slow.

Barney stopped walking and lowered his shotgun. All the fight and anger had drained from his face, and Mercer figured the guy had decided avenging his favorite goat Helen wasn't worth dying for. The old man's eyes darted around the forest, wide and fearful. "I've worked these woods for years! Nothing like this has ever happened. That thing... it shouldn't exist." He was half yelling, his breathing rapid and shallow, clouds of steam piping from his mouth.

Mercer's eyes narrowed, and he whispered, "Snap out of it, Barney. We're all in this now, and if you panic, you're dead. We need to—"

A guttural inhuman wail carried through the redwoods, followed by a deep, rumbling growl, like thunder, but much closer. Too close.

Mercer turned just in time to see the enormous shape of the Saberonis burst from the shadows of the redwoods, its yellow eyes glowing with malice. It had circled around, silently stalking them in the dense undergrowth.

"Get behind me!" Webster shouted, raising his rifle, but the old man was frozen in place, eyes wide.

In a flash of gray, the specimen sprang, a blur of muscle and fury.

Barney let out a strangled cry, stumbling backward, as he fired his shotgun, but there was no time to aim, and the blast cut through the tree canopy.

The beast's front claws raked across Barney's chest and its powerful jaws clamped down on his shoulder, its massive saber-like fangs sinking deep into the flesh.

"Barney!" Webster screamed as he fired wildly at the beast.

The Saberonis didn't release its grip on Barney as the creature shifted, ducked, and danced—a blur of gray, a roiling mass of fury. It snarled in rage, shaking Barney like a rag doll, whose screams echoed through the forest, blood mixing with the rain as it splattered the ground.

Mercer dove for cover.

Webster yelled, "Attack!"

Rocket wasn't an attack dog, but the smart animal knew what his owner meant. The dog vaulted through the air, jaws open, gums pulled back.

Tiny canine teeth punctured one of the specimen's rear legs, jaws locking as the canine thrashed its head, his body leaving the ground with each powerful swing.

But the Saberonis was too powerful. With a shake of its head, it tossed Barney's limp body aside and turned its attention to Rocket.

Mercer's mind went numb, disbelief taking over as he watched his friend fall. "No!" he screamed.

One of the specimen's front paws lashed out, its three-inch claws slicing Rocket's flank.

The dog yelped as his jaws released and he fell to the wet ground in a bloody heap.

Webster screamed, and Mercer thought he would hear the man's wail in his dreams for the rest of his life.

The beast snarled, blood dripping from its fangs as it retreated into the shadows, disappearing as quickly as it had come, vanishing among the towering redwoods, leaving only the sound of the rain and Barney and Rocket's dead bodies behind.

Mercer rushed forward and knelt by Barney's side. The old man lay motionless, his face pale, eyes staring blankly into the rain-filled sky. Mercer felt for a pulse and said, his voice tight, the edge of battle-hardened experience cracking, "He's gone."

Webster staggered, his eyes locked on Rocket's corpse. "We... we need to get out of here," he said, his voice hoarse. "We need to get help."

"Understatement of the year." Guilt seeped through Mercer. Now he had blood on his hands, and the situation had veered out of his control.

Webster swallowed hard, and said, "We need to make sure it doesn't kill anyone else."

Doubt filled Mercer, but he said nothing.

Mercer and Webster were almost afterthoughts in the ensuing chaos.

An ambulance arrived and Barney was pronounced dead, and because of the remote location, the EMTs were given permission by the sheriff's office to transport the body to the morgue.

Helicopters circled overhead, but they found nothing and were soon called off. But that wasn't the end of it. The staties were on the way, and the feds were sure to follow.

Mercer and Webster were questioned, and both men stuck to their story. Webster was helping a colleague and responding to Barney's call, and Mercer was following up because of the incident of the prior day. Talk about withholding information from the police during an ongoing investigation. If he and Webster told the truth now, they'd be in all kinds of trouble. It was bad enough that they were complicit in Barney's death, but lying to the cops never led to anything good, even if your accomplice was a member of the blue religion.

Barney and Rocket were dead, and everything was about to change. Mercer couldn't help but wonder what that would mean for him. Would his failure lead to the exposure of his secrets? He found he hardly cared anymore, yet guilt from the deaths he'd allowed to happen would never leave him, and they would be added to the series of open wounds Mercer carried wherever he went.

But he did care. The specimen was working its way closer to civilization, and when it got there...

Everyone cleared out, and Webster and Mercer said their goodbyes, the two men forever connected by their secrets. Mercer sat on a bench at the side of the parking lot, the storm fading and the clouds clearing as night approached.

As the last echoes of the storm faded into twilight, Mercer sat alone as the redwood forest transformed into a realm of serene beauty. The sky, streaked with clouds and painted with God-like brushstrokes of deep orange, purples, and fiery reds, cast a warm glow that danced upon the glistening rain-soaked leaves. Shadows lengthened as the sun continued its descent, creating a play of light and darkness that added depth to the towering trees.

Mercer sat there a long time, alone, and as the sun dipped below the horizon, the sky deepened to a rich indigo, and the first stars twinkled above the redwoods. When his stomach began protesting enthusiastically, Mercer pushed to his feet and headed for home, the sorrow of two deaths pressing down on him and threatening to break him.

18

Mercer slipped from his house into the early morning mist. Jenni had worked overnight and was going to bed as he was getting up. Two ships passing in the night... the morning, but it was for the best. He was consumed with the Saberonis, and his life problems—though tragically connected to his predicament, would have to wait.

The air was a crisp fifty-four degrees, though it would be seventy by lunch. A heavy layer of dew coated every surface, and the scent of pine and eucalyptus filled the air. Birds argued, and a crow's screech echoed through the stillness.

He took a sip of coffee as he thumbed the Jeep's fob. The vehicle chirped, and its lights flashed as the car's locks snapped and disengaged. As he opened the driver's side door an uneasiness worked its way from his brain to his stomach. Mercer sensed he was being watched, and his hand fell to the Sig Sauer in its holster.

Images of the Saberonis stalking through his backyard rattled his nerves, and he took a deep breath. The beast had last been seen way east of Tall Pines, and even if the specimen had made a one-eighty, what were the odds it could cover so much distance in such a short time and end up on his doorstep? Unless... No, the idea that the beast might be hunting him was insane.

But the mind is a wonderous thing, and as invisible ants burrowed just beneath his skin Mercer climbed into the driver's seat. He closed the door, pulled the pancake holster off his belt, and placed the gun on the passenger seat as he started the car.

He peered into the rearview mirror at his dark house, and a tremor of worry and angst worked through him. Maybe the beast wasn't stalking him, but soon the creature would reach Santa Rosa, and if that happened...

It was a weekday, and Tall Pines was bustling. He waved as he passed neighbors he hardly knew and smiled at the faces of children who looked like they'd rather be any place else in the world other than on their way to school. Most folks who lived in Tall Pines weren't from the area, and most left upon retirement, so there were no seniors walking dogs and no old dudes playing chess in the park. Many of the folks worked at Evolve, and other local businesses that had migrated to the area for the same reasons Evolve had. Though it enhanced the solitary nature of his life, Mercer made an extra effort to stay away from the Evolve people. Friends at work that bled into one's personal life always caused trouble, especially for a security chief.

Mercer was making his way down Occidental Road, sipping the last of his coffee, when he adjusted the rearview mirror and noticed a car coming up fast behind him. It was a blue sporty thing, and Mercer recognized the vehicle as Dr. Ozzie and Dr. Miranda's car. As the vehicle got closer Mercer saw it was Dr. Ozzie driving and he was alone.

When he was on Mercer's ass, the scientist began beeping his horn, his hand out the window signaling for Mercer to pull over.

Mercer waited for a turnout and pulled off the road.

Dr. Ozzie pulled up alongside Mercer, window down. "Sorry about this, Chad. But I wanted to talk with you without an audience and I didn't want to disturb you at home."

Mercer's anger drained away. Once he got to the office Jinx would be on his hip all day and reporting everything he said and did back to Twerp. "No worries. Let's head up the road to the TG trailhead. Nobody will see us there."

The duo continued down Occidental Road and made their way to the agreed-upon spot, Mercer's gaze shifting to the rearview every few seconds like Ray Liotta at the end of Goodfellas. His nerves jumped with anticipation and excitement. Currently, he had no leads, no way forward except to wait and react, but maybe whatever Dr. Ozzie had to tell him would change that.

Both men parked at the far end of the parking area within a thick copse of eucalyptus trees. Most of the morning fog had dissipated, and faint traces of mist snaked through the finger-shaped leaves, thin rays of sunlight casting a puzzle of shadows on the Jeep's hood. There was a sign announcing the Dewy Gress Trailhead, a path that ran through the hills of what used to be a cattle ranch but was now a bed and breakfast surrounded by a nature preserve.

"Shall we walk?" Dr. Ozzie said as he buzzed down his window.

"I've done enough hiking lately, and I need to get to the office," Mercer said. "What's up?"

"What do you know about our technology division?" Dr. Ozzie asked.

Mercer shrugged. "They design, maintain, and troubleshoot the biotech interfaces of the specimens. The neural implants, the controls, the monitoring systems."

Dr. Ozzie nodded. "That's mainly what they do, but would it surprise you if I told you that's not all they do?"

"No," Mercer said. "It wouldn't." He smiled smugly.

"And why is that?"

"Research and development leads to

innovation, and sometimes that innovation is unrelated to the actual product being developed. Like how the space program gave us GPS and memory foam."

"You're on the right track, but in the wrong lane."

Mercer said nothing.

"The Evolve Enterprises tech division also spends a lot of time—almost half, actually, trying to hedge the company's bets and develop new and concurrent streams of income."

"English?"

Dr. Ozzie sighed. "My wife and I did a little digging, and we were surprised to discover that there were several research projects that we didn't have access to. When I asked Dax about it, he said I didn't have clearance to see the projects in question and that I needed to speak with Mr. Thorpe."

Mercer couldn't stop his eyes from going wide. He didn't think there was anything that O&M wasn't allowed to see. It made him wonder what he wasn't permitted to see.

"Yup," Dr. Ozzie said, reading Mercer's mind. "As you would imagine, my wife wasn't pleased. She wanted to run up to Twerp's office—"

Mercer snickered.

"What? You think we don't know about that nickname?"

Mercer said nothing. He perceived the docs as management—above him management, and he'd never felt comfortable around the couple.

"Anyway, she wanted to confront Thorpe, but I talked her out of it," Dr. Ozzie said.

"Good. That's good." If O&M had gone to the boss, Twerp would know the scientists were digging into things, and whatever element of surprise they might have would be lost.

"She was suspicious, so she didn't fight very hard."

Mercer waited. The doctor hadn't flagged him down on the road to tell him he'd failed.

"We've got our own data people," said the scientist. "They work for Dax, but it's only a formality. My wife and I complete their performance evaluations, if you understand me. One of these folks, who I'll leave nameless because, well, you're Director of Security, and plausible deniability is your friend. Through this person, and a back door and current code provided by said person, I hired a hacker." Dr. Ozzie leaned back in his seat and put his hands on the sportscar's steering wheel as if preparing to run.

"A hacker? You?"

"I will, of course, deny said act, but..." Dr. Ozzie tilted his head and smiled like a child who'd gotten away with not eating his dinner but had still managed to finagle dessert.

Mercer sighed. "I thought Dax's firewall was tiptop?"

"It is."

"Our system was hacked to release the specimen. I don't think that's even debatable at this point, and now you get in with a phone call?"

"It was more than that," Dr. Ozzie said. "And don't forget, my hacker had inside help."

Just like the first one, he wanted to say, but he stayed silent. This recent revelation knocked O&M way down the suspect list.

"Long story short, after we went through all the data, we discovered what Thorpe was hiding from us," Dr. Ozzie said. He paused and smiled smugly. "Dr. Gibari is developing—no, scratch that, *has* developed special high-resolution goggles that block certain spectrums of light while enhancing others, allowing their wearer to see things not normally seen by the naked eye."

"Like a creature with crypsis abilities."

"Bingo."

Mercer shook his head in disgust, though he couldn't help but admire the brilliance of it. The company could sell the weapon, and then after the fact, the slick salesforce could sell the product to the enemies of whoever buys the specimen, thus making its crypsis abilities beatable. As to why Twerp wanted to keep the goggles secret—who would pay big money for the Saberonis if they knew there was technology that would make it obsolete? Companies did this type of thing all the time, but somehow the stakes in this case seemed higher—they *were* higher. Lives *were* on the line.

"I see you're working it out," the scientist said. "You're probably thinking it's not a bad idea—but it is. What happens when word gets out? Where the goggles came from? People who spend the kind of money needed to procure a specimen like the Saberonis don't typically take too well to being swindled."

"Why are you telling me all this?" Mercer said.

"So you can get the prototype and use the goggles to kill the Saberonis," Dr. Ozzie said.

It occurred to Mercer then that his life wasn't the only one hanging in the balance. If things continued on their current course, everyone employed at Evolve would be looking for work. "I get why he'd keep it secret, but with the beast on the loose, why wouldn't he have given me the goggles straightaway? I could've gotten the thing before it escaped the property."

"My guess is he didn't want you, or anyone, to know he was playing both sides."

Mercer harrumphed. "Any idea which lab specifically the goggles might be in?"

Dr. Ozzie shook his head no. "Dr. Gibari is in nodes seven and eight, so I'd start there."

The assumption made Mercer chuckle. To obtain the goggles, he'd have to search after hours, and even then, it would be difficult to keep his activities secret from Twerp who had the facility on lockdown mode. "Your... person, can provide codes? I have a feeling I won't be able to access Dr. Gibari's labs."

Dr. Ozzie smiled. "Yes, and don't worry. There are plenty of holes in your security system."

Mercer arrived at work to find Jinx waiting for him, and the woman fell in alongside him as he strode through the front entrance.

"Any word from Cheri?" Mercer asked, though he knew there'd been no progress.

"Searching for the trail, but they're coming in tomorrow. At least that's what I hear."

"So now they're admitting they lost the trail?"

"Not exactly," Jinx said.

"Is the boss here?"

"Up in his office," Jinx said. "And he wants a word when you have a minute."

"Thanks." Mercer made his way to his office, Jinx's shadow alongside him. When he reached his assistant's desk he said, "I need a few minutes to go through email and stuff, so..." He rubbed his hands together. Veronica, his assistant, usually shooed away unwanted guests, but she'd picked the perfect time to go on maternity leave.

"What do you want me to do?" she asked.

"You're done meeting with all the employees? Making your list and checking it twice?"

"All done. I sent you summaries, but I don't think there's anything there."

Mercer said, "What does the boss think?"

Jinx hiked her shoulders. "You should ask him. Like I said: he's waiting on you."

With a curt smile, Mercer disappeared into his

office. He sat in the stillness, mentally preparing a list of things he would need if he wanted to search the Evolve labs unseen. The names of the night security shift, maps of the entire complex including the mechanical drawings, his current security codes, and a dummy ID card. He spun in his chair and tapped his keyboard, and his screen came to life. His fingers hovered over the keys for three heartbeats before he pushed back his chair. Every keystroke could be traced, and he was sure Jinx and Twerp were watching him.

The names of the night shift were easy to get, and Mercer had a final set of stamped architectural drawings from when the building was constructed. As Director of Security, he had several accounts, and he used an old one to create the dummy ID card. Most of the locks in the building were electronic, but the boss could make changes without his knowledge.

There was a briefing during which nothing was learned, and Mercer's meeting with Twerp was as predictable as a sitcom. They were running out of time, pressure was building, and Barney's death was glossed over like a bad sales quarter. Soon the feds would be calling, and Twerp wanted to have something to tell them.

It was all bullshit, and as Mercer left for the night, the search was at a standstill, though Dax had extended the perpetual carrot that his people were getting closer to bringing the tracker online. When he was safe in the Jeep Mercer called Alex.

"Are you fully convalesced? I need backup."

"Where and when?" Alex said.

19

With the moon glaring down like an accusing eye, Mercer traversed the Evolve Enterprises property without incident. He knew where to breach the fences and his radio told him exactly where each patrol was, and he emerged from the forest exactly where he'd intended, on the south side of the building.

An owl cooed softly as he sprinted across a thin band of open area and disappeared into the gardens that separated order from disorder. There he paused behind an ornamental shrub with yellow leaves and peered at the building. Mercer had walked the exterior of the facility at night many times, and he knew every blind spot in the camera system and every sliver of shadow and darkness. Eight floodlights mounted to the sidewall cast wide sprays of light that illuminated most of the side of the building, but there were dark spots and areas dominated by shadows.

More lights on motion sensors were scattered about the manicured gardens, but he knew exactly where they were. Mercer avoided the lights as he threaded through the blackness and sprinted across the strip of turf separating the building from the garden. When he reached the building, he put his back to the wall and waited as a guard loitered at the corner of the structure.

The next step was one of the most crucial because it required a coordinated effort. He glanced at his watch as he pushed from the wall, hiding in the shadows as he ran to the rear of the building. It was 11:06 PM. He still had a few minutes.

Mercer crouched in the darkness next to the loading dock's tall rollup door, which usually stood open, but was closed. His dummy security access card would—should, open any door. If push came to shove, and Dax and his people got involved, the record would show that he created the card, though he'd covered his tracks using the ID of a former employee. The goggles would be missed, and it was only a matter of time before he was discovered. He figured by that point the Saberonis would be dead, or he'd be unemployed and looking for a divorce lawyer anyway.

The seconds ticked away, and at 11:11 PM a faint staccato burst of gunshots carried on the wind. Shift change was midnight, and he and Alex had just ruined a few evenings.

His radio was connected to wireless earbuds, and Mercer listened as his security team mobilized to deal with the shots. No drill was scheduled, and the building's alarm had yet to sound, but given the heightened state of readiness and the underlying pressure being applied by Twerp, Mercer was certain there would be an overreaction, and soon.

Heart beating in his chest, his nerves burning the tips of his fingers, Mercer waited. He knew all eyes would be focused on the problem at hand, but the diversion wouldn't last long. The plan was for Alex to fire shots at the entrance and then follow Mercer's path onto the Evolve grounds, where he would take up position at the main power transfer box, which, thanks to Mercer, his partner had a key for. There he would wait for the signal to kill the power before fleeing to the pickup point. With any luck, all Alex would have to do is wait there for Mercer to arrive with the prize.

Thing was, most plans didn't survive implementation, and when Mercer used the dummy ID card to open the regular-sized door next to the big rollup, he pushed inside to find a guard sleeping. The guy's snores—Mercer thought it was Rodriguez, echoed in the confined space, drowning out the blare of the man's radio, which sat atop a box twenty feet away.

Rodriquez was propped up against a pallet of paper products that had been dropped but had yet to be unloaded and dispersed to the various cleaning closets around the building.

Mercer closed the door gently and made his way to the backup generator, which sat on a containment pad next to the loading dock. Like any engine, wires connected various parts of the machine, and he pulled one free. Mercer looked back at the sleeping guard as he sprinted up the loading dock stairs, and he was halfway to the door that led into the building when the general alarm sounded.

The guard bounced up like he'd been poked.

As the man rubbed sleep from his eyes, Mercer dove behind a stack of compressed boxes awaiting pickup for the journey to the recycling plant. The guard retrieved his radio, bolted down the steps into the main bay, sprinted to the exit, and disappeared out into the night.

Mercer let out a breath he hadn't known he was holding as the door slammed closed behind the man, the loud buzz and click of the lock reengaging bouncing off the concrete walls.

He used his card to enter a short hallway that led to the service elevator. Mercer pulled up the hood of his black sweatshirt, but it was more of a precaution against future reviews of the security video than anything else.

All eyes would be trained on the scene unfolding at the gates, and the camera above the service elevator would be, at a minimum, neglected. Still, he was a blur of motion, a shadow, and as he burst into the fire stairwell next to the elevator his heart was pounding, and sweat dripped down his forehead into his eyes.

To the left, the emergency stairs went down, and to the right, they went up. The plan had been to go down, take care of business, and retreat the same way he'd entered, but yelling carried up the stairs from below, and shadows danced on the walls.

He went right, taking the steps two at a time as he climbed until he reached the first landing, where he paused. The alarm made hearing anything difficult, but between bleats, Mercer heard voices and footsteps coming up the stairs. He ran on, leaving the entrance for the first floor behind. There was sure to be a guard sitting at the main desk, despite the diversion, and he'd be visible to the guard as he exited the stairwell, so the second floor it was.

That was the backup plan, anyway. Other than the camera above the elevator, the executive wing and administrative offices didn't have many cameras, which made it a perfect place to hide while things settled down. Once everyone was back to their predictable routine, it would be simple business sneaking down one of the other emergency stairwells into the basement.

Mercer's cellphone vibrated as he bounded up the steps. It was a text from Alex that read simply, "All G. In pos."

When he reached the second floor he paused on the landing, the alarm still ringing. The stairs switched back and continued up to the roof, and the red light of the emergency exit sign glowed above the door that led into the admin wing. A shard of light cut across the silent elevator vestibule as Mercer inched open the door. Nothing moved in the darkness, but he knew as soon as he entered the space motion activated lights would spring to life.

Memories of the HVAC drawing he'd studied elbowed their way to the forefront of his mind, and he looked up and saw an air intake. He shook his head. Climbing through the ductwork would take forever, if he could even fit, so he'd wait and head back down to the—

Light filled the vestibule, and Twerp appeared. He was wearing jeans, a t-shirt, and he stared at his phone as he waited for the elevator.

Mercer inched the door almost closed, holding it slightly open so the lock didn't engage and click.

The elevator chimed, the doors rumbled as they slid open, and then a bell rang as the doors closed.

Mercer pushed through the door just as the elevator doors closed, hood up as he bolted through the vestibule to the safety of the hallway beyond. The alarm stopped wailing, but the ringing in Mercer's head continued. The hum of the elevators ceased, and a faint bell rang. It sounded like the boss had stopped on the first floor, most likely getting an update from the desk guard on the situation at the gates.

Twelve minutes had elapsed since the shots, and he was sure the Evolve security crew was buttoning things up by now, not that there was anything to button up. Alex had fired into the sky, so there'd be no damage, and other than a report that would find its way to Mercer's desk by morning, that would be the end of it.

He moved down the hall, Twerp's office suite to the left, the other admin offices to the right. The hallway ended at a cube farm, and Mercer crawled through the cubicles because there was a camera mounted above the payroll supervisor's office door that covered most of the open area at the center of the ring of offices. Everything was dark, save for the glow of an occasional computer monitor and the daggers of light from phones and power indicator lights.

There were a series of safety lights around the cubes, but their cones of light were limited, and it was easy business making his way to the emergency stairwell on the opposite side of the floor. It was odd crawling through the cubicles and seeing the lives of people who worked at the company. He knew some of them, but not well enough to know which ten by ten cell belonged to who without looking at nameplates. Faces stared out at him from family pictures, work was abandoned half completed, and knickknacks and souvenirs from vacations adorned shelves along with children's artwork, birthday cards, and important memos that were tacked to the fabric-covered walls.

The lights came on and Mercer dove into a cubicle.

Someone was whistling, most likely a guard doing rounds. Mercer checked his watch. The guard was early, but he guessed that was to be expected given the night's excitement. He wedged himself under a desk and pulled the cube's chair in close.

The whistling got closer as Mercer stared out at the cube's credenza, which was covered in pictures and mementos. A family photo caught his eye and Mercer sucked in a deep breath and held it, afraid that the sound had alerted the guard, but the square badge didn't stop tooting his merry tune.

His skin went cold, then hot. The woman in the picture looked like Annabelle. Sweat ran down his back, and Mercer felt like he had a fever. Sorrow and shame leaked through him, the memory of the devastating night that changed his life coming back like a raging storm, Mercer unable to pull his gaze from the picture as the past replayed.

Mercer was so content he was worried. He'd never cheated on Jenni before—had never wanted to, but…

"Feeling guilty?" Annabelle asked.

The couple was wrapped in their post coitus embrace, the pleasure of release already pushed aside by Mercer's conscience. He nodded. "You?"

"Yeah, but it fades," she said.

"You've done this before?"

"Technically, many times. Why, did it seem like I didn't know what I was doing?"

"Ha, ha."

"Not many times, but a few," she said. "You?"

"First time."

"A virgin. How delicious."

Mercer frowned.

"Oh, come on now. We're just having a little fun. Sex. What's the big deal? It's not like I'm asking you to leave your wife."

Mercer sighed, regret seeping from every pore. "The memory of it... She's going to smell the guilt on me."

"Stop it. Don't ruin a nice night." She reached over and rubbed his crotch.

Little willy responded, but so did Mercer. He had no intention of compounding his mistake by having another go, and he pulled back.

Annabelle made a face like she'd smelled bad cheese.

"I should go." Mercer got up, grabbed his uniform pants, and as he pulled them on there was a knock at the door and he froze one leg in, one leg out.

"Does anyone know you're here?" Annabelle asked as she vaulted from the bed.

"No. You?"

She shook her head.

Both of their gun belts were slung over the bed's headboard, and Annabelle grabbed her Glock as Mercer pulled on his pants, approached the door, and put his eye to the peephole.

"I can see you, asshole, and you're lucky I didn't just put a bullet in your head." A cop dressed in blue stood outside the door, and Mercer recognized the man as Annabelle's husband.

"It's Ray," he hissed.

"What?" Her eyes went wide, and suddenly she looked like a scared little girl. "How? Why?"

"Open the door or I'm going to kick it down, Anna! Now!"

"What should I do?" Mercer said. He searched the room for an escape route, recalled there was a small window in the bathroom, but then remembered he was on the second floor. Besides, this was Annabelle's problem—*not true, sport*, came the rational voice from within his head. Jenni could find out he'd cheated on her, and what could be worse than that?

The door thudded as Ray kicked it, and the safety chain rattled.

With Ray drawing attention and no options left, Mercer grabbed his gun and undid the chain. "Opening up. Step back. I've got a gun and if you try anything…" What? What the hell would he do?

"I just want my wife to see something. Please. I won't hurt either of you. I promise."

Mercer looked toward Annabelle, who made no sign, so he opened the door.

Ray was a mountain of a man, and though he wasn't fat, he filled the doorway. His uniform shirt was wrinkled, and Mercer had just enough time to notice the man's badge wasn't pinned to his breast before Ray brought up his service pistol and pointed it at his own head.

"I love you, Anna," Ray said, and pulled the trigger.

Annabelle shrieked as blood, brain, and bone filled the air with a cloud of crimson mist as Ray's body fell to the ground like a sack of potatoes.

20

Annabelle's scream coalesced into the guard's whistling as the man retreated. Mercer wiped his brow, the afterimages of the suicide and the thunder of the gunshot still ringing in his head. He stared at the picture, and he felt bad for Annabelle. For Ray.

The department, ever eager to cover a mess made by its own and thus protect the blue religion, suppressed the investigation and used Annabelle's statement to gloss over the facts. The story was that Annabelle had been exhausted and too tired to drive, so she took a room for a few hours when she got off shift. Her husband, who she painted as a jealous drinker, had come looking for her because he thought she was cheating on him, and killed himself when he didn't believe Annabelle's story.

The price for this fiction was Annabelle and Mercer were required to resign from the force and sign nondisclosure agreements. Mercer could have fought the punishment—technically he'd broken no laws except God's, and he forgave everything, but the lie was necessary to keep

Jenni from discovering his indiscretion. He took a scene from a Harry Bosch book and told his wife he'd punched his sergeant during a heated argument, and he'd been fired with cause, though the union negotiated a parachute, and he was allowed to resign.

His shame superheated his stomach as he stared at the picture, still crouched in the footwell of the desk. When the affair had been settled, he'd never seen Annabelle again. Never cheated on Jenni again, but he was still paying the price, and on some level, agreed that he should be.

The lights went out from lack of movement and Mercer climbed out from under the desk and continued his crawl through the cube farm, his nerves strumming his unease. He reached the end of the row, crawled past the Director of Human Resources office, and pushed into the north emergency stairwell.

Mercer headed down and paused on the first-floor landing and listened hard, the memory of the alarm still ringing in his head. He eased open the door to the first floor and peered out. Nothing moved in the long hallway beyond. All the doors were closed, the red indicator lights of their electronic locks sword fighting in the darkness.

The lab section was secure, and Holloway, the night tech, was most likely in one of the labs checking experiments and monitoring specimens. He wanted to search the Saberonis's lab and holding area again without Jinx looking over his shoulder, but Holloway usually didn't take a break until midnight, so now wasn't the time. He waited in the stairwell, catching his breath and getting his nerves under control as he gathered his courage and prepared to head down into the basement, the netherworld of Evolve Enterprises, where specimens were harvested and grown.

Mercer didn't normally get involved with the scientific aspects of the company, and rarely did he know exactly what was happening within Evolve's labs. Given his current situation, he'd asked around, read some files, and he'd learned that in addition to the many side products being worked on by the tech division, and the DNA crew, which was always splicing stuff together like chefs in an experimental kitchen, there were currently five specimens, including the Saberonis, that were viable enough to advance to the prototype testing stage.

Three of the creatures were military grade: the Saberonis, the Iron Wasp, and the Strider Mite.

The Iron Wasp was the size of a human hand, with a bulky, armored exoskeleton that had a metallic sheen, resembling tarnished bronze. Translucent wings were reinforced with a lattice of organic metal fibers, allowing the specimen to withstand high-pressure environments. Its mandibles were strong enough to shear through light metal, and its stinger, made of a metallic alloy, was retractable and capable of delivering both venom and small explosive charges. Tests showed that the Iron Wasp's mandibles could cut through light armor plating, making it ideal for sabotage missions where it could infiltrate enemy vehicles, machinery, or structures.

On the opposite end of the marketing spectrum, but just as dangerous, was the Strider Mite, a tiny, spider-like cryptid, no larger than a thumbnail, with six long, segmented legs that allowed it to move swiftly across uneven terrain. Its body was transparent, with crypsis abilities that mirrored its environment. It had a central, single eye that glowed blue when active, and its legs secreted an adhesive substance that let the specimen cling to walls and ceilings. Strider Mites could infiltrate buildings, caves, or bunkers without being detected, and they carried tiny payloads of nanomaterial, capable of corroding wires or mechanical systems once embedded inside an engine or electrical grid. The specimens reproduced rapidly by deploying nests that generated hundreds of offspring in a short period.

The two non-military projects were the Scrubgulper and the Furnafluff, final names subject to change after the completion of a marketing review. An amphibious cryptid made from salamander and octopus DNA, the Scrubgulper had flexible limbs and soft, absorbent skin. It fed on grime, dirt, and pollutants, which it absorbed through specialized pores on its underside. Used for cleaning and environmental maintenance, the creatures slid across floors, walls, or ceilings, absorbing dust and spills. The industrial applications were endless. They could be employed to clean hazardous materials, oil spills, or polluted waterways, and to unclog pipes.

The Furnafluff was a dog-sized, quadrupedal creature that was a cross between a giant rabbit and a sea turtle. Its body was insulated with thick, woolly fur that trapped and radiated heat, allowing the creature to emit a low, constant warmth from its core, which could be regulated depending on environmental conditions. In cold climates, the Furnafluff was a natural heating system. It could warm rooms, replacing traditional power-sucking space heaters. Based on the numbers Mercer saw, the Furnafluff had worldwide marketing appeal and could become the company's most profitable product because of its potential in undeveloped countries.

A door opened, and Holloway appeared in the darkened hallway as the lights came on.

Mercer eased the door closed and continued down the steps to the basement. As he went, he texted Alex, "Almost time."

The lower level contained two surgical suites, growth rooms, testing labs, and an array of clean rooms that housed equipment Mercer barely understood. A gene-editing microscope

—which the bigheads called a CRISPR Station, allowed researchers to view and edit genes at a microscopic level. The system had laser-guided precision tools for cutting, splicing, and editing DNA sequences in living cells. Dax's folks managed the computer interface that helped map gene alterations and simulate potential outcomes before the actual editing process began.

A series of automated cell incubators provided precise control over temperature, humidity, and gas composition to mimic the optimal conditions for cell growth and differentiation. It included sensors and real-time monitoring to ensure that the cells were thriving and adjusting to the controlled environment, whether for stem cell development or organ growth.

Mercer found the bioreactor the most confusing, and thus the most interesting. It had been designed specifically for growing synthetic organisms, and it provided the necessary nutrients, oxygen, and waste removal for growing tissues or even whole organisms. There was a bioprinter room, which created tissues and organs layer by layer, and the electromagnetic chamber for life activation which generated controlled electromagnetic fields that activated dormant cellular processes and jump-started the cryptid life forms.

It was all confounding to Mercer, and as he reached the bottom of the emergency stairs, he asked himself for the tenth time if what he was doing was in his best interest. If he was discovered, or caught with the goggles, he'd be done. He and Jenni would be done. But that argument didn't hold water, because if he didn't kill the Saberonis, all those things would happen anyway.

Mercer tapped his phone, getting his camera app ready. He would have to move fast, but a picture was worth a thousand words and video was worth more, so he intended to record his search. He tapped out a simple text to Alex: "30 seconds."

There was no response as Mercer pressed through the door into the passageway beyond. Once the power was cut, emergency backup power would normally come on within a fraction of a second after power loss, but thanks to his handiwork it would take time for the security personnel to troubleshoot the problem. Most of the emergency lights ran on batteries, but the servers, security systems—including all electronic locks, which would be stuck in the locked position—and other essential systems would remain down until the backup generator was repaired.

He'd made up his mind to try node eight first, and when he reached the lab, he put his hand on the door handle, the count in his head reaching twenty-six. Mercer took a deep breath and put some pressure on the door handle.

The power went out, the hallway went dark, and the lock's red indicator light winked out.

Mercer pushed down on the handle and the door opened.

A heartbeat later the emergency lighting in node eight came to life.

Mercer closed the door.

The lab was awash with LED light from the emergency lights. There were all kinds of electronic equipment, several benches covered with wires, circuit boards, tape, and various metals. The place stank of burnt metal and melted plastic.

There were monitoring collars, robotic insects —everything except the goggles. With his cell light blazing, he took video as he searched, but after five minutes it became clear he had chosen incorrectly.

Mercer pictured the security guards pouring over the emergency generator, and as if she was reading his mind, Mercer's cellphone vibrated, and Jinx's name appeared above the camera view. He didn't answer it. Twerp was probably going batshit, and Jinx was trying to update him.

He recalled the mechanical drawing he'd seen, and starting from a corner, he counted ceiling tiles and mounted a bench on the southern side of the room. Node Seven was the lab directly to the south. Mercer lifted the ceiling tile and peered into the gap between the dropped ceiling and the deck above. As the drawing had shown, there was a two-and-a-half-foot gap above the ceiling providing a plenum for air circulation.

Mercer pulled himself up and made fast work of squeezing himself through the confined space. Laying prone on his stomach, his weight on the top of the wall, he lifted out one of node seven's ceiling tiles and put it to the side before dropping through the opening onto a desk.

As in node eight, emergency lights glowed, but unlike node eight, no search of node seven was necessary, because the goggles were in a fume hood-like display case. Like high-dollar sunglasses, the frames looked to be made of brushed aluminum, and the lenses glowed like those crazy pinwheel glasses clowns wore. The arms were reinforced with carbon fiber, and embedded within there were micro-adjustment sliders that let the user fine-tune vision modes.

The glasses were connected to a series of wires that led to a computer, and there were other units on benches at various stages of construction, and a schematic of the latest design filled a wall. There were lens grinders and cleaning wheels, and it looked to Mercer as though the anti-Saberonis glasses were the node's only project.

Mercer jumped from the lab desk, his heart pounding as he went to the display case. It wasn't locked. He opened it, stripped off all the wires attached to the frame, and removed the goggles. He lifted them to put them on, then glanced up at the emergency lighting. He realized at that moment that he had no idea what he was dealing with, and he'd taken a huge risk for an advantage that might not work.

There were papers all over the place and other prototypes, but none of them were connected to computers. Shame washed through Mercer. All this hadn't been for nothing. It hadn't.

Mercer put on the glasses.

21

Node Seven, Evolve Enterprises, Inc.,
Occidental, California, U.S.A.
12:03 AM PST, Day Five

Shadows burst to life and every angle grew blurry as Mercer entered a world of heightened awareness. The emergency lights blared white, and everything in the lab appeared more vibrant, but also distorted, as if the natural environment was breaking down under the weight of unseen forces. A chilling, primal perception leaked over him, and he looked around, searching for phantom beasts lurking just beyond the edge of sight. He ran his fingers over the micro-adjustment sliders, but he took off the goggles instead. There had to be some information on how the unit worked in the lab.

Mercer felt each tick of the clock, and he figured he had five minutes left before the generator was fixed and the backup power came on. He searched the lab bench closest to the fume hood that had held the prototype and found a series of old-school three-ring binders. One was the SpectraShade Goggles Logbook, next to that were two thick volumes of design specs showing previous versions of the product, and the last binder was labeled SpectraShade Goggles User Manual.

"Bingo," he said to the empty room as he pulled the manual free and opened it.

Mercer scanned the book, pulling the pertinent information. The unit's lenses were composed of an iridescent material known as Prismix Crystal, a synthetic compound that refracted light across unseen spectrums. When inactive, the lenses glistened with faint, multicolored veins of light, and when powered on the colors became much brighter. The glasses used advanced multi-spectral scanning technology designed to detect wavelengths of light that the human eye couldn't naturally see. This allowed the glasses to reveal patterns in light refraction, heat signatures, energy fields, and subtle disturbances in the surrounding air caused by camouflaged adversaries.

He flipped pages, skipping a bunch of technical information as he searched for the mode setting descriptions. When he found the section, he let a low whistle escape his lips. The prototype had four modes that could be changed via the micro-adjustment slider on the left temple arm. The slider on the right was the manual focus adjustment. The four modes were listed as Infrared, Ultraviolet, Thermal, and Spectral Scan.

There was no need to read the detail on the infrared and ultraviolet sections—infrared detected heat signatures and would reveal creatures that absorbed or reflected UV light, causing their outlines to glow or pulsate while the surrounding environment would appear bathed in soft violet hues. Mercer had used binoculars that achieved both these enhanced states of vision.

The Thermal section was filled with technical information, so Mercer skipped to the final and unknown mode.

When in Spectral Scan mode, the glasses filtered the environment through multiple light spectrums at once. The world around the wearer would become a swirling, semi-transparent landscape of distorted colors. Trees, rocks, and buildings would blur at the edges as the glasses isolated living things. Creatures with crypsis capabilities would appear as flickering, unstable forms. Mercer figured it would be like watching static on an old television, the faint images of a program bleeding through.

The manual mentioned two more modes that didn't require action from the user to change. Pulse telemetry occurred every few seconds, and the glasses sent out a weak electromagnetic pulse, forcing camouflaged creatures to briefly reveal themselves as shimmering silhouettes, visible only to the wearer. The prototype also had adaptive lenses that automatically adjusted their focus depending on the intensity of light or darkness.

Mercer put the glasses back on and toggled through the various modes, his vision going from reddish brown to brilliant white, to a blurred landscape where there were no right edges, and finally to Spectral Scan mode.

The world became a churning mosaic of fragmented hues and shifting transparency, and the boundaries between objects blurred and warped as if reality itself was unraveling. Colors bled into one another in a kaleidoscopic whirl, with shades of neon blue, deep violet, and phosphorescent green pulsing like an electric current. The air was thick with distortions, and Mercer pulled the glasses off, folded them, and slipped them into his breast pocket. He scanned the wires he'd disconnected from the unit, but if one of them charged the battery he couldn't tell.

He quickly took videos of the manual's pertinent pages and was climbing through the ceiling when the power came back on. The emergency lights beeped and went out, and the hum and buzz of equipment coming online filled the lab, but the lights didn't come on because no motion was detected.

Mercer put the ceiling tile back in place, nudged himself over the top of the wall, and army-crawled back to node eight. When he dropped through the ceiling the lights came to life. He carefully replaced the ceiling tile, jumped from the bench, pulled up his hood to cover his face, and left the lab. The electronic lock buzzed as he approached, the motion sensor above the door unfreezing the lock.

The passageway was awash with light, and Mercer became aware of the camera mounted above the elevator. He pressed himself to the wall, slinking in the shadows, wanting to run for the emergency stairwell but knowing stealth was more important. He was almost there when the elevator chimed and the white light above the doors came to life indicating that the car had arrived.

Mercer pulled out his dummy ID card—it worked, and he entered the lab closest to him. It was a bioreactor node, and its purpose was to grow synthetic organisms, providing nutrients, and oxygen, and removing waste for developing tissues or entire specimens. He heard voices in the hallway and doors were opening and closing. They were doing a room-by-room check. That was standard procedure.

As the lights came on Mercer noted that the lab looked like most of the others, and most of the gear was foreign to Mercer. There were benches, shakers, centrifuges—nowhere to hide. Then he saw the desk and sighed.

A loud buzz echoed through the room as Mercer ran across the lab and took up his now familiar position beneath the desk in its footwell.

The door opened, shuffling feet, a murmur, a cough, and then the door closed.

Mercer held his breath, but he heard no footsteps, no breathing. Whoever the guard had been had done a looksie and moved on. With the lights still blaring—the guard incorrectly would have believed he caused the motion that turned on the lights.

He crawled out from under the desk, got to his feet, and was heading for the door when he noticed a yellow file atop the desk that read Saberonis. Mercer looked over his shoulder as if expecting to see Twerp watching him, and he flipped the file open. The first page was a summary, and it read: "This report details the process and reasoning behind the impregnation of the Saberonis. The goal of the experiment was to study the specimen's unique reproductive biology, hoping to unlock its regenerative capabilities and understand its evolutionary traits. Using advanced biotechnological methods, including a bioreactor for controlled growth and an electromagnetic chamber to stimulate dormant cells, the researchers successfully fertilized the Saberonis. This experiment was part of a broader initiative to explore genetic manipulation, hybridization potential, and the species' adaptability in extreme environments. The report also emphasizes the ethical implications and future applications of these findings."

Mercer's mouth fell open. Just when he thought things couldn't get worse.

The beast was pregnant.

He took a picture of the page and called Alex.

"Yo. Are you O.K.?"

"Great. I'm going to plan two, so you can pull out."

"10-4. Did you get them?"

"I did."

"Nice," Alex said. "Do you need me to do anything?"

"Yeah, when I call, I'll need to be picked up, remember? I'm going to tell everyone my car broke down like we planned."

"Got it."

Mercer hung up and stripped off his sweatshirt and the oversized black sweatpants. Beneath he wore a black golf shirt and lightweight dress pants. He stuffed the sweatpants and hoodie into a trashcan, covered it with trash, and pushed out into the hallway like he owned the place.

There was one truth Mercer had stuck to his entire life: look like you belong, and nobody will question your presence, especially when one's presence is expected.

He stayed out of sight of the camera and entered the emergency stairwell, and from there he went to the first floor and headed for his office. Nobody saw him except the electronic eyes in the sky. As he walked he called Jinx.

"Boss, where are you? We've got—"

"Easy. I'm on site."

Air moved through vents and the hum of the building's life-support were the only sounds.

"When did you get here?"

Mercer strode down the hallway toward his office. Faint chatter echoed from the lobby, and the red glow of a spinning emergency light coming in through the lobby windows painted the gloom crimson. "A couple of minutes ago."

"You're car isn't in—"

"It's in the shop."

"I didn't hear anything from the gate guards about a strange car coming through."

Anger surged through Mercer. "I'm sorry, but why would the gate guards report my activities to you?" He knew this was a hole in his story, but it was unavoidable, so going on offense was the only option.

"I was just—"

"Don't just," he snapped. "Do you have anything new to report?"

"I'll be up in five."

Mercer killed the connection and smiled.

Jinx arrived with draft reports detailing the gunshots and the loose wire. He chuckled. That's how she described the wire he'd pulled in her summary of the building search, during which nothing out of place was found.

Mercer chuckled. Not yet, anyway.

When Jinx was gone—most likely beelining to Twerp to relay her suspicions about his story, Mercer put the goggles in a lockbox and hid it above the ceiling. He couldn't rule out the possibility that once the prototype was discovered missing, every nook and cranny of the building would be searched—under his command.

It was 1:27 AM and Mercer was having trouble keeping his eyes open when he dropped on his office couch and was asleep in minutes, visions of his success dancing in his head like candy canes.

Sunlight streamed through the office window, rousing Mercer from sleep as a knocking echoed through the room. He sat up, rubbed his eyes, and looked around. He was spending a great deal of time sleeping on the couch for a guy who hadn't done anything wrong—lately.

"Give me a minute," he said as he pushed to his feet, looked into his desk mirror, and flattened his hair before opening the door.

It was O&M, and they looked pleased.

"Thorpe is wigging out," Dr. Miranda said.

"About what, specifically?"

"Not sure," Dr. Ozzie said.

"Did they notice the glasses are missing?"

"Not yet," Dr. Miranda said.

"But by 9:05 they will," Dr. Ozzie said.

Mercer glanced at his watch. It was 8:13 AM. "You guys shouldn't be here," he said.

"You're right, but we had to give you this," Dr. Ozzie said. He handed over a picture.

"Dax's people retrieved a trace of data from the specimen's collar," Dr. Miranda said.

Mercer leaned forward, his enthusiasm growing.

Dr. Miranda put up a hand. "Don't get excited. What you see is all we got. No GPS location. No time stamp."

The picture showed the bottom portion of a large dark circle, and several shadowy shapes distorted the image. It looked like the Saberonis had been hiding under something.

"We'll have an enhanced version for you by the end of the day," Dr. Ozzie said.

"Why didn't Jinx or the ESS people tell me about this?"

"We have no idea who knows what," Dr. Ozzie said.

"Great."

"You should get out of here before..." Dr. Miranda looked at the floor.

"I will," Mercer said.

He called Alex and then instructed the gate guards to let his friend through without questions, and they were to tell nobody. His thought was that maybe when the guards were interviewed, they'd mix up that instruction with the prior night. He doubted it, but the threat of termination was a powerful motivation to lie, or at a minimum, leave out crucial facts.

There was no update on the beast, and Thorpe had called an all-hands meeting for the next day, including the ESS head honcho, Grey. Mercer figured it was 50-50 that he'd be in attendance. He left word at the front desk that he was going home, and that he should be contacted only if there was a new development. Then Alex drove him home.

It was 8:14 PM, and Jenni and Mercer were watching TV when his phone chimed noting the receipt of an email. There were no new developments concerning the Saberonis, but a digitally enhanced copy of the photo provided by the specimen's monitoring collar was attached.

He stared at the picture all night—on his phone, datapad, and TV, and he showed it to his wife, but neither of them could make heads or tails of it. Even with the magic of enhancement, the photo didn't show much.

The black round thing took on a wooden patina and a leg could be seen holding up... what they didn't know. The only useful thing was what looked like a symbol in the lower right-hand portion of the quarter circle. It was an upside-down cross in a circle, that was clear, but internet searches revealed nothing of use.

Mercer was ready to pack it in for the night when Jennie screamed and Mercer spit-up red wine that stained his new Giants t-shirt. He ran into the kitchen and found his wife staring at a wine bottle. "Are you O.K.? Is everything alright?"

She handed him the bottle.

They'd been drinking a local shiraz, a five-year-old Freely. He scanned the label, saw nothing unusual, and turned the bottle in his hands. "What?"

She took the bottle from him and pointed at the label. It was a painting of a wine cellar, and many wooden barrels were stacked atop one another. The logo at the bottom of the label was an upside-down cross in a circle.

22

Tall Pines, Occidental, California, U.S.A.
6:12 AM PST, Day Six

It was too late to accomplish anything meaningful, and Jenni convinced Mercer that he wouldn't be of any help to anyone if he couldn't even stay on his feet, so he crashed. His sleep was fitful, and at 4:40 AM he came awake from his recurring nightmare—the night Ray shot himself in the head, and he was unable to go back to sleep. He got up, took a long shower, dressed, and made coffee.

Stray beams of moonlight streamed through the thick mist that filled the darkness, and everything was coated in a layer of glittering moisture. Most of Tall Pines was still asleep, and only a few windows glowed from early risers as he left the development.

Though he was no fan of his wife's Prius, he and Jenni switched cars for the day because his Jeep was well known, and he had a feeling he was going to require anonymity very soon. Eucalyptus trees lined Occidental Road, an occasional house, business, or cattle ranch emerging beyond the thick greenery that lined the road. Mercer had the car's windows cracked, and the sweet scent of pine and eucalyptus filled the vehicle.

The sun came up as the road wound steadily east, and with each passing mile, his trepidation grew as his fears about the specimen's path came to fruition. If the beast had been at Freely Winery, it was moving east, and if the Saberonis continued in that direction it would reach the town of Barlow. He couldn't let that happen.

Mercer wasn't sure of Webster's schedule, and with Barney's death and the incident at the abandoned farm, the deputy might be stuck behind a desk. Still, Mercer decided to call the deputy anyway. He'd asked too much of Alex already. Things were about to get hot, and his friend was his ace in the hole, and he intended to keep him there as long as possible.

"Mercer. My favorite new friend. How did you know I'd be up?" Webster said.

"I didn't."

Webster said nothing.

"Are you there?" Mercer said.

"That's what one calls sarcasm, Mercer. What do you want? I'm off today."

"Oh, sorry. I didn't mean to—"

"You already did. Since I'm up, what's up?" Webster no longer sounded aggravated.

"I've got a lead," Mercer said. "And I thought

you might want in on it." Mercer had decided not to tell Webster about the SpectraShade Goggles until he had to, because the cop was sure to ask questions, and Mercer didn't like lying to the man.

"Do tell."

Mercer told the deputy about the picture and what it showed.

"I live five minutes from there."

So it was that when Mercer arrived at Freely Vineyard & Winery, he found Webster parked on the side of the road in his patrol car. In Northern California, departments allowed some officers to bring their patrol cars home as part of the "take-home" vehicle program designed to save money and improve response times in rural areas.

The road was deserted, and Mercer pulled alongside the squad car as he rolled down his window.

Webster wasn't in uniform, but he wore a white golf shirt with a gold star on the left breast and a green sheriff's department ballcap. "I waited out here because I didn't know how you wanted to handle it."

"How I wanted to handle it?"

"It's your lead, right? Can I see the picture, by the way?"

So that was it. Mercer handed a copy of the picture from the specimen's collar through the window. The deputy didn't want to put his ass on the line for what amounted to a hunch, and what could end up being a dead fish. He understood and didn't care. The guy had come to help him, and that's all that mattered. The duo was in deep together and had foundational trust, like a married couple. They shared secrets, regrets, and fears, and a betrayal would expose all these things.

"Sure looks like one of the large barrels in the main cellar," Webster said.

"How could that be? Don't they keep that place sealed up?"

"Not the bay doors. They're open all day and depending on the temperature they might be left open for increased air circulation."

"You're a connoisseur?" Mercer said.

That got a chuckle. "Naw. The wife. But I like it here. It's peaceful, though it gets a steady traffic of folks passing through on their way to and from the coast, but only locals setup camp. You've never been here?"

There were more wineries within a fifty-mile radius of Tall Pines than there were gas stations —and it wasn't even close. "No, but as I said, the wife and I were drinking their shiraz. Good stuff. So, you know folks here?"

Webster nodded. "Everybody."

"It's early, will anybody be here yet?" It was 7:37 AM and the hours posted on the website said the first tasting appointment was 9 AM. Mercer and Jenni had chuckled at that one, and not because drinking wine at 9 AM was less than pleasurable. Back when the tasting craze exploded reservations weren't required, and many wineries offered free tasting, a comical concept in the current business plans of vineyards.

"Sure," Webster said. "I assume you'd like to keep the reason for our presence on the QT? At least until we find something?"

"That makes sense. You're comfortable lying? What's the story going to be?"

Webster said, "No story needed. The site manager, Victor, and the wine maker Fiona will be here, and I know them both well. You're a friend who wants to look at the vineyard and the facilities. That's it. They won't ask why. Fiona will assume you're a wine guy who doesn't want to be around the crowds. If she offers a sniff of her newest concoction, take it."

"Right. You're a cop." It had been a long time since he'd possessed the powers of the blue religion, and he no longer assumed people would do what he asked because of a badge.

The duo drove through the open gates, a large sign with white lettering announcing Freely Vineyard & Winery and the tasting room's hours of operation. Below that in smaller, but bolder type, the word 'No' was painted on a removable placard that hung before the words Reservations Required.

Italian cypress trees lined the long driveway, their tall, elegant spires soaring fifty feet above the road, casting long shadows over the rows of grapevines. Native to the Mediterranean region, the trees thrived in warm, dry climates, and their dark green foliage consisted of dense, scale-like evergreen leaves.

When the pair reached the parking lot they were greeted by three large metal cat sculptures. The felines stood ten feet tall, and as he parked, Mercer recalled reading something on the winery's website about the cats being the mascots of the vineyard. Not only did the cats keep out unwanted rodents, but they were also an alarm system that detected larger problems, like mountain lions, deer, and bears.

The tasting room was located in a house that had once been the manor house of an estate, and behind it there were a series of buildings, both new and old. A gentle breeze stirred the vines, and the sweet scent of musk wafted over the parking lot as the partners walked around the tasting room via a path that led to the back of the house. Over the backdoor, there was a sign that read, "Administration. Employees only."

One car was parked in employee parking, and as the partners approached the back entrance a man in jeans and a flannel shirt emerged from the building.

"That's Victor, the site manager," Webster said as he waved.

Victor was a tall man with thinning black hair and olive skin. A smile split his face as he held out a hand. "I saw the sheriff's car and… well, it's you. Is everything O.K.?"

Webster shook the man's hand as he said, "Everything is fine. This here is a buddy of mine, Chad Mercer. We've got business in Occidental, but not until 9ish. Maybe I could show him around? Is Fiona here?"

Victor's smile doubled in size as the clouds of a potential problem withdrew. "Of course. Look at anything you like. Fiona is in the cellar taking samples. Can I offer you a nip of the new cab? Or do you want to wait for Fiona? I'm sure she'd love for you to help her do her tastings."

Mercer fought back a chuckle. The preferential treatment cops got was amazing.

"We'll wait for Fiona," Webster said. "We've got work so we'll be sipping."

"Of course."

"Listen," Webster said. "Has anything… unusual happened around here lately? Dead animals? Damage to buildings? Rutted or dug-up vines? Anything like that?"

Victor's lips disappeared into a thin red line, his radar back on full. "No. Why? You said there was nothing wrong."

"There isn't," Mercer said. "There's been a few reports of a big cat around these parts, so we're just keeping an eye out."

Webster nodded but didn't look at Mercer.

"Ah, a cat. Their tracks are distinctive, and I haven't seen anything bigger than our own small felines, not that I walk the vineyard every day." His gaze strayed from the two men to the grape vines to the east as if teasing out a memory.

Webster urged him on. "Any odd things at all?"

"Yesterday, I was walking..." Victor shook his head. "It's nothing. Let me know if you need anything. I need to get back to—"

"Please, Victor," Webster said. "Any piece of information, no matter how inconsequential, could be a big help."

"I just don't know what I saw. If anything."

"That's alright," Mercer said. "Try. Please."

"I was walking through the vineyard. The sun was going down, and I saw this—to call it a shadow wouldn't be right. It was like an absence of light, a smudge in the air. It was big. I couldn't believe what I was seeing, and I pulled my phone to take a picture, but when I tried it was gone."

Mercer and Webster exchanged a glance.

"Where did this happen?" Webster asked.

"Northeast quadrant by the chardonnay," Victor said. "You know that spot where we had the tasting BBQ last year?"

"Yes, I recall the area. We're going to take a walk out there and take a look. That O.K.?"

"Sure."

"Has anyone else other than Fiona been in the cellar today?" Webster asked.

"No."

"O.K. Thank you. We'll stop and see you on our way out."

Victor nodded.

The garden surrounding the tasting room gave way to stone paths that led to the various outbuildings, and Webster made a hard right and headed out into the vines.

An earsplitting screech broke the stillness, and the singing birds went silent.

A tabby cat with fur-like shadows dancing in the twilight—dark stripes running across a coat of burnt orange and black—appeared at the head of a trellis packed with vines. Its eyes were molten gold, the pupils narrow gashes. The fur along the cat's spine was raised, and its pointed ears twitched as if registering every whisper of movement. With a grace only attainable by felines, the creature disappeared, a streak of hissing blurred orange.

"That can't be a good sign," Mercer said.

23

The cool embrace of dawn spread over the vineyard, soft mist whispering through the neatly ordered rows. Smokey tendrils embraced the weathered vines as the sky blushed, the sun casting faint hues of rose and lavender across the horizon as if the heavens were in quiet conversation with the land. A breeze snaked through the vines, teasing their leaves into a gentle dance and shaking clusters of grapes that glistened with dew.

Mercer and Webster reached the end of a row, and a clearing stretched out before them. There was a small gazebo at its center, a brick BBQ, and a few picnic tables scattered about. The ground was a patchwork of hardpan and mowed weeds and grass, and as the partners searched Mercer found no sign of tracks.

The pair continued west and reached the edge of the vineyard, where a strip of turf with a fence running down its center separated the vines from the forest. The barrier kept most large pests out, though deer could easily leap over the six-foot height. Douglas fir branches extended over the fence in several spots, reaching out from the dense forest. To Mercer, the towering evergreens seemed small after recently spending time among the giant redwoods.

"This is like looking for a needle in a haystack," Mercer said as the partners walked north along the break line.

"The area Victor described is right ar—" Webster dropped to a knee and examined the ground.

A black mark, like a giant's dark tear, marred a patch of dirt between two tufts of poison-fried weeds.

"Blood?" Mercer asked.

"Hard to tell," Webster said as his index finger hovered five inches above the stain. "It could be oil or any liquid that brought out the color in the dirt, or perhaps whatever it is hasn't fully dried. It could be anything."

"Like blood," Mercer said.

The duo searched the area and discovered dark speckles on the green leaves of a vine at the end of a row. Webster delved deeper into the vines and Mercer peeled off west to examine the fence.

Mercer saw that the fence was undamaged, but fifty feet down the line there was a skeletal tree limb that reached over the barrier and a dusting of pine needles, twigs, and pinecones littered the ground below it.

"Webster," Mercer called. "I think something climbed over the fence here."

"Come look at this," Webster answered.

The chardonnay vines had recently been pruned, and there was a thin strip of brown grass directly under the vines. All vegetation below the vines was treated with weedkiller to avoid excess moisture and humidity which caused noble rot and other grape-killing diseases. A thin black irrigation pipe was attached to the lower trestle wire, and clusters of grapes hung from brown ropy vines. Trimmed grass dotted with dandelions ran down the center of the row, but there were patches of dirt and occasional tufts of untamed grass where the mower had missed.

Webster stood before a thick wall of green gazing down at the ground, his hand on his sidearm.

When Mercer arrived at Webster's side he pointed.

The grass was disheveled, and the round pads of a giant cat paw and the slashes of its claws could be seen in a dirt patch at Webster's feet.

Webster led, and the duo found more partial prints and two more possible blood drips. They followed the trail, a large white metal building framed at the end of the row.

As the duo exited the vines a blue Honda pulled into the employee parking lot.

"I don't want to press the panic button, but we should keep this place clear," Mercer said. "I'm sure the Saberonis is long gone, but it can't hurt to take precautions."

Webster nodded and approached the employee as she exited her car. "Morning, Ma'am. I'm Deputy Webster and I'm with the sheriff's department. Everything is fine, but can you hurry into the building? Tell Victor to lock the doors and nobody should come out until I give the go-ahead."

The woman's face slipped from a smile to a frown. "Let me get Mr.—"

"No," Webster said in that cop tone that demanded respect and compliance. "Please go inside and tell Victor to stay there as well. Everything is fine and we'll update him in a few minutes." He finished with a broad smile that made Mercer uncomfortable.

"Well, O.K., then." She shut her car door and hustled to the rear entrance.

"Let's go see what there is to be seen," Webster said when the woman was gone.

Like several of the outbuildings, the main wine cellar had once been part of a century-old estate. When the structure above it required replacement, the decision was made to preserve the cellar. The corrugated metal building contained the crushing chambers, the bottling equipment, and ten massive stainless-steel casks filled with young wines that were being treated and tested before going to their midwives, barrels of oak or steel, where they would let time turn grapes into wine and money before being bottled.

Large roll-up doors stood open on both the eastern and western ends of the twenty-thousand-square-foot building, and during business hours a steady flow of forklifts, tractors, and delivery trucks would constantly be moving through the building. As the partners entered through the western bay door the temperature dropped ten degrees.

Mercer put on the SpectraShade Goggles and light blared like a blazing sun. The stainless-steel glowed bright as the cement floor grew dark. He ran his fingers over the micro-adjustment sliders and switched the unit to Spectral Scan mode.

Everything dissolved into a chaotic mosaic of fragmented hues and shifting transparency, and the boundaries between objects blurred and twisted. Colors bled together in a kaleidoscopic swirl, neon blues, deep violets, and glowing greens pulsing through the air.

"What are those?" Webster asked.

"Just a little something I picked up on the internets to help me see in the dark," Mercer said. He didn't see the shimmering outline of the Saberonis, but he did see the slender radiance of a woman approaching.

"Webster?" came a concerned voice as gentle as the cooing of an infant.

"Hi, Fiona," Webster said.

Mercer took off the glasses and slipped them into a pocket. "Chad Mercer."

"Do what do I owe the pleasure?" Fiona said.

Her strawberry blonde hair was in a tangle, her powder-white freckled face sunburned, and she wore work boots and overalls with a white t-shirt beneath. She held a wine glass with an ounce of white wine in it.

Before Webster could answer Fiona's radio chirped.

"Fiona. Are you there? It's Victor."

Webster and Mercer both looked at the ground.

Fiona thumbed the comm button on her radio and said, "I'm here, Victor. Go ahead."

"Is Deputy Sheriff Webster and his guest with you?" Victor said.

Fiona looked up at Mercer and Webster, her green eyes going wide. "Yes, they're here."

"May I speak to them?"

Webster shook his head no. "Tell him to stay put and I'll be with him in five minutes."

"You're not here to taste?" she asked.

"Not really, no," Webster said. "In fact, would you mind going to the tasting room and staying there until I come and get you? Please."

She put her glass down, retrieved her purse, and exited the building without another word.

Webster picked up the glass Fiona had abandoned and slammed the white wine therein. "Good stuff," he said as he put the glass back where he'd found it.

Somewhere a pump kicked on, and the sound of rushing liquid drove out the whisper of the wind and the distant arguing of birds. The air was thick with humidity and the scent of damp earth. Several glasses of wine rested atop an empty barrel, each sitting atop a coaster with a number on it.

Mercer didn't know much about wine, but he knew brewmasters tasted their concoctions regularly to ensure quality and to judge when the product was ready for consumption. He assumed wine makers used a similar system.

Webster picked up a glass of red wine, downed it, and said, "White or red."

"White."

Mercer accepted a glass and downed the contents with one pull—it was only an ounce. He said, "Good. Very."

The stairwell that led up into the storage room and down into the cellar was at the center of the space, and a series of thick stainless-steel pipes ran from the metal casks down into the cellar where the transfer to smaller vessels occurred.

Mercer drew his Sig Sauer and Webster his Glock, and the two men prepared the weapons to fire as they stood at the top of the stairs staring down into darkness.

The cement floor was clean, and several areas were wet from a recent scrubbing. There were drains placed at strategic spots, and if the prints of the Saberonis had ever been there, they were gone now.

A gust of wind pushed through the doors.

"The specimen could've gotten in here easily," Webster said.

Sunlight angled into the building, dust motes dancing in the air.

"What are your thoughts on backup?" Webster said.

"For what? We have no idea if the thing is in here," Mercer said. His skin was crawling, his nerves gyrating and poking at the underside of his skin, and he felt—though he didn't know how, that the Saberonis was close, yet still he resisted the idea of bringing in more people.

Webster said nothing as he cracked his neck.

"Let's take a look," Mercer said. "We can always retreat and call in the contractors Evolve hired and let them handle it. No need to put ourselves in the limelight."

Webster nodded emphatically "I like that. A lot."

The partners searched the wine-making and bottling areas and found nothing out of place. Webster started down the steps, gun in a twohanded grip as he ranged the weapon around.

Mercer followed, and when the pair was halfway down the stairs the lights in the subterranean chamber blossomed to life. The steps ended on a platform where the winery's guests could view the cellar without entering its hallowed grounds. Shadows danced, and the humid air was crisp and carried a rich, earthy aroma, a blend of damp stone and oak, with subtle notes of yeast.

The stairwell was open and all sides, and a brushed metal railing and redwood stations boxed in the steps. Ahead a series of stainless-steel workbenches sat in shadow, atop which were hydrometers, test cylinders, tasting glasses, and pipettes for drawing small quantities of wine. Shelves held pH meters, testing kits, cleaning supplies, and a variety of logbooks and paperwork.

To Mercer's right and left the cellar was filled with standard fifty-nine-gallon oak barrels, each with a number burned into its face. The barrels were set in permanent cradles and were stacked three high. A forklift sat at the end of one of the aisles, and Mercer traced the thick pipes coming from above to the two holding casks that were used to transfer the wine into wooden and stainless-steel barrels.

Mercer turned one hundred and eighty degrees and whistled. Behind him, four rows of huge wooden casks lined the southern wall.

"Those big ones hold the cheaper stuff," Webster said. "The wine you'd buy in a liquor store or order at a restaurant. The aging process is much shorter, the wines less complex, so it's more cost-effective to use bigger vessels."

Mercer pulled a copy of the picture captured from the specimen's monitoring collar. He held it up, trying to see what the Saberonis had seen. The rows between the regular-sized barrels were tight, but the bigger vessels had passages between them wide enough to accommodate the moving of the larger casks.

Webster unfastened a gold chain that blocked the short staircase leading from the viewing platform down into the heart of the cellar. The deputy's steps rang on the metal stair treads as he descended into the maze of barrels, gun up.

The picture crinkled as Mercer made a fist, the shrill sound echoing through the cellar, his heart racing. Suddenly things had gotten very real. The cellar was the perfect place for the Saberonis to lay low. It was cool, dark, free of other creatures, and there were plenty of places to hide, even for a huge sabertoothed cat chameleon cryptid.

Mercer rolled his shoulders, put his phone on vibrate, and slipped on the SpectraShade Goggles. He grew dizzy as he traversed the steps, a chill running through him as the shadows became deep dark patches, and the metal bands around the wine barrels glowed gold.

"You go right, and I'll go left, and we'll meet back here at the base of the stairs," Webster said.

Normally, Mercer would oppose splitting up, but the cellar was an open space with only barrels and worktables obstructing the view, allowing the partners to keep an eye on each other. He nodded and raised the Sig Sauer, imaginary ants marching up and down his spine.

24

Even with the lights on, the cellar was a dark place. Abrupt changes in heat, humidity, and light changed the complexity of wine, usually for the worst. The SpectraShade glasses dulled the room, erasing much of its detail—the sharp edges of the stair rails, the sleek, glowing lines of the worktables— all fading into blackness.

Something shimmered at his feet, an amorphous blob that glowed bright and was outlined in glistening silver. The undulating mass moved as if alive. Mercer lifted the glasses and placed them atop his head.

A small puddle gleamed under a closed spigot.

Mercer searched for Webster and found the deputy creeping through a row of wine barrels directly opposite him, the stairwell in between them. With the glasses still resting atop his head, Mercer stopped under a ceiling light that reminded him of something you'd see on a submarine. The bulb was covered in a metal cage and cast a dull yellow light. He scanned the picture again, slowly turning in a full circle as he tried to locate the vantage point from which the photo had been taken.

The partial barrel in the picture didn't show a number because there wasn't one. Larger casks had clipboards hanging from hooks on the faces of the barrels. He slipped the glasses back on.

When Mercer reached the section with the larger barrels, he paused. Shadows danced in the corners of the room, thick patches of darkness ten feet away that could hide a small dinosaur. The low rumble of the HVAC system moving air was the only sound.

Mercer folded the photo and put it away as he pulled his cellphone. He tapped its screen and used the light app, holding it like a flashlight next to the Sig Sauer as he broke left, casks towering over him on both sides of the aisle.

Now that he was moving through the space, the photo made more sense. The Saberonis had most likely wedged itself between two of the large barrels and the image captured was the beast staring at the cask across from its hiding spot. He was now certain of that. That meant there should be some sign in the thin layer of dust that covered the sides of the aisle and the floor between the casks.

Mercer saw that an attempt to clean between the barrels had at least been made at some point in the recent past. Here and there a boot print could be seen where an employee had ventured off the beaten path to clean a cobweb or shine a light into a dark space checking for leaks or mold. He reached the end of the row, the world a churning, semi-transparent landscape of bright colors, but there were no flickering, unstable forms.

He headed back the way he'd come, and in the distance, Mercer saw the glow of Webster's light. Mercer clenched the Sig Sauer so tightly his hand cramped, his breathing shallow, his eyes still adjusting to the chaotic landscape revealed by the glasses. His pulse throbbed in his ears, the echo of liquid running through pipes like blood coursing through his veins.

Mercer scanned the large wooden casks as shadows clawed out from between barrels searching for light. He reached an aisle that ran left and he continued straight, Webster's cellphone light fading. Mercer saw the shadowy form of his partner every few seconds as he passed through cones of light.

Then he was gone, and there was no sign of him or his cellphone light.

A strangled wail shattered the stillness, and Mercer broke into a run. "Webster?"

No response.

"Webster?"

Two gunshots rang out, and the sound of splintering wood and gushing wine carried through the cellar, followed by a string of curses.

Mercer looked back at the staircase. He should go topside and get help. Call for backup. The ESS folks could have a team on-site in minutes via chopper. But he couldn't leave Webster. Not after all they'd been through together.

"Is everything O.K. down there?" shouted Victor.

Mercer held back a string of profanity. The beast was close, and he didn't want to give away his position, but he couldn't let the man enter the cellar. He yelled, "Don't come down here. No matter what. Go call the police. Now!"

No response and Mercer figured his frantic tone had been enough to tell the man danger was afoot. Mercer sprinted down the aisle, gun at the ready, tall wooden casks towering over him.

A low growl reverberated off the stone walls.

Mercer slowed to a walk, the shimmering outline of the Saberonis twenty feet away. It was on all fours, its front legs flickering with movement as the beast clawed at the lower edge of one of the large barrels.

There was movement, a shadow sliding between the casks. He felt his heart rate spike as he edged forward, going slow, making sure his boots didn't whisper against the stone floor.

Mercer caught sight of Webster. He was wedged into the tight space between the wall and one of the massive wooden casks.

The Saberonis still hadn't noticed Mercer, and it continued to hiss and grunt as it clawed at the oak barrel and the concrete floor, splinters flying as the beast tried to get at the deputy.

Dust clouds filled the air as Mercer aimed and fired. The bullet punched into a barrel and a thin stream of wine doused the Saberonis as it dodged Mercer's second and third shots.

The flickering image of the Saberonis was so fast, like smoke eddying in a chaotic airstream, and Mercer couldn't get a bead on the creature. Gun smoke filled the air as the shadow of the Saberonis crawled across the floor. It was massive, its long fangs curving from the specimen's upper jaw, each nearly as long as Mercer's forearm.

With his nerves crawling and his stomach churning like molten lava, Mercer aimed the Sig Sauer at the spot where he believed the specimen lurked, guided only by the location of its shadow.

Webster picked that moment to emerge from his hiding spot into the aisle, gun up, his right side torn open and bleeding.

Mercer held his fire. If he missed, or his shot ricochetted or went through the creature, the bullet could hit Webster.

The Saberonis appeared between the men, crouched tight to the ground on all fours, the fur crawling up its back blazing white, the creature's image blinking like a warning signal. Its eyes appeared gold, and they gleamed with an unsettling intelligence as they locked on Mercer for a heartbeat before launching into the air.

With its huge wingspan and baseball mitt-like paws, the Saberonis climbed atop one of the huge wine barrels and disappeared into the shadows, its pulsing form vanishing from Mercer's field of vision.

Suddenly the stairs seemed very far away. Mercer searched for the glow of an emergency exit sign and found one at the far end of the row. He forced his breathing to slow, crouching low, trying to make himself smaller. Mercer whisper-yelled, "Are you alright?"

"Not really," Webster said. "I need an ambulance. The damn thing slashed me."

Mercer bit his lip. Exactly what he didn't want to hear. "O.K." He couldn't see his partner, but he felt the specimen's presence and understood the beast hadn't been defeated, but simply discouraged.

Recalling the powerful sense of smell that guided the Smilodon as it hunted, Mercer looked around for something to disguise his scent, and the pissing flow of wine jetting from bullet holes gave him an idea.

"Are you near that spouting wine?"

"Yeah." Webster didn't sound good. He wheezed between breaths and Mercer could sense he was holding back grunts of pain because every few moments the man squeaked like a rubber duck.

Claws scraped against wood and a jolt of adrenaline coursed through Mercer. He was outmatched in every conceivable way—strength, speed, ferocity—but he had one advantage: his mind. At least he thought he did.

Mercer said, "I want you to—"

The Saberonis launched from its hiding spot, a knot of fur and fangs.

Mercer threw himself to the side.

The beast crashed into the spot where Mercer had been standing, its massive paws raking the stone floor, the cellar trembling from the impact. Dust rained down as Mercer hit the floor hard, and his head bounced off stone as the Sig Sauer flew from his grasp, skittered across the floor, and disappeared under one of the huge barrels sitting in its stand.

Mercer crawled between two of the casks, his head ringing as he searched for his gun. Jagged lines streaked his vision, and the air blurred with a myriad of colors, the creature's form pulsating.

"Let's do this, bitch." Webster limped out from between two barrels, gun up. "Take cover. Mercer, take cover!" The beast roared as the deputy fired, but the Saberonis was already moving, and his shots punched into wood and more geysers of wine jetted into the aisle.

With another shriek of dominance, the specimen closed the ten feet between itself and Webster in a flash of twisting movement and churning legs.

Webster screamed as he fired, but the beast was like smoke, and it hit the deputy head-on. He folded, the massive beast's flickering visage like an afterimage burned into the underside of

Mercer's eyelids.

Panic squeezed Mercer's stomach like a grape as he searched for his gun. Backlit plumes of gun smoke clogged the air, and the sounds of Webster's screaming, tearing meat, and cracking bones drove out the ringing in Mercer's head.

The glasses revealed a surreal image of the specimen's huge cat-like head as it thrashed and tore. Its flexing jaws glowed as they churned like the guts of a woodchipper, the creature's strobing image on fire, its crypsis camouflage laid bare. Webster's final scream was cut short as powerful jaws clamped down, crushing bone and flesh. His body went limp, his struggle ending in a swift and brutal crack as his spine snapped.

Mercer's hand found metal and he screamed as he gripped the Sig Sauer and yanked it from beneath the cask.

The Saberonis shrieked as it moved, an amorphous blur of blinking light.

A thunderous crash reverberated through the cellar as the Saberonis pushed off one of the huge casks. The sound of cracking wood and rushing wine drove out all other sounds. Splinters flew and the rivets holding the giant barrel's loop strapping in place shot from the oak like bullets, and the air vibrated as the barrel came apart.

Mercer and the Saberonis were washed away in a sea of crimson shiraz as a wave of wine rolled through the cellar. Mercer fought to stay above the flow, but after a few seconds, he sucked in a mouthful and swallowed. The wine was young and bitter, like his life, and neither he nor the vintage would survive to maturity.

Cheri and the ESS folks arrived first by vehicle eighteen minutes later, but the party was soon joined by several members of the sheriff's department, including the sheriff himself. An officer of the law was dead, and though Barney's death had caused the dust-up, now a cop was dead, and that would stir a shit storm of epic proportions.

Mercer had crawled from the wine cellar like a drenched Frenchman, leaving a trail of wine behind him, as had the Saberonis. The specimen had given him the slip again, and this time it had cost him dearly.

Thankfully for Mercer, the murder scene was clear as day, and he had Gray and the ESS people to help handle the sheriff. There were paw prints, blood splatters, clawed barrels, the tip of a broken claw, and even a few tufts of fur from the beast's long mane of hair. The sheriff didn't buy the story that Mercer wasn't sure what had attacked Webster—some kind of animal, or a mutant he had said. Mercer was chief of security for a mysterious biotech company and had been involved in multiple incidents involving an unknown creature, but it was his confidentiality agreement, the pressure of the ESS folks, and Thorpe's local power that kept the water at a simmer instead of a full boil.

Webster's corpse was taken away, and the sheriff announced angrily that he was off to talk to the man's wife. Mercer felt like he was the one who should do that, but he wasn't a cop anymore and was barely the man's friend, so it wasn't his place. Mercer was allowed to go home, but the sheriff made it clear that they would need to speak again soon. The winery would remain closed due to the ongoing investigation, and Mercer was certain the police wouldn't rest until they nailed down all the details of the death of one of their own.

The beast had gotten away, again, despite Mercer having the goggles, and now it was just a matter of time before the Saberonis reached Barlow, and there was nothing he could do about it.

25

By nightfall, Mercer was officially a highly sought-after man. Not only did Twerp want to meet with him, and his hired ESS guns, but the sheriff wanted a follow-up interview, and the feds had requested a briefing with all relevant parties. From what Alex was able to gather, Mercer hadn't been charged with any crime... yet, but given his recent track record the authorities had follow-up questions and the words 'withholding evidence in an ongoing investigation' had been mentioned, but it was semantics. Potato, patato, or creature, specimen.

Mercer abandoned Jenni's Prius in town, and Alex picked him up. He turned off his cellphone after calling Jenni to explain as much of the situation as he could while still maintaining plausible deniability for his wife. Pillow talk was a thin line, but he didn't want his wife getting caught up in what was to come. Regardless of how things turned out, Mercer had accepted the reality that he was screwed, and the only path forward was to kill the Saberonis, regardless of the personal cost.

A deputy sheriff showed up at Alex's house unannounced, but the partners had anticipated this, and Mercer hid in an old barn on the back of Alex's property. It didn't feel right hiding out like a criminal, or asking his friend to perjure himself, but Alex knew the stakes and he'd volunteered without being asked. There was no way to prove Alex had been involved in anything, and if it came to it Mercer would make sure his friend came out clean.

The pair sat in the barn's loft where they had a good view of the driveway, Alex's lone lamppost like a beacon in the darkness.

"What did you tell Lorili when she got home from work?" Mercer asked. He knew if Alex brought a friend home without advanced warning a series of tactical questions would be asked.

"Nothing. She doesn't know you're here, and that's how it's going to stay."

Mercer said nothing as he bit his lip. He hated putting his friend in this position.

"She thinks I'm out here drinking beer and working on the tractor mower."

"At least the drinking beer part is true," Mercer said. "Thanks, man. Really. You're all I got."

"Bullshit, but O.K."

The pair clinked bottles of Modelo.

"I hate to ask... but what's the plan here, Chad? When the sun comes up..." He took a long pull of beer.

Mercer nodded. "I guess it's time to find out where I stand."

"The cops want to see you, the feds... Maybe called Twerp first? I'm sure he's got a team of lawyers."

"My concern now is innocent people getting killed," Mercer said. "Trying to keep things contained and low profile was fine when the beast was running around in the woods, but now?"

Alex nodded. "You could pass on what you know without going in."

"Go on."

"Leave messages, or a note somewhere, an anonymous phone call..."

Mercer chuckled, his third beer forcing his mood into brighter lands. "Do those exist anymore?"

"You know what I mean. Push the panic button from afar."

Mercer's heart sank. "That would mean the story would get out, all of it."

Alex said nothing. Mercer had shared his motivation for being a good soldier, even the really bad stuff Alex hadn't heard before. His friend had understood, but Mercer could tell he hadn't agreed with the decision.

"Jenni and I would be over."

"Maybe you should get in front of that. Explain things. It was a long time ago."

Mercer knew that once trust was broken,

rarely could it be reestablished, and with all the couple's other issues, Mercer didn't see a scenario where the marriage survived. Still, perhaps that was where things were headed anyway, and he owed Jenni the respect of not learning of his indiscretion from a stranger. "Yeah," he finally forced out, but a frog had climbed up his throat and was swinging on his epiglottis.

"You could use my phone to call her?" Alex said.

Mercer held out a trembling hand.

The call was short and brutal. Jenni didn't cry, or say she'd had suspicions. She stayed silent as she listened to Mercer apologize and explain how he would have rather had this conversation in person. He detailed his brief relationship with Annabelle, how Ray had killed himself, and how he'd carried the guilt of it because he loved her and knew immediately that he'd made a mistake. He told her about Twerp using the information, about the Saberonis, and his role in two deaths, not counting a dog.

"Where are things now?" Jenni asked with no emotion when he was done.

"That's why... one of the reasons I called. I have to tell the cops everything I just told you, and it's only a matter of time before word gets out."

"My mother is going to hear about all this?"

Mercer almost laughed. Their marriage was leaning over a thousand-foot precipice, with no parachute, and she was concerned about what her mother might think. "Probably not. Once the feds get involved—"

Alex was making a slashing motion in the air.

"Can we talk later? I owe you a long, deep apology, in person, regardless of what you decide to do," Mercer.

Alex smiled, nodded, and then mouthed, "Give her some time."

"What to do? What are you going to do?" she said.

"Kill the damn thing. I'll see you later. Hopefully not from behind bars." Mercer hit 'end call' and he felt like a great weight had been lifted from him, despite not knowing where he stood with his wife. "Now Twerp?"

"I would think so."

"The cops can't trace my cell without jumping over all the legal hurdles first, so I should be OK," Mercer said. "For the present, anyway." He gave Alex his phone back and pulled his own.

Alex nodded. "They'll surely want it after the fact."

Mercer video called Twerp, and he picked up on the first ring.

"Where the hell are you?"

Mercer was standing before a white wall, and the boss was sitting at his desk in front of his computer. "We need to talk. Are you alone?"

"Yes."

That was bullshit because, in addition to

the primordial cat tooth sitting in its display holder on a credenza behind the desk, Mercer saw Jinx and Gray in the reflection of a picture over Twerp's right shoulder. He decided not to protest. What did it matter? Thorpe would tell them everything anyway.

When Mercer stayed silent, Twerp said, "Do they work? The goggles?"

So there it was. Twerp knew he'd broken into the Evolve labs. No sense lying, but he didn't need to tell the truth, either. "Did I forget to tell you I was borrowing them? You know, to catch the Saberonis."

"We'll deal with that later. I need you here. There's a big briefing in the morning and you are a central participant."

"We'll see about that," Mercer said.

"Listen—"

"No, you listen. I'm going to the feds and the cops and telling them everything—and before you spout off about what you will and won't tell my wife, she knows the entire story."

Silence.

"So, unless you have something to offer, I think we're done."

"We're done when I say we're done," Twerp screeched.

"I quit," said Mercer, and he stabbed 'end call'.

"When you handle all family business you really handle all family business."

Mercer grunted.

Alex retrieved an email address for the local fed office, along with a few names he got from contacts, and by 11 PM Mercer had comprised a detailed email which he sent broadly to the sheriff's department and the feds. Then he called the local fed office and left a message of him reading the email. When he was done, he sat back and took a long pull of beer.

"Feel better?"

"Yeah, I do. I'm still in the shit, but at least I feel like I've taken steps to be on the right side of things if such a side exists," Mercer said.

"Now you're a full-on rogue."

The pair sat in the dark loft, sipping beers, and when Alex's wife came looking for him, he told her he'd be right in.

"You fall asleep up there? Why is the light off," she said.

"Motion sensor. I'll be right down." Alex flicked on the light. "We'll start fresh in the morning."

Mercer nodded. "You hunt up Barlow's way, right?"

"Yeah."

"Do you have typo maps of the area?"

Alex nodded.

"Can you get them for me? I'm not going to be able to sleep, so at least I can chart a search pattern for tomorrow."

Alex went to a chest and retrieved the maps without a word.

Mercer knew what his friend was thinking. Finding the specimen's trail would be next to impossible without a lead. "Can you keep your scanner tuned? I want to know about every call in and around Barlow tonight."

"Done. I can put out a word or two also now that things are in the open," Alex said. "What about weapons?"

Two compound bows hung above the chest that held Alex's hunting gear, and Mercer knew the man had a stocked gun cabinet in the house. Mercer had his Sig Sauer, and he had a spare full magazine and there were nine bullets still in the gun's current mag. "Can I borrow your Benelli M4?"

"Nice choice. Consider it done. Anything else?"

"You're not coming with me tomorrow." Nothing else needed to be said, the reasons obvious.

"We'll talk in the morning," his friend said.

Mercer nodded. He'd intended to slip away before sunup, but now that Mercer had laid down his cards, his friend wouldn't be bringing the Benelli out to him until morning. Then there was the fact that Mercer needed the man's car and contacts for leads. But all that was for another day.

"Nite, Mercer."

"Nite."

There was an old, battered couch in the barn's loft, and Mercer stretched out, sipping on his last beer and eating Cheetos, the night symphony ringing in his ears as it leaked into the old barn. He stared at the maps, the wavy lines mesmerizing as his eyes slipped closed and his body settled down. An intense weariness pushed him toward sleep, and he didn't fight the inevitable.

Thorpe stabbed his keyboard so hard it jumped. "That fool is going to ruin us all."

Gray said nothing. His ass was only on the line as far as his contract went. He'd withheld evidence, but he'd been clever with his words, and specimen and creature were the same thing.

Jinx was screwed. Though she operated under the same NDA as Mercer, such things didn't hold water when the cops were investigating two murders. Yes, Apple Corp. had fought off the federal government's request for its encryption algorithm, but Jinx wasn't Apple, and local authority marched to a different drumbeat.

"Jinx, get with the PR people and get our spin ready. I have no doubts that Mercer will do as he says and within the hour my phone is going to start ringing. Gray, what the hell do you have to offer? This thing has barreled out of control, despite your assurances that you could handle this. Your people haven't helped at all, and you haven't even sniffed the creature."

"We're doing the best we can, Mr. Thorpe," Gray said, his tight smile faltering for an instant.

"We're dealing with a creature that's never been hunted before and it's practically invisible. Now, if you'd offered the goggles—"

"Shut it," Thorpe said. "I don't give a shit. Mercer is the only one who can corroborate his story. Did you notice there was no mention of evidence?" Thorpe knew that wasn't necessarily true. He was sure Mercer had taken pictures and saved documents, but they were all illegally obtained and most likely couldn't be used in court. The challenge was to control public opinion in the early hours of the situation and if need be, he could hide behind his thick legal shield.

"What do you want me to do after I speak with PR?" Jinx said.

Thorpe sighed and threw up his hands. "And you. I thought you were the future of this place. Guess I was wrong."

"What is it you want of me?" Jinx said a little too fast and a bit too harshly.

"What do I want you to do? Get the specimen and Mercer."

"Get him?" Gray said. "You mean bring him in for questioning?"

Thorpe clenched his teeth as he smiled, then said, "Dead men tell no tales."

26

Manzana, California, U.S.A.
5:24 AM PST, Day Seven

Mercer clocked some solid sleep before Alex woke him in the wee hours before dawn with the lead he needed.

"It just came over the wire. A car was dispatched to Coast Miwok Indian Rancheria in response to a call about a head of cattle being killed and mutilated."

The partners checked their weapons, loaded up on water and power bars, and Mercer left Alex's place in the vehicle's cargo area just to be safe. When Alex was certain he wasn't being followed he pulled into a turnout and Mercer joined him in the front seat of Alex's wife's Chevy Tahoe.

Occidental Road wound through fields, the sides of the road lined with Douglas fir and eucalyptus trees. Gentle dusk spread over the land as Alex drove, dark shadows fading to green as the duo made their way east.

The rancheria was just west of Barlow, and

it was surrounded by forest and homesteads. In the mid-19th century, the influx of non-native settlers in California displaced many native tribes from their homelands. In 1901, Congress passed the Homeless Indian Acts, leading to the creation of Indian colonies and rancherías—plots of land set aside for Native Americans.

Spinning red lights cut through the darkness, and Alex brought the car to a slow stop on the side of the road. Up ahead, two patrol cars were parked, half on the road and half off, and flashlights cut through the grazing field to the south.

"Get us close so I can take a look," Mercer said.

Alex turned off the Tahoe's headlights, inched the truck around the police cars, and stopped a hundred yards up the road.

Mercer pressed his eyes to his binoculars, and the officer's flashlights provided enough light for him to see.

A cattleman stood with two sheriff's deputies staring down at a mound of meat and bones. The steer's head was intact and still attached to what was left of its body, and other than a missing rear leg, the beast's limbs had been overlooked. Its torso was a hollowed cavity, and everything was drenched in blood, which looked black in the gloom. Glowing shards of shattered rib bones protruded from the carcass, and entrails glistened in the fading moonlight.

"There's only one animal I've ever seen that

can rip something apart like that," Mercer said as he let the binoculars drop to his chest.

Alex didn't ask to take a look.

The partners sat there, watching the sun peek its head over the mountains to the east, and when it looked like the party was breaking up Alex asked, "What now?"

"All we can do is stick with what the Saberonis has been doing so far," Mercer said. "For whatever reason, the specimen has been traveling toward the sunrise, pretty much since the moment it escaped."

There were more grazing fields to the west, and to the east, a thin copse of evergreens gave way to Coffee Lane, which ran north to south and cut across Occidental Road.

"O.K. Sticking with that premise, let's go see if there are any signs of the specimen on Coffee Lane. There's no way the thing can go east without crossing the road."

Mercer nodded because he didn't know what else to do. If there was a blood trail from the slaughtered head of cattle, the police would surely follow it, so he needed to get ahead of them.

Alex put the Tahoe in drive and inched past the driveway that led into the ranch. There were more cops up at the house. An unmarked car was flanked by another patrol car and a white Jeep with the California rabbit ranger logo on its side.

Occidental Road wound around a large grassy

berm dotted with the dark shadows of cattle before straightening out. A band of evergreen forest packed both sides of the road, and the grazing fields beyond faded as the woods thickened. Half a mile up the road Alex made a right onto Coffee Lane.

"How far?" Alex asked.

"Stop here."

Alex pulled off the road—there was no shoulder, and huge Douglas firs towered over the street and blocked out the rising sun. Shadows danced just within the forest, flashes of light breaking through the thick foliage like sparks.

Nothing moved on the road ahead.

"I'm going to walk up a ways and check things out," Mercer said.

"We'll both go."

The partners walked the road for a quarter of a mile, thick forest on both sides of the street. There wasn't even an echo of a vehicle, the lane nothing more than a cut through the forest that only locals used. The transient tourists rarely strayed from Occidental Road.

Mercer saw nothing out of place, and the weeds and grass separating the trees from the blacktop were undisturbed. The pair trekked back to the Tahoe, dejected and sullen.

When they were back in the car Alex pulled up the digital map on the Chevy's navigation screen. The image showed Coffee Road meandering through green and intersecting Occidental Road, the forest and rancheria to the west, and the outskirts of Barlow to the east.

Barlow was a tiny town, and Gravenstein Highway cut through its center. Directly to the east, beyond the forest and a smattering of farms, was the Redwood Farm Creamery, a church, and a series of small shops anchored by Andrew's Market.

Mercer saw one of the sheriff's cars pass the turnoff for Coffee Road as it sped east. "Things are breaking up. Maybe we should—"

A white rabbit ranger Jeep turned onto Coffee Lane.

Though he doubted there had been enough time for his picture to filter down to the chicken police, Mercer hid himself anyway, ducking down as the Jeep passed without giving the Tahoe a second glance.

The next vehicle that turned onto Coffee was more trouble.

"What is this now," Mercer said as he eyed a white Ford Taurus in the rearview.

"Should we split?" Alex said as he started the car.

Jinx was at the wheel of the Taurus. She gunned it, the car's tires squealing as the Ford fishtailed, went around the Tahoe and came to a stop angled across the road.

Alex dropped the truck into drive, his foot hovering over the gas pedal.

Jinx burst from the Ford, hands up in a sign of

supplication.

The Tahoe inched forward, Alex's foot still floating over the gas pedal.

Mercer saw no gun, and though there was another person in the car, Mercer didn't feel threatened. Maybe it was all the time he and Jinx had spent together, or that he knew where she'd come from and how she'd ended up in northern California. He said, "Hold up a second."

Alex shifted his foot to the break and the vehicle lurched to a stop.

Mercer rolled down the window and yelled, "Tell your partner to get out of the car. Hands up."

"Mercer, I'm here to help you, I need—"

"Do it. Now!" Mercer yelled.

Jinx waved a hand and her top guard, retired Marine Ricky Cokely, emerged from the Taurus with his hands in the air.

Alex and Mercer drew their weapons as they got out of the car and approached the newcomers like they were serial killers. Not that Mercer would be able to shoot either of them, that was unless they tried to shoot him.

"What are you doing here, Jinx?" Mercer asked.

"Like I said, I'm here to help," Jinx said, hands still in the air.

"How did you know where I was?"

"I staked out Alex's house."

Mercer spit out air. "You what? Does Twerp

know what you're up to? Where I am?"

Jinx shook her head slowly. "No. I've... fallen out of favor."

"I still don't see what you want with us," Alex said.

"Nobody else has even gotten close to this thing," Jinx said. "I want its pelt, or at least a piece of it, on my wall."

Cokely's gaze shifted back and forth like he was watching a tennis match, but he said nothing.

"Mercer, if I don't get the Saberonis I'm done. Like, maybe jail done. We can worry about all the bullshit later," Jinx said.

Teaming up with someone who had been informing on him for years wasn't his idea of an ally, but beggars can't be choosers. "Let me see your phones and weapons."

Jinx and Cokely exchanged a glance, and Jinx nodded.

After verifying they'd been no recent communications with Twerp or Gray, Mercer locked the phones in the Tahoe's glovebox. The guns were standard issue Glocks, and he returned them to their owners. It was a leap of faith, but a small one. He believed Jinx, and in his experience Cokely had always been a straight arrow. He had young children and that... Well, that reduced the urge to take stupid risks.

"What now?" Jinx said.

"Didn't you ever hunt before? Now, we wait,"

Mercer said.

And wait they did. The quartet sat in the Tahoe and watched the road for over an hour. Boredom took over, and the group decided to search the surrounding woods. As Mercer reviewed the map so he could give out assignments, he caught a flicker of movement on the western side of the road.

"Did you see that?" Mercer asked. "A hundred yards up on the right."

Nobody answered.

Mercer slipped on the goggles.

Jinx said, "The boss is REALLY pissed you stole those. He gave orders to..." Her voice trailed away, and she looked at the floor.

"What? Orders to do what?" Alex asked.

"Retire him," Jinx said. "I might be a kiss-up, but I'm not a murderer. And for a job?" She spit out laughter. "But they'll be coming for you, Mercer."

The SpectraShade Goggles were already in Spectral Scan mode, and Mercer's field of vision changed from vibrant greens and deep browns to a shifting landscape of semi-transparent distorted colors. The road, the trees, and the rocks blurred at the edges as the glasses attempted to isolate living things.

An ill breeze puffed as the Saberonis crawled onto the road, its body flickering and unstable, the specimen unable to maintain its cloak against the bombardment of multiple spectrums.

"Do you see it?" Mercer asked.

A chorus of no.

"It's on the right edge of the road, under that large tree limb."

Harsh breathing and the hiss of the breeze pushing through the cracked-open windows filled the vehicle.

"Let's roll," Mercer said as his hand gripped the Tahoe's doorhandle.

Alex grabbed his arm. "Careful with gunshots. There are still cops around."

Mercer nodded as he burst from the Chevy. The companions checked their weapons, and Mercer grabbed the Benelli and Alex his rifle before the foursome started up the street.

The smear that was the Saberonis darted across the road and disappeared into the forest.

Mercer and the others broke into a run.

Flattened weeds on the roadside marked the specimen's passage. No blood was visible, but large paw prints were pressed into the sand where the blanket of bronze pine needles had been disturbed.

The party plunged into the woods and the temperature dropped ten degrees. Shadowy darkness filled the forest beneath the dense tree canopy, but with little undergrowth the party moved fast, Mercer on point, the specimen fleeing before them. Tree branches snapped, and pine needles eddied like snow, the path over the bronze carpet easy to follow.

Heart pumping, Mercer and crew ran for almost a mile, weaving in and out of trees and avoiding pricker vines, stones, and depressions in the forest floor.

A roar pierced the day, and the shrill cry carried into the woods as the party broke free of the trees into a pasture.

The specimen galloped across the field, heading for the parking area behind Andrew's Market. Dirt and grit clung to the Saberonis as it ran, dampening its crypsis coat. The monster bounded for the rear of the market, its long fangs gliding up and down and almost scraping the ground. A thick dust trail followed the beast, and Mercer stopped and took aim at the creature, but held his fire.

Cars were parked in the rear lot of the market and several workers prepared for the store's opening.

The beast flitted in and out of dust clouds as shots rang out. Jinx was firing, and then Cokely opened up, and soon the *pop* and *snap* of gunshots drowned out all other sounds.

A guest of wind gathered the dirt and grit, driving it upward in a swirling tornado. The market's rear loading dock door was open, and a truck was being unloaded. Two men stood on the dock staring out at the chaos.

With a crunch of bending metal, the Saberonis leaped onto a car, its massive head moving side-to-side as its jaws slid open.

Mercer ran with the Benelli aimed at the Saberonis, but there was #4 Buckshot in the gun, and at this distance, the pellets in the shell would scatter too widely. He was so close, but so very far. It had been a long time since he'd run so hard, and he felt the heat of his past on his heels, and his lungs burned with regrets.

One of the men on the loading dock screamed, and the Saberonis jumped from the roof of the car, its pulsating form a blur as it charged straight for the loading dock.

27

Mercer **sprinted through the field and** passed between two cars as he ran across the market's rear parking lot. The M4 was heavy, and he thumbed off the safety as he closed in on the flashing image of the Saberonis.

The workers on the dock were still staring east, unmoving, unable to see the Saberonis clearly, their gazes transfixed on the brown smear that flashed over the lot. Patches of dirt and grime clung to its hide, though the specimen's passage through the forest had wiped away some of the dust. Its hindquarters remained mottled brown, but the creature's front flanks and head had regained their natural camouflage, blending seamlessly with the surroundings. As it juked and sprinted, the effect was uncanny—almost as if the forward half of the beast had vanished into a time hole, leaving only its rear visible.

A double mauling was imminent. Mercer stopped running, braced himself, and took aim. He focused on firing low, hoping that if he missed the creature, the pellets would ricochet off the parking lot and hit the side of the loading dock.

The rest of the crew took cover behind parked cars and opened fire.

One of the men on the dock, hearing the gunshots and realizing that the two gleaming eyes charging at him through the haze wasn't a good thing, dropped to the deck. His partner soon did the same, but their actions were too little too late.

The Saberonis dodged, bullets spraying asphalt and igniting sparks. With a shriek of fury, the specimen jumped onto the loading dock, its right front paw, claws extended, raking across one of the men as the beast's fangs sank into the other.

Mercer stopped firing, the men and the Saberonis a jumble of swirling colors and flashing light.

The Saberonis grunted and blood sprayed as the beast thrashed and mauled its victims. Bones snapped and cracked, muscle ripped and tore, and Mercer saw the specimen's head outlined in blood before the beast crashed through the swinging doors into the food mart.

Jinx and the others joined Mercer, and he said, "Jinx, you and Cokely go around the sides to the front. Don't let it out. Alex and I will head inside."

Sirens wailed in the distance, and Mercer thought he heard the distant thumping of airfoils slicing the air, but there was no time for that now.

Andrew's Market opened at 7 AM and the market was sure to be crowded with eager beavers looking to knock one of the day's chores out early. Mercer's stomach ached with the thought of it as he climbed the short staircase up to the loading platform where he found what was left of the two men who only minutes before had been chatting and unloading the delivery truck.

The intoxicating scent of freshly baked bread mixed with the deathly scent of blood enticed the power bar and coffee Mercer had for breakfast to make a curtain call. He gagged, the scent of blood sticking in the back of his throat, his eyes watering as pain knifed up his back and knotted his neck, but he didn't hurl.

Both dead men were of Spanish descent, and their faces were frozen in horror, eyes open wide as they stared into the next world. One of the men was torn to ribbons, the corpse's chest cavity slashed open, ribs cracked, organs spilling onto the concrete deck. The other was missing chunks of meat, and those pieces were scattered about the loading dock as if the Saberonis had lost its taste for human flesh.

Mercer and Alex did their best to avoid the blood as they made their way through the swinging doors into the backroom of the market. Mercer had the Benelli's stock pressed to his shoulder, and Alex held his pistol in a doublehanded grip, his rifle slung over his shoulder.

Screams leaked from the front of the market, but Mercer saw no employees in the backroom. The specimen left a trail of bloody prints, and they meandered through stacks of boxes and cases of soda toward the front of the store.

This was Mercer's worst nightmare, a trail of dead people and him with no sensible reason for allowing it to happen other than saving his own pitiful life. Jail was suddenly a possibility, but he didn't care. The heat of anger pressed through him as he darted forward, following the tracks. Maybe if he could limit the damage... but it didn't matter. Regardless of what happened, he'd have to live with it. As before, Mercer might not be the killer, but that didn't mean his hands were free of blood.

Content to let him lead, Alex fell in behind Mercer as the pair threaded through the boxes and loaded U-boats waiting to go out into the store so the shelves could be restocked. The crew passed the beer cooler, and the frozen food cold box, and burst out through swinging doors into the frozen food aisle.

Screaming and the hiss and roar of the Saberonis filled the market as people fled and took cover. The beast's tracks cut left, and an endcap of potato chips had been knocked over and bags of chips covered the floor.

An old woman huddled beneath the meat display that ran along the back of the store, the deli counter and butcher stations empty of employees. Mercer wanted to help the woman, but he ran on. She was fine where she was, and the specimen had passed her by.

A thunderous crash echoed through the store. A woman screamed and the Saberonis roared.

The gentle classical music playing over the PA system sputtered to a stop with a burst of static and a man's frantic voice blared through the market. "Please find the closest exit and leave the market. Please do this in an orderly fashion and ever—" The man screamed, and the sound of the PA handset hitting something hard echoed through the chaos, and the deafening buzz of reverb rang through the store.

Mercer crunched over the bags of chips, the blood prints fading, but as he made a right and charged down the soda aisle, he was met with new horrors.

With the SpectraShade Goggles still on Mercer saw the Saberonis at the far end of the aisle, bright sunlight streaming through the large windows at the front of the store illuminating the creature in a dazzling pulsating glow.

A woman sat propped against a display of soda holding her bloody stomach, her right leg twisted at an angle it wasn't designed to allow. A large African American man lay face down, his back a tattered mess of red flannel, blood, and the white notched bones of his tattered spine.

Alex coughed and almost hurled. His friend had seen many nasty things over his years as a cop, but Mercer guessed he'd never seen carnage like this, at least not of the human variety.

Mercer looked back. Alex was the only one behind him and he went on, shotgun at the ready, ignoring the pleas of shoppers, some of which were more scared than hurt.

As he reached the end of the soda aisle, a sudden spray of liquid hit Mercer. Soda gushed from punctured bottles of Mountain Dew, where the creature had slashed its claws across the shelf, leaving jagged tears and holes in the plastic bottles. Mercer paused, lined his mouth up with one of the spurting geysers of green sugar, and took a long pull, the soda spraying his face and drenching his shirt, which was already soaked with sweat.

Shoppers hid between the registers, and people ran for the exit as they screamed, but Mercer was thankful he saw no children. In Sonoma, most kids had long bus rides to school and shouldn't be in the food mart at 7 AM on a school day. Thank someone for small favors.

The Saberonis stood amidst a fallen display of paper towels. It moved with a liquid grace as it lunged at a young man in a postal uniform hiding behind a shopping cart filled with items. Metal sang as the beast knocked the cart away and the man screamed as he threw a can of baked beans at the beast. It hit the Saberonis squarely on the snout and the specimen jerked its head back, its eyes going wide with astonishment as its jaws slid open, displaying rows of sharp teeth bookended by two long fangs.

Muscles rippled beneath the creature's shifting translucent skin, brown patches of skin blending into the white of the paper towels and the light brown of the boxes.

Gunshots rang out as Alex fired, but that didn't stop the Saberonis. The beast pressed itself to the ground as it juked and advanced on the mailman. Yellow eyes glowed, and the beast pawed at the linoleum floor, the sound like nails being pulled over glass.

Shoppers were backed up at the front entrance, and they screamed and yelled as they fought for freedom. The register aisles had emptied, and Mercer saw the chaos in the parking lot through the large plate glass windows at the front of the market.

Without his cart for protection, the mailman crab-walked backward through the paper towel wreckage.

Mercer aimed the Benelli, but the scattershot was too risky, so he swung the weapon onto his back and drew his Sig Sauer, which was in a pancake holster clipped to his belt.

Alex moved in alongside Mercer, and both men aimed their weapons.

The Saberonis was a blur of motion, its claws

raking over the mailman's face and neck. Blood spilled from the wounds as the man collapsed to the floor and the beast disappeared down an aisle.

"Alex, guard those people and help them get out of here in an orderly fashion," Mercer said. The shoppers needed the help, and things in the market were getting close, and he was concerned that with bullets flying around a customer or a staff member would be collateral damage.

Alex opened his mouth to protest, but a sharp look from Mercer made his friend think better of it. That, and Mercer knew the retired cop had no desire to end his retirement early, certainly not at the claws of a mutant.

There was a break in the chaos as Alex went to work ordering the panicked customers attempting to flee the market.

A crimson puddle spread around the postman, and Mercer's frenzied mind produced a joke that only a distraught brain could create: Spill on aisle five.

The crash of shelving falling over carried through the store. Mercer tracked the sound and ducked around an endcap of cookies.

With a shrill cry that Mercer would hear in his dreams, the Saberonis appeared atop the shelving above Mercer. It threw back its head and roared as it leaped over the gap between aisles, its body partly visible above Mercer for a heartbeat as he tried to bring his gun to bear on the creature.

The Saberonis landed atop the shelving on the opposite side of the row, and canned goods spilled like a wave onto Mercer. As he lay buried beneath servings of canned spaghetti and meatballs, he caught a flash of the beast looking down at him—its jaws hanging open in a toothy smile, its radiant yellow eyes gleaming, its head blackened by the blood that covered it.

Mercer tried to shake himself free of the cans as he fought to aim the Sig Sauer, but gunshots rang out and peppered the shelving next to him.

The beast launched itself over into the next aisle and was lost from view.

Mercer screamed in fury as he shook free of the cans and pushed to his feet. He climbed the can pile, searching for a shot, but hissed in disappointment. The heat of failure leaked over him, a feeling to which he was becoming too accustomed.

The sound of breaking glass, crunching metal, and the screams of patrons still hiding in the market set the imaginary maggots in Mercer's stomach to churning, nausea creeping through him as he ran for the end of the aisle, his leg muscles screaming, his head ringing. Desperation had taken hold, and doubt consumed him as he shook off his angst, and went in search of the Saberonis, death be damned.

28

Mercer skidded to a stop, the chaos of the market fading but leaving the faint echo of terror behind. The air reeked of fear and spilled blood mixed with the sour stench of rotting produce. A growl-hiss echoed through the aisles, a jolt of adrenaline stinging the tips of his fingers and toes.

The Saberonis was close. He felt the predator shadowing its prey, and sweat dripped down his brow, Mercer's breaths coming in ragged bursts as his gaze swept over the chaotic remains of the market. Somewhere in the mess of overturned stalls and wrecked shelves death stalked him.

A loud metallic click reverberated through the market and Mercer looked over his shoulder.

Jinx and Cokely had entered the food mart via the front entrance, and they'd locked the door behind them.

"Front is secure." It was Jinx. She and Cokely took positions behind registers next to Alex, who peered over a display of candy.

The sound of approaching sirens leaked into the store, and Mercer felt his time running out.

When the cops arrived, the ESS folks, it was game over. His first thought was for Alex. If his friend was on the scene when the fuzz started taking names, there would be no way to keep the ex-cop out of things. So far, he hadn't broken any laws per se—other than aiding in the break-in of the Evolve offices, but nobody knew about that except Mercer and Alex, and neither of them were going to tell anyone.

A wall of cereal boxes tumbled from a shelf next to Mercer, Tony the Tiger and Toucan Sam staring up at him from the wreckage. As he turned his attention back to the row of breakfast items and coffee, a low gurgle carried through the market.

Nothing moved along the breakfast aisle except the occasional tottering cereal box.

The world changed color like a malfunctioning television as Mercer cycled through the SpectraShade Goggle's modes.

"Mercer!" it was Jinx, and Mercer saw her white aura in his peripheral vision as she appeared at the end of the aisle. Gunshots split the stillness—*pop, pop, pop*. A scent like burning sulfur filled Mercer's nostrils as bullets punched into cereal boxes and shreds of cardboard and clouds of sugar dust filled the air.

The Saberonis leaped from its perch atop a row of shelving as Jinx fired again.

Head ringing, Mercer's chest tightened like a fist as the creature soared past—jaws wide, claws extended, tail out straight. Its long fangs narrowly missed him, and the air crackled, the heat of a phantom wound cutting across Mercer's face.

Mercer fell back as he swung his gun and fired, but he was off balance and the shots punched into cereal and shelving.

Jinx screamed as she fired, the release of her primal rage carrying over the carnage.

The Saberonis shrieked as a bullet thumped into its hindquarters. Blood splattered the carpet of groceries covering the floor and disrupted parts of the creature's crypsis camouflage. The Saberonis moved with the fluid precision of a swirling cloud as it charged Jinx, dark blood spots betraying the beast.

Mercer could only guess what Jinx was seeing without the SpectraShade Goggles, but it was clear she was struggling to track the beast because her shots were missing the mark.

Bloody footprints and a line of crimson drips marked the specimen's passage, and the Saberonis pulsated with white light as it attacked Jinx. With a horrifying realization that pinned his feet to the floor, Mercer realized Jinx was going to die and there was nothing he could do about it. With the creature nothing but a blur, and Jinx in the line of fire, Cokely and Alex also held their fire.

Jinx went rigid as the Saberonis bounded at her.

But then fate stepped in, and Jinx drew a full house.

The Saberonis bounced off an endcap of dried pasta and sauce, jars popping and splattering tomato mush as they hit the floor. A shifting blur of conflicting light knocked Jinx to the ground, crossed the main aisle, and launched atop a candy display. The giant meta-cat paused, its massive, blood-soaked head scanning its surroundings. Then, with a sudden leap, it hopped onto a conveyor belt behind a register and crashed through one of the large plate glass windows at the front of the store, leaving a trail of bloody pawprints in its wake.

Mercer stood frozen, his brain still processing what he'd just seen, the ringing in his head driving out the echo of shattering glass.

Jinx sat up, rubbed her eyes, and said, "Well, shit."

Mercer went to the woman and helped her to her feet. "Thanks," she said.

"No, thank you," Mercer said. "You saved my bacon." Right then and there he decided to call things even with Jinx. "Are you alright?"

She nodded. "A little shaken, but I'm O.K." A wicked smile leaked over her face. "I hit it."

Mercer nodded but said nothing. She had wounded the creature, but it hadn't slowed the beast down. He recalled the specimen's advanced healing properties, remembered that the beast had been shot at the start of the hunt and it hadn't made any difference. Not one bit.

He stuffed more shells into the Benelli's magazine tube as he and Jinx joined Alex and Cokely. Both men stared out the broken window like children who had just heard a teacher go on a rant for the first time.

"Everyone O.K.?" Alex asked.

"Thanks to Jinx," Mercer said.

"More like luck," Jinx said.

The parking lot was chaos. Two police cars had arrived, and the cops were doing their best to control a knot of scared customers, some in their cars trying to squeeze out the clogged entrance, and some fleeing on foot.

Mercer stared through the broken window, jagged tooth-like shards clinging to the metal frame. He scanned the lot for the Saberonis, and when he found the specimen, he sucked in a sharp breath.

The beast was crossing the road that ran through town, the cops unaware that the creature had already moved past them. There were shops on the opposite side of the road, and beyond them a ribbon of forest wrapped Atascadero Creek in a green cocoon. The eight-mile stream surrounded by woods ran due north into the wilderness of northern California.

One of Mercer's mantras fought its way through the fuzz of indecision, reminding him that if you acted like you belonged, nobody would notice you. "Weapons away," he said as he slung the shotgun over a shoulder.

"What—" Alex held up his rifle.

"I know. Come on." Mercer tracked along the front of the store and unlocked the main entrance.

Cokely and Jinx holstered their weapons, and the foursome strolled out of the store like they'd just picked up a sixer of Modelo and were headed for the park.

People were yelling and screaming, and the cops were doing their best to work through the chaos toward the market. Two more police cars arrived, one skidding to a stop behind the others. The second, an SUV, jumped the curb and drove on the ribbon of grass separating the market's parking lot from the lot next to it. The truck kicked up grass and dirt as it fishtailed and headed for the rear of the store.

Mercer made a right and walked along the front of the market, tracking through the shattered glass that covered the walkway. Alex and Mercer carried their rifles discreetly, slung over their right shoulders, keeping them concealed from the people in the parking lot. When the foursome reached the end of the store, they made a hard left and trailed through the chaos toward the road.

It took every ounce of patience Mercer had left to keep himself from running.

The beast had crossed the road and disappeared into a grass alleyway between a shoe store and a tasting room for a local winery.

Like ghosts, the foursome blended into the chaos and slipped by the police, who were doing their best to control a frightened mob and help anyone who was crying or shrieking. An ambulance arrived, and the police shifted their attention to getting the paramedics to the scene.

Mercer broke into a run, threading through the cars jamming up the road as he followed the beast's trail. His lungs burned as he looked over his shoulder, and he couldn't help but smile. Alex was right behind him, followed by Cokely, and Jinx was watching their backs.

The companions ran between Dizzy's Shoes and the Gulf Coast tasting room. When Mercer reached the parking lot behind the buildings, he pulled up short, focusing the SpectraShade Goggles as he searched the area.

Beyond the lot, there was an open field boxed in by a thick line of Douglas fir trees. The strobing white image of the Saberonis raced across the open field. It stood out like a cockroach on a birthday cake, and there was nothing else to see. Mercer raised the Benelli, but he was out of range. "Alex!"

His friend stepped forward, his face etched with concern and streaked with dirt.

Mercer pointed. "It's almost to the edge of the trees. Can you get a bead on it?" The rifle had better range and accuracy.

"I don't see—"

Mercer tore the glasses off and handed them to Alex, who put them on.

The retired cop's head jerked back, the influx of color and light stunning him. Alex shook it off and raised the rifle, but then dropped his aim. "It's in the forest."

Mercer darted forward, running between two parked cars and sprinting across the field. Tall grass tore at his legs, and clouds of gnats and flies filled the air as the greenery was disturbed. He blinked and rubbed his eyes, the sunlight blinding. He'd worn the goggles for so long that his eyes needed extra time to adjust, and he slowed down because he was afraid of tripping.

As the foursome entered the forest the temperature dropped, and the bird song went silent. The gentle sound of water rushing over stones filled the woods, and broken branches, flattened undergrowth, and drips of blood revealed the beast's passage. Mercer wanted to run after the specimen, but he'd learned the hard way that the creature was intelligent. It understood how and when to lie in wait, and there was plenty of cover within the dense copse of trees that ran along the stream. Caution was needed.

"Alex, stay with me," Mercer whispered. "Cokely, you peel off left, Jinx right. Stay behind us and watch our flanks."

The day chorus came back online, and the arguing birds were accompanied by the gurgle of the creek. The air was crisp, and sunlight peeked through the dense canopy, spotlights angling through the trees, the stream sparkling. The specimen's trail disappeared in the clear water of the river.

"Shit!" Mercer screamed. The thumping of the helicopter and the singing of the creek and the birds filled the stillness. He paused to catch his breath, and Alex handed him a water bottle. He took a long pull and asked, "Where did you get the water?"

"Borrowed it from the market."

"Too bad we didn't go down the beer aisle," Cokely said.

"Which way?" Jinx asked.

That was the million-dollar question. A fast scan of the eastern riverbank revealed no paw prints or blood.

"It's using the stream as a path," Cokely said.

The creek was tight, only ten feet across, and pricker vines and weeds encroached to the edge of the water. To the south the vegetation was undisturbed, but to the north several branches that had spanned the stream were broken and leaves and twigs floated downstream.

Mercer and crew headed north, trailing along the edge of the forest, Mercer and Alex on the eastern side of the thin river, Jinx and Cokely on the western side. The pounding of helicopter airfoils reminded Mercer he wasn't far from chaos, but as he listened hard, he heard no wailing sirens. Things back at the market would be settling down. The danger was gone and there were people who needed help, and that would occupy the police. Shame heated Mercer's stomach, but given the number of people in the market, Mercer thought things could have been much worse.

The quartet worked their way up the river, and as the creek got wider and deeper Jinx and Cokely joined Mercer and Alex on the eastern shore. A thick field of water reeds blocked their way, and it was difficult to tell how deep the water was, so they backtracked and followed the opposite shoreline.

Mercer's heart pounded. The specimen's trail was almost nonexistent. Though there was an occasional splatter of blood on a stone, the stream had washed the beast and diluted any blood that dripped from its wound, or wounds. Mercer hoped the Saberonis had taken more than one shot, but hope played by its own rules.

29

As the sun crawled toward its zenith, Mercer and crew trekked through the knee-high vegetation that packed the creek. Cokely was on point, Jinx following up the rear. Alex still had the goggles on, and he walked with the rifle's stock pressed to his shoulder, one eye fixed on the sight.

Mercer's phone vibrated and buzzed, and he pulled the device. It was O&M. Mercer bit his lip. He had the Benelli slung over his shoulder, the Sig Sauer in one hand, and he put the cell on speaker and dropped it into his breast pocket.

"Mercer, are you alone?" It was Dr. Miranda.

"I can talk. I'm hiking through the forest." He didn't need to tell his companions to stay quiet.

"Are you alright?" Dr. Ozzie asked.

"Yes, but I'm in the shit, here, up a creek you might say. What's up?"

"They're coming, Mercer. The ESS people. They left by chopper fifteen minutes ago. They know about the ranchería and the market."

"So will half the state by tonight, so what?" Before O&M could answer Mercer said, "Listen..."

He ducked under a tree branch, the stream only two inches deep. "The Saberonis has been heading east. We figured toward the sunrise, but now it's heading north along Atascadero Creek. Any idea why it might have changed direction?"

"We've got more pressing matters," Dr. Miranda said.

"I don't," Mercer said. "This thing isn't far, and I need any information you have."

Dr. Miranda sighed. "You're probably right. The specimen may very well be heading toward the sunrise."

"Many species, including birds, bees, reptiles like salamanders, and you guessed it, mammals, utilize the sun as a reliable reference point to maintain direction over long distances," Dr. Ozzie said.

"This involves an internal clock that compensates for the movement of the sun across the sky throughout the day," Dr. Miranda said. "For example, a migrating bird can adjust its flight path based on the time of day, ensuring it stays on course. Some animals even combine this technique with other navigational cues, such as landmarks or the Earth's magnetic field."

Dr. Ozzie, not to be outdone, added, "The sun compass is especially important for species that travel vast distances because it provides a consistent, natural guide, helping the animal find food, mates, and nesting sites."

"As to why it's going north now," Dr. Miranda

said, "it's most likely fleeing the population, the noise, the buildings."

"And the creek is the perfect cover," Dr. Ozzie added.

"For now," Dr. Miranda said. "If you're right, and I believe you are, the specimen will head east again as soon as it feels comfortable."

Mercer splashed through a deep section of the river, and Cokely held back a series of branches for him as he slipped under them.

"We don't have time for this, Mercer. There's been some developments you need to know about," Dr. Miranda said.

Mercer said nothing.

"The feds have arrived, and well, the shit has hit the fan," Dr. Ozzie said.

"Turns out Mr. Thorpe was behind the specimen's escape. Just like you thought, Mercer," Dr. Miranda said.

So many questions ranged through Mercer's mind he asked none of them.

"Apparently, the boss and the CFO have been overly creative with the company's books. Something about research funding, bribes, and falsified trials. You know, the standard accusations," Dr. Ozzie said.

"Things went off the rails when one of the board members, who so far has gone unnamed, threatened to take the company from Thorpe. Call a vote of no confidence at the next board meeting and accuse him of mismanagement, misappropriation of funds, and a slew of other charges," Dr. Miranda said. "There are many examples of founders losing their babies, but Twerp was determined to not have that happen to him."

"But…" Even though he'd known deep down Twerp was behind all the mischief and had a good idea how he'd done it, Mercer still couldn't believe the boss had pulled it off. "How?" he sputtered.

"He knew the system's weaknesses, and he tampered with controls and sensors. He hired the hacker… it's a long story I'm sure you're going to hear a thousand times."

"You're telling me the boss let the Saberonis go? To what? Buy time with investors? The military? To show off the beast's abilities? It sounds ridiculous."

"That's the basic theory, yes," Dr. Miranda said.

"And the feds are buying it," Dr. Ozzie said.

"What could Twerp possibly have hoped to gain?"

"Gain?" Dr. Miranda chuckled.

"I think he was desperate, and what did he have to lose, really?" Dr. Ozzie said.

Mercer said nothing. The stream had grown wider, and the buzz of cars carried over the creek.

"He had you on a leash and he had the ESS crew. The military threatened to close our contract and withhold a huge final payment. Either way, the Saberonis, along with all its data and failures, needed to be gone. He figured that at the very least, we'd have a PR nightmare that would scare away anyone who might want to orchestrate a hostile takeover of the company."

Mercer had to admit there was a certain twisted logic to the way Twerp had hedged his bets. "Where is Thorpe now?"

"That's the main reason we called," Dr. Miranda said. "The feds want to question him, but—surprise, he can't be found."

There was one certainty of human existence: shit flowed down, not up, and with Twerp in the wind, the splatter was sure to be wide. "What about you two? Are you bugging out?"

"We're at the office," Dr. Ozzie said. "We're not being detained, but we're not free to leave, either, if you understand me."

He did. "Do they know you called me?"

Both doctors blurted, "No."

"Thank you."

"Good luck, Mercer," Dr. Miranda said, and she broke the connection.

Mercer stopped trudging down the stream as a chill spread through him, the thought that he was never going to see or talk to O&M again, except maybe in court, settled in his stomach like bad clams. He said, "You guys heard all that, right?"

Nobody spoke. Alex examined a water bug, Cokely was gazing upstream, and Jinx studied her gun.

"If you want to call it quits, I understand," Mercer said. "I can't ask you to go further because I don't know what will happen from here on out. Leave now, and it won't be me who mentions your name."

Jinx looked up, a glimmer of hope in her eyes that soon faded. "I'm not going anywhere," she said.

Cokely said nothing as he turned upriver and continued working his way through the thick vegetation, following the path of broken branches left by the Saberonis.

Alex clapped Mercer on the back. "A little bit longer and all this will be over."

Mercer didn't think that was true, but he lurched into motion anyway.

The party hadn't gone far before the screech of tires carried over the creek, followed by a roar that sounded like a pissed-off lion.

Cokely doubled his pace, the road visible through the trees ahead. The stream ended at a galvanized pipe that went under the road, and as the companions broke free of the forest, they climbed up the small embankment to the road.

A car was stopped diagonally across the street, and the Saberonis loomed before it.

Without the SpectraShade Goggles, the specimen was difficult to see. Light refracted off its skin, its form blending into the greenery along the side of the road.

Alex planted his feet, aimed, and fired, the

glasses providing him with a target. The shot rang out, followed by the ringing of metal sliding over metal as Alex ejected the spent bullet, pumped another into the firing chamber, and slammed the bolt home.

The driver of the stopped vehicle—a young woman with long blonde hair, burst from the car and ran for the cover of the woods.

A flash of blurred light, and then the crunch of metal as the Saberonis jumped onto the car's hood.

Alex fired again, but the shot plunked into the car.

Cokely appeared on the roadside next to the vehicle, gun up.

The Saberonis screamed as it jumped, twisting in the air, its form nothing but a wisp of distorted color.

Alex pumped another bullet into the rifle as he bolted toward the chaos.

Mercer searched for Jinx and found her standing next to him like a shadow.

Cokely fired a steady stream of 9 MM parabellums, his gun in a doublehanded grip.

The car's windows exploded as the Saberonis pounced onto the vehicle's roof, Cokely's shots peppering the car. The specimen coiled, jumped, and twisted, spinning through the air. It landed on all fours in front of Cokely as effortlessly as a cat that's been dropped upside-down.

As Cokely aimed the Saberonis came at him,

claws distended. The beast juked at the last second, avoiding a volley of gunshots and raking its paw across the guard's chest.

Cokely shrieked as he fell backward, blood spurting from his wounds as he fired wildly. He hit the road hard, and the gun went silent.

A gust of wind plowed down the street, and the hair on the back of Mercer's neck stood on end. The Saberonis galloped into the underbrush on the northern side of the road, the sound of cracking branches, splashing water, and the screams and wails of Cokely driving out the distant sound of sirens.

Evolve Enterprises was many things. Cheap wasn't one of them. Cokely wore a ballistic vest, and the Kevlar had absorbed much of the specimen's strike. A deep gash ran across the vest, but unfortunately for Cokely, the tear extended onto his shoulder and waist. Blood leaked from the wounds and puddled on the road.

Alex wore a shirt over a t-shirt, and he pulled off his top layer, ripped it in half, and he and Jinx used the fabric as bandages to try and stop the bleeding.

"I'm... alright. Leave me."

The driver of the car wandered back onto the road, her startled gaze shifting from her bullet-ridden crunched car to the foursome.

"We can't..." The sirens were getting louder, and the Saberonis was getting away. "Help me,"

Mercer said.

Alex and Mercer carried Cokely to the side of the road and propped him up against a Douglas fir. Then Mercer called the driver of the car over.

The blonde was sheepish, clearly in shock, and as she approached, she asked, "What... What the hell was that thing?"

"There's no time," Mercer said. "What's your name?"

"Gloria."

"Can you keep an eye on Cokely here until an ambulance arrives, Gloria? Make sure he doesn't fall asleep or pass out?"

Gloria nodded solemnly, the sound of sirens growing louder.

Normally this would be the end of the line. Cokely would live, but the guy was in bad shape, and abandoning a teammate on the side of the road wasn't something Mercer would normally do, but... There was no time left.

Cokely grasped Mercer's leg. "Go. I'll be fine. Help will be here soon." He smiled. "And now I'm out of it."

Mercer nodded, searched the faces of Alex and Jinx, and found nothing but resolute determination.

The trio used the pipe that directed the stream for support as they climbed down into the creek. Thick greenery made seeing the river difficult, the stream nothing more than a trickle in spots. As the companions followed the trail of flattened plants through the greenery, Mercer called up a mental map of the area.

Graton wasn't far to the northeast, and Atascadero Creek became Green Valley Creek as the river turned due north and dumped into the wilderness of northern California.

Mercer didn't know how much longer he could go. His stomach was bitching, his knees ached, and his mouth was dry as paper. He judged the party had traveled at least four miles along the stream, and as buildings began to appear beyond the trees on both sides of the creek an extreme heat melted over Mercer.

There would be no retreating to regroup. No explaining things to the feds and forming a hunting party. The beast would be long gone by then, and once he lost its trail…

The wailing of the ambulance alarm snapped Mercer from his reverie. Through the spattering of trees on the eastern side of the creek Mercer saw the western edge of the small town of Graton.

"Here!" Alex yelled. The retired cop, still wearing the SpectraShade Goggles, peered north, the rifle aimed at something Mercer couldn't see. Alex lowered the gun and continued picking his way through the overgrowth along the widening stream.

With a sense of foreboding that told him things were about to get hairy, Mercer holstered his Sig Sauer and swung the Benelli into his hands.

The path of the Saberonis was clear, which meant so was Mercer's. He felt pressure building all around him. Cheri and the ESS crew would catch up soon, and Mercer was surprised they hadn't already. What would happen then, he didn't know. With Twerp MIA and the company in turmoil, Gray was sure to be concerned about the shit splatter, not to mention not getting paid.

A guttural roar of warning pealed through the stillness.

30

The threesome followed the trail of broken branches, overturned stones, and floating twigs with green leaves still clinging to the fresh wood. After a couple of miles of traversing ponds, pricker vine thickets, and patches of water reeds, Alex took the lead, being the most experienced hunter and already accustomed to using the glasses. The afternoon was waning, and Mercer was starting to worry. He no longer saw many of the *signs* Alex saw, and the fact that he heard no sirens and the ESS crew hadn't shown up made him wonder if he and his merry band had lost the specimen.

Alex put up a hand and dropped into a crouch as Mercer and the others pulled up short.

The whoosh, rumble, and creak of a moving car could be heard just below the buzzing, hooting, and chirping of the day band. A strange scent, reminiscent of scorched earth, drifted over the creek as thin tendrils of white smoke curled through the undergrowth ahead, gently stirring the vegetation.

Pocket Canyon Highway meandered east-west,

tracing the southern edge of Green Valley Creek, where the stream's flow came to an end. The group huddled in a patch of tall weeds as a large growling semi rolled along the highway. Mercer knew the road well. It was like most roads in northern California; it was a two-lane snake with no shoulder.

The party secured and holstered their weapons before climbing over a crumbling stone railing that ran along the street. A gap in the tree line on the opposite side of the road revealed the source of the burning smell.

Across the street, looming over the landscape, stood the Blue Stone Quarry and Concrete Plant. The quarry was carved from the mountainside, a rugged expanse of exposed rock, while the concrete plant sat like a fortress, its towering silos and machinery dominating the skyline. The rhythmic hum of heavy equipment and the occasional rumble of pinballing stones from the quarry echoed across the highway, and Mercer's urgency and fight drained from him.

A huge concrete truck, its payload spinning, rumbled through the plant's main entrance, kicking up grit. The air was heavy with the dust of pulverized limestone, giving off a dry, chalky scent that mingled with the faint metallic tang of machinery and tools. There was also a persistent undercurrent of sulfur and burnt minerals, adding a sharp, slightly acrid edge to the air.

Mercer ran across the road and examined the ground. The driveway was made of hardpacked concrete-like gravel, and even the giant trucks left no tracks.

Alex and Jinx joined Mercer, and the trio stared dejectedly at the churning plant.

"I'm going to walk through the quarry, but…" Mercer didn't want to say he wasn't hopeful because O&M had said the beast was running from people and noise, but…

Jinx said, "I checked the sides of the road to the east and west… not far, but there was no sign the Saberonis pushed through the thick vegetation, so th—"

A cacophony of deep, resonant thuds followed by a sharp, thunderous boom exploded from the quarry, and the ground trembled and shook. The shriek of bending metal rose above the clamor of the plant, followed by a loud whine as a piece of metal bent and snapped.

Jinx was the first to break into a run, and she bolted through the plant's entrance and ran between parked trucks waiting to receive their payload.

Mercer and Alex exchanged looks of apprehension and doubt, but then Mercer nodded, and Alex lurched into motion.

The screech and moan of equipment shutting down, mixed with the shouts and pleas of workers, drowned out the sounds of cracking stone and rumbling engines. An excavator clawing blue stone from the mountainside had tipped over, and employees were working to get the operator out of the cab.

Alex scanned the scene with the SpectraShade Glasses. "There's too much grit and smoke in the air, it's distorting everything."

The plant's administration building was to the left, and there was a large sign out front that said, "131 days since our last accident." What were the odds that a company with a solid safety record would have a major accident five minutes after the Saberonis fled the creek?

"It's this way," Mercer said as he slung the Benelli off his back and headed for the crumpled excavator.

The companions threaded through the trucks, passing the kiln area where cement was processed. Despite not being very close to the kilns, the heat was intense, and a thick soupy smoke reminiscent of burnt wires wafted over the area.

Workers managed to get the operator of the excavator free of the cab, and the guy looked like he'd seen a ghost. Mercer nudged his way into the crowd surrounding the wreckage, but he couldn't hear the answers to the many questions being hurled at the distraught man.

A supervisor arrived in a golf cart, the distant warble of a siren reminding Mercer time was short. The crowd parted for the boss like he was Moses, and the workers fell silent.

Mercer leaned toward a tall man wearing a yellow hard hat, his brown face streaked with perspiration, dirt, and grease. "What happened? I mean, how did this happen?"

The man never took his eyes off the boss as he questioned the operator and he said, "Don't know. Kirny is the best we've got. Someone said he saw something weird, and he… I don't know, man. Sounded like he panicked." The worker looked Mercer's way, but Mercer and his companions were on the move, skirting the edge of the crowd and trying to get a better view.

A gunshot rang out, and Mercer tracked the noise and headed for a large metal warehouse just east of the main quarry. The warehouse doors were open on both ends, and abandoned forklifts were scattered about, some with material still on their forks.

Inside the expansive warehouse, the air was thick with a gritty haze, and the faint scent of chalky limestone permeated the space. Towering stacks of raw materials dominated the walls, each section meticulously organized to facilitate the concrete-making process. To the left, large bags of pulverized limestone were piled high, their grayish-white exteriors dusted with fine powder. Adjacent to them there were containers of clay and shale, their earthy tones contrasting with the brighter hues of the limestone.

At the center of the warehouse, large silos stood like sentinels, their metal exteriors gleaming under the harsh fluorescent lights. The silos were labeled identifying the various materials therein, and they included gypsum and sand, critical ingredients for regulating the concrete's setting time and adding strength. Pipes and conveyor belts crisscrossed overhead, and at the opposite end of the warehouse, an abandoned mixing station hummed as it blended the raw materials. The hum of the machinery was steady, and Mercer's heart pumped as he pushed through the dust that swirled in the rank air.

Alex scanned the area with the SpectraShade Goggles.

Jinx asked, "Is there anything in here that can't take bullets, because—"

"Shush..." hissed Mercer. "There. In the reflection of the stainless-steel silo ahead."

A distorted image of the Saberonis shimmered and shifted in the mirror-like side of the storage tower.

Mercer looked at the ground, searching for dark crimson drips and paw prints, but there was nothing. The companions hadn't seen blood in over an hour, and Mercer wasn't surprised. Surely the wound had begun to scab —or... He recalled the beast's enhanced healing capabilities, and for the thousandth time, wondered what he was going to have to do to kill the Saberonis.

An answer came immediately. Bury the bitch

in concrete, but he didn't see how that was possible. The plant wasn't a movie set. There were no open vats of chemicals or concrete. Everything was secured and covered.

The Saberonis yelled, its wails fading to a cackle.

Mercer recognized the sound. The beast was cornered, and a trapped animal with no way out becomes exponentially more dangerous. Desperation pushes even the most passive creatures to act unpredictably, driving them to tap their primal strength to survive. He signaled to Alex to move left, while gesturing for Jinx to take the right.

The trio eased through the warehouse, the sound of the mixer drowning out the commotion outside. Mercer's nerves beat his chest like a snare drum, the ringing in his head rising above the mixer.

A screech, like ripping metal, tore through the warehouse, and the beast's reflection disappeared.

Alex fired, slung the rifle over his shoulder, and drew his revolver. He chased a blur of motion as it streaked across Mercer's field of vision.

Jinx surged into motion.

Mercer followed, his body weighed down by the exhaustion of what felt like an endless day. Every step and action felt like a monumental effort, Mercer's muscles protesting with the strain of overexertion.

The pair caught up to Alex and he whispered, "It's through there." He pointed between two large metal storage towers.

There was yelling and screaming behind the companions as workers entered the warehouse. As the trio eased around a large silo the ratatat of gunshots drowned out all other sounds, and bullets peppered the floor and punched into the silo.

Mercer dropped and Alex did the same.

Jinx fell back as she fired, the crack and pop of her shots deafening in the confined space.

There was a wail of pain, and a man screamed.

The ESS crew stood before Mercer and his companions, staring down at Cheri, who was bleeding out on the ground. She wore body armor, but one of Jinx's shots had caught her in the face, and blood gushed from where the left side of her head had been.

Three mercenaries in full body armor turned their rage toward the trio, and one of the men dashed forward, his gun aimed at Jinx, his face twisted with rage.

"Wait!" Mercer yelled.

The guy's aim shifted to Mercer.

"It was an accident, the beast—"

A roar thundered through the warehouse, and the Saberonis—nothing more than glowing yellow eyes, a blur of color, and exposed teeth—ran between two of the silos, bouncing off the stainless steel as it twisted and writhed through the air.

The specimen crossed between the two parties, and it took every ounce of effort Mercer had left not to open fire and risk more senseless deaths. With a heavy huff and the rapid thudding of paws, the creature darted down the main aisle between the rows of supplies and equipment toward the open bay door at the eastern end of the building.

Mercer, Alex, and Jinx stood frozen in place, their guns aimed at the three ESS men, who had their weapons trained on the trio. The tension in the air was palpable, each group waiting for the other to make a move. Chalk dust filled the air, and the rumble of approaching voices grew louder.

Cheri had gone silent and stopped moving, a crimson puddle leaking over the floor around her head.

Alex lowered his weapon, pulled off the SpectraShade Goggles, and strode toward Cheri.

"What do you think you're doing?" the lead ESS guy asked as he trained his gun on Alex's head.

Alex pushed the man's weapon to the side as he said, "Helping her."

Mercer looked toward the open door at the east end of the warehouse, and he no longer saw the streak of nothingness that was the Saberonis.

Alex knelt beside Cheri. "Give me something to..." He fell back onto his ass and let his head fall into his hands.

"The lead man pointed his gun at Alex and yelled, "Help her! You said you'd help her!"

"She's gone," Alex said as he pressed to his feet.

Jinx's wail of anguish broke Mercer's heart. He'd killed, but it had always been military-related. Snuffing a life is a crime against nature, but when there is no reason, no way to justify what's been done, a deep scar is left that never fully heals.

"Stay here with her until help arrives," Mercer said.

All the fight had gone out of the lead man, and he dropped to his knees next to Cheri's corpse and lifted the woman in his arms. Mercer realized then that there was more between Cheri and her number one than work.

The other two ESS men stood back—they were only hired guns after all, and nobody tried to stop Mercer and his companions as they left the ESS crew behind with their dead leader.

Jinx wept like an infant, and Mercer put his arm around her and said, "It was a mistake. Bullets were flying. They shot at us."

The words did nothing. Jinx looked like a balloon that had never been filled with air.

"Help me now. Don't let her death be for nothing," Mercer said.

Jinx nodded, wiped her face, and the trio went in search of the Saberonis for what Mercer hoped would be the last time.

31

The trio double-timed it through the open bay door at the eastern end of the warehouse, Mercer's knees throbbing, Jinx squeaking like a child whose been reprimanded, Cheri's death still only minutes in the past. Alex wore the SpectraShade Goggles, and his head jerked back as the companions burst into the late afternoon sunlight.

Work at the plant was at a standstill, and Mercer figured it would be until a full safety inspection was performed. The weary hunters wound through forklifts, excavators, dump trucks, and waiting eighteen-wheelers with huge payload trailers as workers stood around smoking, drinking water, or playing with their phones.

The eastern portion of the quarry climbed the mountainside in a series of steps that were crisscrossed with work roads, and a service road ran to the top of the quarry and looped around its upper edge. Alex was heading for the service road, his gaze locked straight ahead.

White dust clouds billowed over the yard, the

specks of quartz and fool's gold within sparkling like diamonds as the falling sun cast daggers of light over the quarry. Mercer's visibility was limited, but he saw the ghostly rooster tail of dust that trailed up the road.

The plant was surrounded by sparsely populated woodlands to the north and west, and Forestville was to the east, but beyond Forestville… Mercer didn't want to think about it.

Alex was no spring chicken, and Mercer's buddy slowed to a jog, and then to a fast walk, his breaths coming in ragged fits and bursts accented by an occasional cough or gag. Mercer and Jinx adjusted their pace and fell in on each side of him. Alex said, "Fricking cigarettes."

Mercer was also breathing heavily, and every joint in his body screamed for a shutdown.

Jinx wasn't winded at all, but her eyes were puffy with tears, her face dusted with white powder, and her shirt was speckled with blood.

"Alex, you don't smoke," Mercer said.

"Not anymore—not for forty years, but a pack a day for almost twenty years creates a lot of tar. And you know, I still crave one every once and a while, and if I get a whiff of smoke…" He waved his hand. "Forget about it."

The trail of dust followed the service road as it ascended to the quarry's highest point, where it veered north and curved around the upper rim of the newest excavation site. Slowly the clamor of the plant came online, and Mercer looked over his shoulder and saw the spinning lights of an ambulance beyond the warehouse. The law was nowhere in sight, as far as he could tell.

A gust of wind stirred the clouds of cement dust and grit, scattering the specimen's trail as it entered a glade of Douglas fir trees. The towering specimens, though unable to rival the immense redwoods, were over a hundred feet tall. Bronze needles carpeted the ground, but there was little underbrush due to the dense canopy, and there was plenty of space between the telephone pole-like trunks of the massive evergreens.

The creature's dust trail vanished in the woods, and there were no broken branches, but patches of sandy soil peeked through the layer of pine needles where they had been disturbed. The specimen's massive, baseball-mitt-sized paws had brushed them aside, offering the only trace of its passage.

An eerie silence fell over the forest, the distant clamor of the plant fading. Mercer's heart pounded in his chest, each beat sending sharp, icy pain radiating through his limbs like spidery daggers. His sweat-soaked skin grew cold, a creeping chill settling over him as he looked at Alex. His friend was pushing himself, and Mercer saw the fatigue etched in his face. The retired cop was slowing down, and Mercer knew it was only a matter of time before he couldn't keep up.

The shrill scream of a woman, followed by a

gurgle-roar, pierced the day as the forest gave way to a homestead carved from the forest. A ranch house with a makeshift carport sat in the middle of a dirt clearing that housed a corral, a dilapidated barn, and a small field of marijuana plants that was protected by a camera and a six-foot fence.

There was also a vegetable garden, and a woman standing at its center brandished a shovel as she fought off the blurry form of the Saberonis.

Alex aimed the rifle and cursed. He was too far away and there were several obstructions between him and his target.

The Saberonis was a shifting mass of muscle and teeth. With the sun inching its way to the western horizon, dusk crept over the clearing, the tall trees blocking the sunlight, and the specimen's crypsis abilities were failing. With the green backdrop of the trees, the cedar-clad house, the burnt metal roof of the carport, and the variety of multicolored plants filling the vegetable garden, the beast's camouflage was a shifting mess of brown, orange, and an entire palette of greens that outlined its form.

Mercer and his companions were getting close, but it was clear they weren't going to arrive in time.

The gardener brought her shovel around like she was swinging for the fences, but she missed, lost her footing, and fell to one knee as the shovel was knocked from her hands. She bent the knee for a second, staring at the Saberonis, the specimen's jaws flexing open, its tail out straight, yellow eyes burning as it sprang at the woman.

Alex and Jinx fired, and a tremor of anxiety rolled through Mercer, but the woman was already meat.

The creature's long fangs pierced her body, driving through her as the air crackled. Its powerful incisors crunched through her torso as its front paws drove the woman into her trampled tomato plants.

Mercer screamed, a primal wail of frustration and pain. He fired the Benelli, the thunderous booms scattering the birds perched in nearby trees.

Like an arrow with teeth, a dog appeared at the edge of the garden, its legs cycling so fast Mercer couldn't see them. The canine arced through the air, jaws open, the dog's vicious snarls carrying over the garden.

A smile leaked over Mercer's face. Man's best friend to the rescue.

One of the specimen's huge paws raked through the air and knocked the canine aside. The dog yelped and cried as it flew through the air, and when it crashed into a fencepost with a sickening crack the animal stopped wailing.

The Saberonis bolted toward the house, stomping vegetation as it wove and dodged.

Bullets tore through the garden as the trio

unleashed their firepower on the beast, but it was futile. The creature moved with such speed that Mercer could hardly track its blurred form. With every shot, more ammunition was wasted so he shouted for his companions to stop firing.

Mercer dry-heaved when he reached the center of the vegetable garden, the coppery odor of blood mixed with the scent of fresh-cut grass with hints of spice and bitterness from the crushed tomato plants filling his nostrils. Blood leaked into the rich soil around the woman, her eyes open, her face frozen in a grimace of terror, her organs spilling out onto eggplant vines.

The dog whined.

Mercer coughed and gagged as he went to the beast. The Canine's throat had been torn open by the specimen's savage claws, and no surgeon on Earth could save him. As the dog gasped for air Mercer knew there was only one thing he could do for the animal. He slung the shotgun over his shoulder and pulled the Sig Sauer.

When she arrived at Mercer's side, Jinx said, "Oh, now that sucks."

The dog was a mutt, but it appeared to be a golden retriever mixed with a small breed. Watery eyes stared up at Mercer as he pointed the Sig Sauer at the dog's head, looked away, and said, "Sorry, boy," as he pulled the trigger.

A yelp Mercer would never forget echoed over the garden, the gunshot ringing in Mercer's head like an alarm bell. Anger and rage turned his vision red. He'd been chasing the Saberonis for so long his hatred had ebbed, but as he stared at the carnage his skin prickled with rediscovered hatred.

The trio left the woman's corpse behind. She was dead, and there was nothing to be done except kill the beast that had brutally murdered her for no reason.

No reason? The idea bounced around in Mercer's head as he followed the trail of blood splatters and partial pawprints that led north into the woods. When he rolled the specimen's POV around in his bean, Mercer saw several legitimate reasons why the Saberonis might be angry with humanity. For starters, the beast knew nothing of the environment outside its cell, and it had no idea how to interact with other life forms. It had been bred for violence—it had been created to kill, there was no sugarcoating it, and the bigheads were going to tap its brain so they could control it. The specimen was probably confused and scared, not understanding what it was, what abilities it might possess, how to use them, or what using them might mean.

All that added up to a creature that humans had created, abused, and used, so the beast's attacking everything it came across was an inevitable outcome. The truth was those who had died had no connection to the Saberonis; their deaths were the result of Evolve Enterprises' actions. Mercer bore some of the blame as well, his involvement intertwining with the tragedy. The dead and injured weighed heavily on him, and he would have to try and make amends, but that was for another day.

The trail of blood ran along a deer path that cut through a copse of eucalyptus trees. The land angled up, and huge slabs of stone, like steps, jutted from the hillside. In spots the ground itself was cleaved, leaving narrow ravine-like cracks running through the forest.

Orange light angled through the trees, and though he couldn't see it, Mercer knew the sun was racing toward the horizon, and when darkness fell, he would... what? He turned to Alex and said, "How are you holding up?"

Alex grunted. "I've been better."

"How close are we?"

"I don't know. The last couple of splatters have been dry."

Now it was Mercer's turn to grunt. "How long does blood take to dry?" Mercer felt like he should know the answer, having once been a cop.

Alex hiked his shoulders. "The bigger issue is light. Do the glasses work in the dark?"

"They do, but..." Something ate at Mercer, but he couldn't put it into words. He felt like he'd already lost, and he was just going through the motions to avoid being held accountable for the tragedies he'd left in his wake.

"Yeah," Alex said.

The deer path ended at a narrow cut in the

land that was only fifteen feet deep, but there were steep scree piles on both sides of the gap. The tumbled stones ranged in size from gravel to small boulders, and everything looked loose and ready to topple.

Alex led, followed by Mercer, and then Jinx. Saberonis prints led into the tiny ravine, but the trail died after ten feet as if the beast had disappeared. Alex knelt and examined the ground.

The Saberonis attacked without warning, swooping down from above. A sharp hiss reverberated off the walls of the gully as the monster swiped at Jinx with one of its powerful front paws. The beast reared back and pushed onto its hindlegs, the specimen towering over Jinx. Brown skin shimmered and shifted, and dagger-like claws glistened as they sank into flesh.

Jinx screamed, but her wail of pain was cut short by the sound of cracking bones.

The giant cat jumped and twisted as Mercer and Alex opened fire, the pop of gunpowder expanding and the whoosh and hiss of bullets leaving steel barrels filling Mercer's head.

Jinx fell to the ground, where she lay motionless, blood pouring from wounds on her chest and head, and spurting from a vein in her neck.

When Mercer reached her side Jinx was already staring into the next world. He dropped onto his butt, all will to live draining from him like so many failures. She'd saved his bacon... today? Could it be? Mercer's day had started before sunrise, and as he pushed to his feet, he knew the day was far from over.

32

Dust crept through the forest, and the deer trail petered out. Mercer found himself in a familiar position. He and Alex were in the middle of nowhere, night was coming on, and wolves howled as owls hooted. The partners were hungry, tired, nervous, and yeah, a little scared.

Sound carried long distances in the stillness of the forest, and the snap of a tree branch reminded Mercer the Saberonis wasn't far ahead. Grunts and panting echoed through the woods, and splinters of pain knifed up Mercer's legs as he ran. The forest was growing tight, and Alex slowed, not only because he was ready to collapse, but because he hadn't seen the pulsating flashes of the specimen in more than fifteen minutes.

"Anything?" Mercer asked.

Alex shook his head no without speaking.

Both men were still shaken up about Jinx's death, and Mercer felt the constant itch of guilt for leaving her behind. If the beasts of the wood got to her, Mercer would never be able to forgive himself. Alex had agreed that they had to go on, but two wrongs didn't make a right, and with each step, he felt the weight of Jinx's death and saw her shattered face in his mind's eye.

The last seven days replayed like a dying man seeing his entire life. A late night call from Twerp, the breakout and all that it meant, Barney's death, Webster's, the massacre at the market, the creek, Cokely's injuries, Cheri's death, and Jinx's. It all led to here and now.

A spattering of weeds filled a gap in the forest where a giant Douglas fir had given up the ghost. The last rays of the setting sun angled into the narrow clearing, and Alex put up a hand. As the two men took cover behind the trunk of the fallen tree Alex said, "It's perched on a thick branch straight ahead."

Mercer gazed into the thickening gloom, but all he saw were bare tree limbs and a backdrop of tall weeds.

"Here." Alex handed Mercer the SpectraShade Goggles.

Mercer put the glasses on, and the familiar world of shifting colors, dark hues, and overly bright accents was overwhelming, and it took a minute for his eyes to adjust. Mercer's eyes hurt —like the rest of him, but as the fallen tree and surrounding weeds came into focus two yellow orbs blazed through the gloom.

"See it?" Alex hissed.

"Yeah." Mercer saw it, but a tangle of tree

branches protruding from the rotting trunk obscured the line of fire, and…

"Give me the glasses," Alex said. "I'm a better shot."

"You can hit it from here?"

Alex said nothing.

Mercer stared at the pulsating form of the Saberonis in the distance, the yellow eyes unmoving. There was intelligence in those eyes, and something else Mercer was loath to accept. He sensed the creature's apprehension and understood that it was just as weary as Mercer and the many people on his trail. The trail…

The land to the north was a varied landscape made up of dense redwood forests, rolling hills, and winding rivers. As the Saberonis traveled further north the terrain would become more rugged, with hills giving way to mountains that were part of the Coastal Range. Many streams and creeks snaked through the forest and provided fresh water, and thick underbrush offered constant cover.

Mercer had been up that way many times, and Alex had hunted deer up there. Most of the region was remote and wild, and there would be no need for the Saberonis to attack humans or cattle because it would have everything it needed. Mercer felt his hatred roll away like the tide and it didn't return.

The Saberonis blinked, and the orbs of yellow light floating in the gloom disappeared. Mercer took off the glasses and dropped them in a pocket.

Alex nodded, a slow up and down that grew in speed as his resolve and acceptance grew.

The sunset filtered through the towering silhouettes of Douglas firs, casting long, slanting shadows across the thin clearing. Above, the sky glowed in a palette of warm oranges and purples, fading into deeper shades of indigo as the sun sank lower on a horizon Mercer couldn't see. Golden light streamed through the gaps in the surrounding forest canopy, illuminating patches of ferns, weeds, and underbrush with a soft, ethereal glow. The tall firs stood as silent witnesses to Mercer's decision, their branches swaying gently in the evening breeze.

Mercer and Alex stood there a long time as the dying light knifed through the higher branches, the narrow beams creating a luminous haze that softened the sharpness of the forest's edges. Pine needles shimmered in the fading light, their deep green hues turning to shadow. The air was filled with the scent of resin and earth and hope, and the distant calls of birds settling in for the night echoed faintly through the trees.

On the trek back to civilization Alex asked, "How do you see this going? I'll do whatever you want."

Mercer hiked his shoulders and said, "All I know is we did our best to kill the thing. As to the facts..." He stopped walking and pulled his cellphone. "I'm going to say as little as possible, and you didn't help me until the end."

"They'll want our phones and—"

Mercer smashed his phone with a stone, and he was surprised at how much fun it was. Not only was it like severing the line to a former life, a life he wanted to forget, but he'd had enough of technology. The tech companies knew more about him than he knew about himself, and freedom and relief flooded through Mercer as the cellphone screen cracked, and he pounded the device to wire and broken circuitry.

Alex was hesitant, but he also got in the spirit, hooting and yelling as he destroyed his phone. "I don't think I'm going to get a new one," he said.

Mercer didn't believe that, but he liked the sentiment.

"What about the goggles?" Alex asked.

"What about them?" Mercer padded his pocket. "It's always good to have leverage." He didn't know how much leverage the tech would provide, or if he'd need it, but something was better than nothing.

With that settled the partners ran through their story, making sure everything was in order. When the duo reached the road reality would kick in, and things needed to be set straight right at the start. Content with his decision, Mercer's thoughts turned to Jenni, and he felt a renewed purpose he hadn't felt in a long time.

A howl cut through the night, but it wasn't

fierce or full of rage. Instead, it carried a sense of relief.

Nineteen days later, the wind gently rustling the trees behind his house, Mercer sat on his patio sipping a glass of Freely Vineyard's chardonnay. He was unemployed for the first time in his life, and he had to admit he liked not having to report like a prisoner for roll call each day.

The feds and local authorities were in no rush to resolve Mercer's case, and to date he hadn't been charged with any crime. There was enough egg on enough faces, and he was a small fish, though his day in court would come. He'd hired a lawyer—something he'd sworn he would never do, and the woman was a shark.

Mercer called the attorney, and she showed up at the sheriff's office where he'd just spilled his entire story. Without even shaking Mercer's hand, the woman went to work building a case that painted Mercer as a hero. He was uncomfortable with that, but he was more uncomfortable with the possibility of going to jail. The law didn't care about Mercer's NDA, but he was a former cop, and the blue religion still protected its own, even those who had been excommunicated.

Then there was the fact that Mercer had blown the whistle, and the facts pointed to him doing everything within his power to kill the specimen. That, coupled with his standing in the community, Alex's support, and the fact that he'd agreed to testify against Twerp, had bought him a fair amount of goodwill. Mercer's lawyer was confident he'd get nothing more than probation for withholding critical information during a murder investigation. There was no way around that, and Mercer was willing to pay that price.

The downside of his freedom was that his entire life story was now in the public domain, and as predicted, Jenni was forced to fight off sorties from her mother who said, "You should drop that son-of-a-bitch like a bad habit."

Mercer smiled as he sipped his wine, the breeze refreshing, sparkles of sunlight glowing through the trees like a dying flame.

The Twerp didn't get far. In a display of irony that even a politician wouldn't scoff at, the feds picked Thorpe up in central Florida where he was enjoying a day fishing on the Santa Fe River. He'd lawyered-up immediately, but given all the evidence and testimonies, Mercer's version of the facts wasn't in dispute. Video evidence and random eyewitness accounts supported Mercer's statement, as did the accounts of Dax, O&M, Gray—who sold Twerp out as soon as the feds arrived, Declan, who was doing well, and a slew of others. Based on all this, the founder of Evolve Enterprises was being held without bail pending his trial and the company was shuttered until further notice.

Jinx had broken a few more laws than Mercer, and it seemed to Mercer that, despite his best efforts, she'd fallen on the wrong side of the sheriff's opinion. But she was gone, and if there was any truth to the old legends she would have to stand before the toughest judge of all. Redemption is powerful, and Jinx had done more than seek forgiveness. She'd done everything she could to right the wrongs of her past, and Mercer felt she'd reclaimed her integrity, and he hoped she would rest in peace.

Local authorities bent the knee to the feds, and unsurprisingly, there had been no media coverage about the Saberonis. The murders made national news after conspiracy nutters manufactured a theory that Bigfoot was behind the carnage—and media outlets picked up the craziness faster than news of an actor tripping on the red carpet.

It was odd to Mercer that the element of the caper that he felt was the most important was getting the least amount of attention.

Everyone accepted Mercer's story that the beast had given him and Alex the slip, and of the Saberonis there was no sign. Helicopter searches revealed nothing, and the tree canopy of the vast wilderness was impenetrable from above. The sparsely populated wilds of northern California gave way to the vast nothingness of the Sierra Nevada range in the east, so when the beast headed for the sunrise, there would be no finding her, or her newborn calve, which, based on the documents Mercer had discovered, wasn't far off.

Funerals and memorials were held, and Mercer visited all the local cemeteries, but he found little animosity among the mourners. The story about what had occurred, how the dead had perished, had blossomed in a positive direction for Mercer, though it made him sick to think about it. Somehow society's game of telephone had produced a story in which he'd fought against the creature to help the people of northern California and to avenge those who had died. This was far from the truth, but when people talked, they talked. What could he do?

Mercer held up his glass and stared through the white wine, the last rays of the setting sun painting the vino sparkling gold.

What the future would bring, he didn't know. Mercer and Jenni had been talking. A lot. Much ground was covered, and a lot of grass was mowed. The couple found common ground, and things were looking up, though he knew it would take time for his wife to get over his indiscretion and forgive him, but he was willing to wait.

As for work, Evolve Enterprises would most likely go out of business, and there would be no security or law enforcement in Mercer's future. He sipped. Maybe he would go back to Freely Vineyard & Winery and ask Victor if he needed help. How hard could working at a winery be? If things got tough, he could always have a glass of chardonnay.

ABOUT THE AUTHOR

--

Edward J. McFadden III is a prolific author with over thirty-five published novels spanning the thriller, horror, science fiction, crime, and adventure genres. His works TRAGIC, Wolves of the Sea, Terror Peak, Crimson Falls, Drop Off, Shadow of the Abyss, and The Breach received Amazon #1 Best Seller tags. Famed author F. Paul Wilson praised Terror Peak, saying "Terror Peak pits you against not only murderous creatures lurking in the snows, but a hostile environment so real you'll come away with frostbite. A triumph of terror." Ed resides on Long Island with his wife Dawn, their daughter Samantha, and their cats Snoop and Skittles.

BOOKS BY THIS AUTHOR

Terror Lake

The Inuit people call it Akhlut, and legends tell of a horrific monster, a freak of nature from the depths that appears every six years in search of flesh and blood.

Mount Aire is a secluded enclave on the Kenai Peninsula where folks do their best to live quiet lives away from the chaos of civilization. The town's peace is shattered when a musher is killed during the annual Terimore 200 sled dog race, and signs of a strange creature are found at the murder scene. Murmurs recalling the year of the beast percolate through town. Six years ago, three died, five the cycle before that.

Wildlife Trooper Terry Wyatt had seen and heard it all before. His father and uncle were lost on the lake when he was a boy, and it had been a year of the beast.

And it was all happening again.

Tragic

Borderland Pass is a desolate ravine in the Ozark Mountains that only the strongest dare to call home. It's an ancient place of battle, struggle, and survival where the past and present collide, and the spirits of the fallen roam in search of vengeance.

The legend of the Ozark Howler is as old as the mountains themselves, the bloody tales of terror, mutilation, and murder a foundation block in the region's folklore. Skeptics dismiss the Howler as nothing more than tall tales and the work of overactive imaginations, but those who have seen the monster tell a different tale.

Carter Renfrow is hiding from his past and living the life of a wanted man when a multi-car pileup interrupts his plans, and two worlds collide in an epic clash with life and death hanging in the balance.

From the author of The Cryptid Club and Crimson Falls comes a new adventure-horror novel. Fast-paced and exciting, TRAGIC is a roller coaster ride through disaster and heartbreak, where the hits just keep on coming, and no one is safe.

Just Beneath The Skin

The monster inside is always closer than it seems.

Peter Lastner's life is ticking away, each borrowed breath a grim reminder of his fragile state. When he stumbles upon an old engine carburetor in the depths of the Klara's Woods Preserve, an insidious obsession takes root. Piece by piece, Peter's discovery of more parts pulls him into a dark spiral where nightmares blur with reality.

The once-peaceful preserve becomes a hunting ground, and every step Peter takes brings him closer to the precipice of madness as a relentless whisper from beyond promises power and eternal life.

As his sanity slips away Peter is haunted by forces beyond comprehension, and the line between man and monster fades.

Will Peter reclaim his humanity, or succumb to the darkness that lies Just Beneath the Skin?

From the author of TRAGIC, Landfill Lizards, and Crimson Falls comes a new horror thriller so dark it will leave readers questioning the line between reality and nightmare.

Time's Claws

Through an ancient gateway the dark universe yawns, casting a group of unsuspecting travelers into the jaws of primordial terror.

A thunderous roar echoes through the ages as a Tyrannosaur fossil is unearthed in the same geological stratum as Native American artifacts, signaling the beginning of Marshall Stanton's transformation from history professor to prehistoric adventurer. He is a stranger in a strange world that time forgot, and his only hope is unraveling the mystery of returning home.

With apex predators lurking at every turn, Marshall must rely on his wits and new companions to navigate this unforgiving land. But even the most cunning strategies can't prepare him for the brutal reality of the dinosaur domain.

As time runs out, Marshall faces the ultimate question: Can he find his way back to where he belongs, or will the ancient world claim another victim? The claws of time are closing in.

From the author of Throwback, Primeval Valley,

Predators & Prey, and Jurassic Ark comes Time's Claws: A Dinosaur Domain Thriller—a relentless, edge-of-your-seat adventure that will keep readers guessing until the final page.

Quick Sands

Money. Love. Murder. Sand?

Ex-FBI intelligence analyst Theo Ramage doesn't want to die in an endless West Texas wasteland, but there's gold in them thar hills... or rather, dunes, and old habits die hard.

The fracking craze in the Permian Basin has made Texas sand worth billions, transforming the endless sea of windswept dunes into a modern day El Dorado. All Ramage wants is his truck and load of fresh cut Christmas trees back, but due process in Prairie Home is a bullet, and Ramage won't stand-down. He joins forces with embattled local rancher Anna Gutierrez, and the duo finds themselves plunged into a world of eco-terrorism, drugs, and murder.

The sheriff wants Ramage gone. The local crime boss, the Sandman, wants him dead, and nobody in the badlands of Texas will give him the time of day, but Ramage can't let sleeping dogs lie. It's not in his DNA.

Fast-paced, humorous and exhilarating, Quick Sands reveals the dark underbelly of the fracking industry, and what happens when you push an honest man too far. If you're a fan of F. Paul Wilson's Repairman Jack, Ian Fleming's James Bond, Lee Child's Jack Reacher, John Sandford's Prey Series, Michael Connelly's Harry Bosch, Carl Hiaasen, and Stuart Woods, then Theo Ramage is your man.

Printed in Dunstable, United Kingdom